MADAME DE CHARRIÈRE

LETTERS FROM SWITZERLAND

The rediscovery of an eighteenth century

female writer of genius is an exciting event. Belle de Charrière was a Dutch aristocrat who wrote in French with a talent for controversial novels that shocked the conventional *salons* of France and Switzerland. Her four best short novels (novellas) are translated here and we can now recognise her piercing talent. Until now we have lacked in one volume a translation into English of these novels which are issued here with a short biography that seeks to place Belle in her rightful place as a feminine (and feminist) writer second to none. Belle has been known principally as the close friend of two famous men: James Boswell and Benjamin Constant. She and Boswell were the same age (23) when they first met in Utrecht in 1763. He was on his Grand Tour in Holland and we have to thank his Journal and letters for a day-by-day account of his hesitant wooing of the beautiful Belle. Could they be happily married? It takes them five years to decide they could not. Belle's own marriage to Charles de Charrière when she was already 31 was generally considered to be something of an anti-climax following the dozen or so exotic suitors who had queued up for her hand when she was in her twenties. Her quiet married life in Neuchâtel, a sleepy little town in French Switzerland, is transformed once she starts to write her polemical novels and other works.

Benjamin Constant and Belle met in Paris in 1787 when he was only 20 and she already 47. There was an instant *rapport* between them despite the difference in their ages. She takes his youthful genius under her wing and prepares him for the role he will play later in the French Revolution – as well as for his torrid relationship with Madame de Staël. Belle's four novels were written in her forties between 1784 and 1788. Belle's heroines are all strong-willed women each of whom suffers, in some measure, at the hands of bigoted males whose own position in society enables them to condemn women to be disadvantaged. Belle's novels contribute some of the earliest feminist writing and speak out in favour of the liberation of women. The literary form she uses is that of an exchange of letters between friends, a form much in vogue in the eighteenth century and which even today carries great conviction.

MADAME DE CHARRIÈRE

LETTERS FROM SWITZERLAND

EDITED AND TRANSLATED
WITH A BIOGRAPHY BY

JAMES CHESTERMAN

CAROLE GREEN PUBLISHING

JAMES CHESTERMAN

For Anna

First published in Great Britain in 2001 by
Carole Green Publishing
4 Station Road, Swavesey, Cambridge CB4 5RA

and

James Chesterman
Knights Manor, Swaffham Prior, Cambridge CB5 0LD

A CIP catalogue record for this book is available from the British Library.

ISBN 1 903479 03 7

Designed and typeset in Fournier 12/14½ pt by
Geoff Green Book Design, Cambridge
Printed and bound in Great Britain by
Antony Rowe Limited
Bumper's Farm
Chippenham, Wilts SN14 6LH

Frontispiece: Isabelle de Charrière. Portrait by Maurice de La Tour, 1766, painted when she was 26. *Musée d'art et d'histoire, Geneva*

CONTENTS

INTRODUCTION AND
ACKNOWLEDGEMENTS

" *Tous ceux qui se sont occupés d'elle se sont pris à l'aimer* [All those who are concerned with her fall in love with her]." This quotation is from Philippe Godet's *Madame de Charrière et ses amis*. Published in 1905 this was really the seminal work to introduce the world to Belle in her life and works. Other books on and about her have appeared since then but none so affectionate as befitted an historian of Neuchâtel where Belle had lived and worked for 35 years. Godet researched his subject on the spot for 20 years and his two-volume work was the result, later to be shortened to one volume which was issued in 1927.

In following Godet and other authors (see Bibliography p. xii) I have wished to offer those readers who do not speak French a translation into English of her best, and best-known, four *contes*. I have also added a short biography of Belle, necessary, I felt, to try and illumine her for the reader and to convey to that reader some of the love affair I have also undergone in absorbing all things Charrière (for a mere five years). I hope the reader will be similarly affected.

Belle was Dutch-born, in 1740 near Utrecht, as Isabella van Tuyll, the eldest of seven children. Her father was a Governor of the local province and a worthy but somewhat dull aristocrat much loved and respected by Belle but with whom she was exasperated in equal measure. Her father had had the wisdom to marry an heiress which increased the comfort of the family but also its dullness. "*Ici l'on est vif tout seule* [Here one must be lively on one's own]." The Dutch dowagers observed Belle with many misgivings as, in her teens, she sailed into a room with her bosom rather too well displayed. Criticism of her displayed beauty was not objected to by Belle herself nor was praise resented by her - rather, the contrary. Fluent in French, proficient in Italian and English by the age of 14, she set herself to learn mathematics by rising at six in the morning to visit her professor in Utrecht. Her precocity contained a strong element of defiance and the dowagers viewed Belle as quite unmarriagable. Sixteen was the age at which marriages were arranged and Belle's own mother had been this age when betrothed to her father. But this did not suit Belle, as we shall see.

Belle's encounter, she aged 20 to his 37, with the dashing though somewhat rakish Baron d'Hermenches resulted in a clandestine exchange of letters which continued for some 15 years. This *liaison dangereuse* was carefully contrived to be hidden from Belle's parents but the rumours abounded in shockable Utrecht. The Baron's marriage was heading for the rocks and Belle's own suitors were to be analysed and dissected in her correspondence with him until she takes her own faltering steps to the altar when she was already aged 31. In her twenties, therefore, we see this queue of mostly degenerate swains attracted by the generous de Tuyll dowry – and in equal measure put off by Belle's straight speech that invariably swiftly exposes her swains' stratagems.

James Boswell appears on her scene when both are 23; he is terrified of her sharp wit and unwifely ambitions and he begs her to control her "*bel-esprit* [lively spirit]" so that he may consider her for a wife able to accept and suffer the rigours of social life in

Edinburgh. Which of course she refuses to do though she strings him along nicely in her letters to let him think that she *might*, just *might* ameliorate her wicked ways. Their last letters are dated 1768 and the correspondence lasted five years.

Her last *inamorato* is not to appear before she is 47 years of age: Benjamin Constant, nephew of the earlier Constant d'Hermenches is to encounter her in Paris in 1787. He is 20. Their instant *rapport* one for the other is to extend 18 years to her death, and indeed the last letter that she wrote was to him. Their often stormy relationship is recorded largely in her letters to him that are still extant (though she begged him to destroy them). His need of her was as mother-to-son; teacher-to-pupil; and perhaps lover-to-lover though we can reliably interpret their letters as expressing love in the boudoir rather than in the bed. Her need of him was the reverse of the above. Her coaching of his mind and knowledge during his formative years leads to his eventual entanglement with Madame de Staël, and ultimately his fame in Paris as a champion of critics of the French Revolution.

Belle's marriage at the age of 31 to her death aged 65 in 1805 has been described by some writers as a sorry affair. She and her husband Charles were to be pitied in their "*mésalliance* [poor match]." Simone de Beauvoir in *The Second Sex* (1976) uses Belle's marriage as a feminist lever against women being suffocated in marriage. Geoffrey Scott used his *The portrait of Zélide* as a catharsis for his misplaced adoration of Bernard Berenson's wife, interpreting Belle's treatment of her husband as the sort of protracted scorn that he himself had suffered at the Villa I Tatti residence near Florence. Both interpretations are somewhat wide of the mark. I believe Belle was quite unfitted to a traditional marriage of the times in which a wife toed the social line and did not write rather risqué novels that reverberated through society. Her *mariage de convenance* to Charles gave her the stability to create her written novels.

Belle admired Charles's legendary encyclopaedic knowledge and enjoyed his undying love and support in all that she did. It is true that she shone in a sleepy little provincial town such as Neuchâtel and that in a more cosmopolitan environment her bright light might have been more subdued. Her childlessness created a void of some sadness but Belle's adoption of bright young women as student-maids gave her solace and them an education.

So if Godet first carried the torch in 1905 for Belle, so have seven editors now assembled her complete works in ten volumes which were published in Amsterdam between 1979–84. Critiques have followed and I would like to pay tribute especially to Dr Cecil Courtney's magisterial biography issued in 1993; *Isabelle de Charrière (Belle de Zuylen)* is his *magnum opus* of some 800 pages. He quotes extensively from her letters in their original French.

In my own short biography (pages 1–66) of Belle I have leant largely on the books of Godet, Scott and Courtney. Other works appear in the Bibliography (xii). I have also quoted extensively from Belle's letters and given my translations of these extracts. The four novels by Belle that I have selected are undoubtedly her best (and best-known) and I have devoted a chapter to their interpretation and place in feminine literature (Chapter XII). Each novel has its own preface.

In their introduction to *Letters of Mistress Henley* Philip and Joan Hinde Stewart interestingly describe Belle's writing as having " ... an exceptional density [and] plain but powerful and often ironic formulations ..." This comes closest to Belle's mode of writing.

Translations into English of *Mistriss Henley*, *Lettres de Lausanne (I and II)* appeared in one volume in 1925, by Sybil Scott (wife of Geoffrey Scott) under the title *Four Tales by Zélide* together with an earlier work *Le Noble*. *Lettres Neuchâteloises* has not been translated before into English. My four novels are all available in French editions.

The translation into English of *Letters of Mistress Henley Published by Her Friend* by Philip Stewart and Jean Vaché was published in New York in 1993 on its own as one volume. It was published by the Modern Language Association of America.

French editions I have used in my translations are as follows:

Lettres Neuchâteloises; *Mistriss Henley*; *Le Noble*. Ed. and Preface Philippe Godet. Published Geneva by A. Jullien, 1908.

Caliste ou Lettres écrites de Lausanne. Ed. Claudine Herrmann. Des Femmes, Paris, 1979.

I have verified the above texts that I used against the definitive versions printed in the ten volumes from Amsterdam. Only very minor differences occurred here and there, mostly in punctuation. I have occasionally cut out short passages in the four novels where Belle is referring to obscure works prevalent at the time.

I have been encouraged in my endeavours and wish to thank: Dr Cecil Courtney of Cambridge; Madame Schmidt-Surdez, Conservator of Manuscripts at the Public Library in Neuchâtel.

LIST OF ILLUSTRATIONS

BIBLIOGRAPHY

Boswell, James. *Boswell in Holland 1763–1764*. London, Heinemann, 1952.

Charrière, Isabelle de. *Letters of Mistress Henley Published by Her Friend*. Translated by Philip Stewart and Jean Vaché. New York: Modern Language Association of America, 1993.

—, *Oeuvres complètes*. Ed. seven authors. 10 vols. Amsterdam, van Oozschot, 1979–84.

Constant, Benjamin. *Le Cahier Rouge*. Paris, Calmann-Levy, 1907.

Courtney, C. P. *Isabelle de Charrière (Belle de Zuylen)*, A Biography. Oxford, Voltaire Foundation, Taylor Institution, 1993.

Godet, Philippe. *Madame de Charrière et ses amis*. 2 vols. Geneva, Jullien, 1905. Abbreviated and re-issued as one vol. Lausanne, Editions Spes, 1927. Reprinted Slatkine, 1973.

Scott, Geoffrey. *The Portrait of Zélide*. London, Constable, 1925. New York, Scribner's, 1926.

—, Sybil. *Four Tales by Zélide*. Translated Sybil Scott. London, Constable, 1925. New York, Scribner's, 1926. Re-issued as *Four Tales*, Freeport, Books for Libraries, 1970. Includes *The Nobleman*, *Mistriss Henley*, *Letters from Lausanne* I and II (*Caliste*).

West, Anthony. *Mortal Wounds*. London, Robson, 1975. New York, McGraw Hill, 1973. Contains a chapter on Madame de Charrière.

CHAPTER ONE

BELLE DE ZUYLEN (ZÉLIDE):
ENFANT TERRIBLE

I SABELLA AGNETA ELIZABETH van Tuyll van Serooskerken was born at the chateau of Zuylen, near Utrecht, on 20 October 1740. Known as Belle de Zuylen in her early years, then as Madame de Charrière after marriage, she had also named herself Zélide in her *Portrait of Zélide* which she had written when she was in her early twenties. But she was known as Belle both by herself and by her intimates and I call her thus in this brief account of her life and works. Her ancient Dutch family name belonged to one of the oldest and most respected families in Holland which dated back to the twelfth century. Her family upbringing was divided between the chateau at Zuylen and a large town house in Utrecht five miles away. The family moved house according to the seasons; the milieu was *ordentlik* [orderly] in the Dutch manner and as a young girl she was to exclaim in desperation *"ici l'on est vif tout seule* [here one must be lively on one's own]."

Her father was a model of propriety as befitted a Governor of the province, a noble and dignified man whom Belle respected and loved with loyalty mixed with exasperation. Her mother had been married at 16 to Jacob van Tuyll; conveniently she was an heiress which must have facilitated the raising of their six children. Belle was the eldest and was followed by four brothers and two sisters (one died in infancy).

French was learned alongside Dutch at the earliest age, according to aristocratic Dutch custom and became, for Belle, her preferred language which she wrote perfectly – Sainte-Beuve described it as "the French of Versailles." At nine years of age she appears to have spent some time in Geneva attending a school where she was scolded for not wanting to learn knitting or sewing. Her first tutor-governess was a remarkable Mlle Prevost who arrived from Geneva in 1748 and stayed for five years, adored by Belle and the source of much of our knowledge of Belle's early years through her many letters to her pupil. At the age of twelve Belle considered her formal education was completed. She embarked on a study of mathematics, rising at six in the morning during the summer to visit her professor in Utrecht. She loved the logic of mathematics, and of physics, but disliked chemistry. English and Italian were added and at 14 years she could conduct a conversation with any of the formal grown-ups who surrounded her. With her precocity comes a certain defiance and she is sensibly warned by Mlle Prevost to accept criticism. She is vivacious but inclined to tackle too many tasks in a day and not to finish them. "*Un seul objet ne pourrait jamais satisfaire à toute l'activité de mon âme*. [A single pursuit could never satisfy all of my restless soul]." She is viewed with amazement by the rather stiff gentry who visit the Tuylls; in her turn she views *savants* in Holland as pedants, the Dutch bourgeois as heavy-handed, and their simple folk as brutish. Yet she mixes with the Tuyll estate workers and sits down to eat with 90 of them at harvest time. She prefers, and often says this, "*les petits gens* [the humble people]." She considers the Dutch language as "*pas encore perfectionée* [not yet perfected]" and it is her intention to leave Holland as soon as she can, preferably to a place where French is spoken.

Plate I: Belle de Zuylen, painted by Guillaume de Spinney in 1759, painted when Belle was 19.
Private collection, Iconografisch Bureau

In her teens she incurs extreme disapproval as she sails into a room with her "*belle gorge, dont elle se pare trop* [with her beautiful bosom rather too well displayed]."

Belle is dutiful towards her much loved parents though critical of their set ways and beliefs. She goes her own way and hopes they won't discover her escapades. Her brothers and sisters may be *ordentlik* but she has the whole world and its wonders in her mind's eye. "*Je voudrais être du pays de tout le monde* [I would rather belong to a country that is universal]."

Music, and her beloved harpsichord follow and are learned with delight and we shall see in later years that both the libretto and composition of the music for operas were both well within her grasp. Private tutors come and go to educate the six children; Belle had a pretty low opinion of most of them and at 16 could run rings round them academically. One, a certain Mme Girard "scarcely knows that two and two make four and that there are seven days in the week. She has never understood that there are 12 months in the year." But she is amiable and has an excellent heart, so Belle likes her for herself. As to religion, Belle was ostensibly Protestant but not a convinced one. She had received poor instruction and found that religion lacked the logic so dear to her tidy mind. Her doubts were with her even to her deathbed.

Although French, as language and literature, was her preferred medium in which she excelled, the gallantries of the French people were not for her. She retained her Dutch disapproval of foppish young men with their routine praises and grandiose wit; sincerity, truth, nature, reason – these all came first. Later she comes to prefer the English way in society where men who have nothing remarkable to say, say nothing. She buried her own romanticism and relied on frankness in speaking which frequently shocked people – but fascinated them. One to whom that applies comes next.

CHAPTER TWO

CONSTANT d'HERMENCHES:
LIAISON DANGEREUSE

"Young people of either sex may learn that the friendship which seems to be granted to them with such facility by persons of bad morals is never anything but a dangerous snare, as fatal to their happiness as to their virtue."

CHODERLOS DE LACLOS, *Les Liaisons Dangereuses*

THE BARON DE REBECQUE et d'Hermenches was 37 and married when he met Belle. She was 20. He was to be the most important influence in her life – not excepting her husband-to-be Monsieur de Charrière, nor James Boswell, nor d'Hermenches's nephew Benjamin Constant, nor any of the dozen or so suitors (*"les épouseurs"*) whom we shall meet in the next chapter.

It was at a ball in the Hague in February 1760 that Belle addresses d'Hermenches, the first to speak, without any introduction, which was unorthodox to say the least. *"Monsieur, vous ne dansez pas?* [Sir, you do not dance?]." She writes him later that she places little reliance on etiquette and that when she sees *"ce qui peut s'appeler une physionomie, j'ai toujours eu la passion de la faire parler* [what one might term a physionomy, I am obliged to speak]."

So the die is cast and they are to correspond for some 15 years. She writes him close on 200 letters that have survived, and there may well be others still undiscovered.

The Baron was a dashing Swiss soldier who served the Dutch Republic; he was the eldest of five sons whose father was even more dashing and rather more successful militarily. D'Hermenches himself suppressed some trouble in Corsica but otherwise seems to have had little to do except pursue the ladies, rather unsuccessfully but which gave him a shocking reputation. He was unhappily married with two children so could never be a serious contender for Belle's hand, though if he could have been she might well have married him. We shall see later that the possibility does in fact present itself.

Her parents viewed him with great suspicion and the pair could only meet occasionally; when they did so both were confused and said very little face to face. They were destined during the 15 years to communicate only by letter. And what letters they are! "*Libertinage* [libertinism]" is one of the words that appears often, especially by her, and one is forced to conclude that the misspent youth she might have had in her 20's is conducted more circumspectly in letter form. Libertinism was safer in written form rather than fact. His letters in this respect are rather more those of a *voyeur* who relishes his clandestine contact with an aristocratic beauty – albeit at arm's length. The letters between them range over the arts, politics and above all themselves for they are both fiercely self-centred. She is fully aware of his rakish reputation and is both frightened and attracted by it. He is her confidant, kept at a safe distance, and in their letters they are able freely to exchange views on every subject imaginable. They have a true affection for each other. Her novels that follow 25 years later, in their epistolary form, must have been influenced by her practised pen honed by d'Hermenches and her other numerous correspondents.

Plate II: Baron Constant de Rebecque et d'Hermenches (1722–1786). He was 37, Belle only 20 when they first met in 1760.
Rijksdienst Beeldende Kunst, Iconografisch Bureau

Belle writes "better than Voltaire" says d'Hermenches – and indeed she meets Voltaire in 1777 though rather unsuccessfully. When d'Hermenches treads a little too close to her physical features she warns him off with "I am not to be confused with other sorts of women". But she obviously delights in his *risqué* innuendoes.

There are some dangerous moments. All the letters are sent via clandestine messengers and one of her letters falls into the hands of her mother – a letter which contains a plea that he should be more attentive, of all things. Her parents are horrified but Belle talks her way out of it. Another of d'Hermenches's letters is delivered by mistake to her father. Belle grabs it and rushes to the kitchens to burn it unopened. She explains that it was a mysterious letter, author unknown, and the mystery was best burned before it could do any further damage. And she got away with it! In truth it seems that her parents treated her very much at arm's length – they must have realised it was the only way.

Belle's affection and need of d'Hermenches (and vice versa) is part-psychological (they explore each other's minds interminably), part-libidinous as we have noted, part joy of words, part loneliness. He is unsuccessful in his career and unhappy most of the time, a failure in his own eyes and in those of others. She chafes at the confines of Zuylen and her need to be married, ever-present in her mind after her eighteenth birthday. Each acts as a valve for the other. When she is to be married in 1771, a decade later, she asks him to burn her letters – or to return them. He prevaricates and does nothing. We have to be grateful to him, for otherwise how could we know so much about Belle?

Their epistolary long friendship through letters is really a *roman épistolaire* and indeed imagination informs much of their exchange over the years. They dissemble expertly so that their messages to each other are often embroidered half-truths – what they would like to believe of themselves rather than as they really are.

CHAPTER THREE

SUITORS

MARRIAGE IN THE eighteenth century was an early affair for women. We saw that Belle's mother was married at 16 and between 16 and 20 was considered the norm for betrothal. Here we have Belle who does not marry until she is 31! We will trace the more interesting of her suitors who paid court to her in that slow, mercenary way of those times. The minuet of matrimony was slow and had its rules. The dowry was all-important. Many of Belle's suitors were impoverished aristocrats or soldiers who obeyed their fathers (and their own impulse) in aiming for the richest possible conquest in any of the countries of Europe whose families were willing, and rich enough, to play this rather desperate game. Their rank of course mattered, as did their religion. The feelings of the young women were definitely secondary to the wish of the parents although some pretence would be given to marriage for love, especially if it coincided with a fortune. There are parallels to this latter thinking in Belle's novels.

We might glance sideways for a moment and identify a very early, short first novel of hers, *Le Noble*, that she wrote and published in her early 20's; this was a satire on parents of noble birth countering the wishes of the young. The heroine at one point flees her father's castle and throws the family portraits into the moat, thereby enabling her to reach her lover with dry feet. The father, suitably softened up by drink, later forgives the pair whilst celebrating the marriage of his son to a girl of a desirable, i.e. titled family. The little novel was published anonymously but her parents got wind of it – how could they not have? – and suppressed it, thereby bearing out the very point of the novel. Belle often denied authorship though she admitted it to d'Hermenches. *Le Noble* caused her to have the reputation of a dangerous rebel against her own class – and to be too intelligent, too self-willed to be a wife. She would hardly have proved to be a complaisant, deferential wife. This becomes clear to Boswell later on. "*Je n'ai pas des talents subalternes.* [I have no talent for being subservient]."

So some of the worthy, or not so worthy suitors were put off making a firm approach to this blue stocking despite the prize of a large dowry and connection with an illustrious family. Any suitor who actually made the journey to Utrecht rather than failing to do so would, on meeting Belle, presumably have noticed that she was not likely to be a sweet and adoring wife.

The first suitor of consequence was to be none other than d'Hermenches's best friend: the Marquis de Bellegarde. This suited d'Hermenches and Belle since such a marriage might result in a sort of *menage à trois*. They could play trios, they said. Much ink was expended as to whether this would be, *could* be *comme il faut* and "*libertinage*" is a word much exchanged. To "play trios" probably meant two things at once. We shall never know how it would have worked out because in the two years or so that Bellegarde plied his lukewarm troth, he only visited

Plate III: Marquis de Bellegarde. Aged 44 to Belle's 24, his courtship was lukewarm and he only visited her once in their 2 years of correspondence.
From an anonymous drawing.
Pollini Album, Gemeentearchief, The Hague

Utrecht once and is finally given his marching orders because he is Catholic and Belle is Protestant. Monsieur Tuyll is steadfastly against such a mixed marriage, especially since the suitor was 44 (Belle 24) and riddled with debt – if nothing worse. He had also asked that the dowry be doubled. D'Hermenches was told to take his friend elsewhere.

Another difficulty in all the scheming for an acceptable suitor during this decade of indecision is Belle's pent-up passion, normal in any young girl but somewhat more marked in her case with her vital "*bel-esprit* [lively spirit]."

Belle is on record as saying she would prefer her husband to treat her as a mistress, and elsewhere that she would prefer her husband to be unfaithful rather than sulky or brutish. She is alert to the danger of a suitor being too old and wanting to "take a wife to help him through the winter, inviting a woman to warm herself before a feeble fire after having spent his springtime and summer picking flowers and fruits without her." All of which clear thinking is somewhat at odds with sedate eighteenth century views. It also helps to make clear just why she suffered a decade of suitors, and rejected them all finally in favour of *un petit bonhomme* [a good little man] in the person of Charles de Charrière to whom she turns in due course.

A certain Christian von Brömbse appears in 1763, later to be a Burgomeister of Lübeck, but at this date "needing improvement". Next, a rather better prospect appears (or might appear) in a Count d'Anhalt who was aide-de-Camp to the King of Prussia, Frederick II. An erstwhile tutor to the Tuyll children, a certain Monsieur Catt, had been invited into the King's court as Reader at Potsdam, and there sang the praises of Belle and offered round her portrait, to the point where d'Anhalt became interested. He wrote that he was coming to see her – but never came. Then there was a rather dim cousin of Belle's, Frederik (Frits) who had admired her from childhood. She turns him down whilst pointing out that she does not wish to spend her life in their country of Holland – it is not to her taste and does not suit her health.

Two more suitors advance, then retreat, probably frightened off by Belle's reputation. These are the English Lord Wemyss – despotic and dissolute – and a somewhat gentler German Count who was impoverished and therefore refused.

Meanwhile she writes to d'Hermenches that she is happy enough at her harpsichord and her mathematics, and that her parents are now accustomed to her daily round , though sometimes she is forced to consort with people "to whom she has nothing to say and who tell her things she knows already". She is 24 and determined to get married one day but for the moment her private studies are sufficient grist to her mill. Now centre stage comes a young Scotsman whom she will know off and on for four years, none other than James Boswell.

CHAPTER FOUR

JAMES BOSWELL

B ORN 1740, Boswell was the same age as Belle and both were 23 when he arrived at Utrecht in August 1763. He had set off on the Grand Tour and Utrecht was his first stop. He had been ordered there (he was willing enough) by his father Lord Auchinlech to study law, now his intended profession.*

Boswell's short life had already had much vivacity in it; his two years in London prior to 1763 had been years when he learned less law than the delights of young ladies, usually of the accommodating sort to be found (and paid for) in the London parks such as Vauxhall Gardens. His *London Journal 1762-1763* recounts these exploits with much delight and vigour. He

---

* Boswell's father was a well known barrister and judge in Edinburgh and had himself studied law in Holland at Leyden. Scottish law was very different from English and had its roots in Roman law which the Dutch observed. To be accepted at the Scots bar it was necessary to have studied in Holland. Auchinlech had promised his son to finance his stay for one year in Utrecht, thence to Paris and Germany which explains Boswell's willingness to cross the Channel. He had really wanted to stay in London and take a commission in a fashionable regiment which his father had wisely refused to pay for.

expresses surprise when a fourth-rate actress imparts to him a common disease, yet engages in similar pursuits once it is cured.

Boswell is known to us both for his wonderful *Journals* and his *Life of Johnson*. He had first met the great author of the *Dictionary of the English Language* in London in the Spring of 1763, not an auspicious encounter with an initial exchange of banter between them:

BOSWELL: "Indeed I come from Scotland, but I cannot help it."
JOHNSON: "Sir, that I find is what a very great many of your countrymen cannot help."

During Boswell's two years in London he had had lodgings mainly at 10 Downing Street (for forty guineas a year) where, happily for us, his landlord had furnished him with "material for writing in great abundance." The address was a popular one with its close proximity to Westminster and Whitehall and we (and the British Prime Minister) must be grateful for its longevity.

Johnson grew to like Boswell, even to rely on the younger man to help him get about London, encumbered as he was by persistent gout. He even comes to Harwich to see Boswell off on his packet boat:

"As the vessel put out to sea, I kept my eyes on him for a considerable time, while he remained rolling his majestic frame in his usual manner; and at last I perceived him walk back into the town, and he disappeared."

At Utrecht Boswell lost no time in calling on the best families, of which the van Tuylls were in the forefront. Monsieur van Tuyll particularly approved of the young Scotsman, probably for his lineage as much as his eligibility as a possible *épouseur* [suitor].

The first meeting with Belle took place on 31 October 1763 and his *Journal (Boswell in Holland), 1763–1764* for that day records:

> "And yet just now a Utrecht lady's charms
> Make my gay bosom beat with love's alarms."

Boswell's *Journals* are of course our means of knowing him so well – a depressive, hypochondriac, naif, self-obsessed, vain and of course a libertine who, to give him credit, tried very hard in Holland to contain these particular impulses. His excesses in London, and resultant diseases, had inspired in him a new caution in these pursuits. He was now more interested in finding a wife who could accompany him in due course in his Scottish castle as Lady Auchinlech. Might Belle be suitable? It takes him four years to find out.

Belle herself seems to have known from the outset that Boswell was perfect for her as an epistolary friend with literary skills, whom she could tempt and mock for his gaucherie, as yet another correspondent for her endless letters. As with d'Hermenches, she preferred distance between her and her suitors. And, also as with d'Hermenches, Belle and Boswell interwove fact and fiction in all they wrote. It was how they saw themselves and not as they really were which is foremost in their letters. Boswell long term was not for her (nor she for him) but Belle tolerates his arrogance and simply laughs at it. Their correspondence is to last four years with many breaks and vicissitudes. He cannot understand why she cannot be more "*retenue* [reserved];" why she has to frighten him with her exaggerated remarks; why she loves metaphysics whereas he likes sober thoughts; why she cannot be more like the frumpish Scottish wife he finally marries and who turns a loving blind eye to his misdemeanours amongst the ladies of Edinburgh.

His *Journal* is full of self-admonishments. Be *retenu*. Be Johnson (i.e. be soberly mature). Pursue Plan (orders that he addresses to himself which more often than not he fails to follow). Much of this moralising is written to Belle when he has left Utrecht for

Germany and he had (at least at this point) put her on his list of possible wives. He is really pleading with her to be more decorous and less outspoken.

All of this she finds vastly amusing, and even more so when he starts to woo her rather more earnestly:

> She writes: "You appeared to me to be experiencing the agitation of a lover."
>
> "You believe that … a woman such as I am, might be weak; I believe you are mistaken."
>
> "If you wish me to love you always, the only way is to be always lovable."
>
> "But I am not in love with you. I swear to you I am not."
>
> "I have no talent for being subservient."

She horrifies him by saying she would prefer a husband who treats her more like a mistress and a husband who beats her rather than one who sulks. She tells him "I have no regard for dignity, and I despise the art which you revere so much." But she also tells him that he is "odd and lovable," and "I have indeed much feeling for you." She is playing the age-old feminine card of attracting and rejecting a suitor, a push-pull action which he finds quite impossible to understand and deal with. She attracts him hugely yet both frightens him and frightens him off.

Boswell even writes to Belle's father with a circumlocutory offer of marriage to her, exacting various conditions:

> "I should require … that she would always remain faithful."
>
> "She would neither publish … any of her literary compositions if disapproved of by her husband."
>
> "But I will enter into an agreement with her to maintain a decent composure, a certain reserve even, before the world."

Belle, not unnaturally, tells Boswell she would not marry him if he were the last man on earth but they agree to continue writing to each other. Belle may let suitors escape but always insists on retaining them as correspondents.

Poor Monsieur de Tuyll, being confronted by Boswell's haughty letter, exercised his great tact and politely replied that he could not judge of their happiness together in the future but that nothing could be done in the matter for the moment because Bellegarde's proposal of marriage was still on the table.

Boswell's father heartily disapproved of Belle, judging accurately that she would have been a disaster in Edinburgh society. He is an ever-present *eminence gris* to the son in his travels and they write to each other regularly. Now that Boswell is leading a more assiduous life, with his legal studies and his search for a wife, so that he may follow in his father's footsteps as a settled man of the law with a reliable wife by his side, so is the father now affectionate towards him. He gives his son good advice but cautions: "Your being a good speaker is of no import if you have nothing useful to say."

On 18 June 1764 Boswell departs for Germany and is now embarked on his Grand Tour. This takes him to many countries: Switzerland, Italy, Corsica, France. In Potsdam he meets the Count d'Anhalt, a rejected suitor and tells Belle he might have provided her with a good husband – very *"prévenant* [obliging]," rather a barbed compliment. Boswell still keeps Belle in mind as a wife although, perhaps released from Utrecht, he contemplates with anticipation "to have fine Saxon girls."

We cannot accompany Boswell further on his travels, nor continue to quote misleading letters from one to the other, but we

Plate IV: James Boswell, painted 1765 by George Willison when Boswell was 25. He and Belle were both only 20 when they first met in Utrecht.
National Gallery of Scotland

may perhaps report that he visits Neuchâtel to meet Belle's old governess, Mlle Prevost, from whom he learns terrible things. In her early years Belle wrote "shocking fables", and later called the libertine d'Hermenches "her generous friend." All of which is too much for the ambivalent Boswell who now sees Belle as "a vapourish, unprincipled girl" and is now "happy not to be connected with her."

CHAPTER FIVE

VISIT TO ENGLAND

I N N O V E M B E R 1766, aged 26 and depressed at the serried ranks of inconclusive suitors, Belle is packed off to England where she is to spend six months; happily, it seems, and accompanied for appearances' sake by Ditie (her much loved younger brother) and a German maid. She has been invited initially by a General and Mrs Eliott of Curzon Street, London who arranged that she should be presented at Court. There she forgets to address King George III as "Sire." In the gallery of the House of Lords she comments that the speeches are "rather adolescent and lacking in eloquence." *Plus ça change?*

Belle much admires the Eliott's marriage – based on politeness one to the other. Belle is particularly impressed by the attention paid to his wife by the grizzled soldier who is amiable and considerate. They dislike society and abhor the beau monde. Belle may be learning something about herself here because it is about now that she starts to view Monsieur de Charrière as a possible husband who seems to have many of the attributes of General Eliott. Dull but polite and reliable and above all kindly to his wife.

She frequents dinners, balls, assemblies. A certain Lord March importunes her and tries to persuade her into his carriage; she is appreciated for her wit and beauty and soon speaks English so well that she is asked whether she can speak French! She is jostled at the opera by raucous young men; she is something of a threat to high society wives because her lively *bel esprit* manner attracts the husbands who misjudge this liveliness as *libertinage*. She is reprimanded and told to be more *retenue*. She likes the lack of gallantry in the men and the fact that people say what they mean and, if they have nothing to say, remain silent. She finds the *grandes dames* to be reserved and sullen, but points out that the men are used to this. One quite sees that Belle must have been a striking antidote to the boredom of the gatherings that she attended. It is said that George III warned an ambassadress that Belle was receiving too much attention from her husband. She sees David Garrick on stage and admires him greatly. She meets and dines with David Hume, the philosopher, and is surprised that he prefers to talk about roast beef and Yorkshire pudding.

Boswell was in Scotland at the same time that Belle was in England and neither tried to contact the other, which only underlines the real distance that has now grown up between them. On the other hand she writes regularly to d'Hermenches and it is these letters that tell us about her English sojourn. He replies rather sourly that he cannot imagine how she can be enjoying herself in such a country.

In March Belle moves to Ongar in Surrey to stay with distant cousins, the Bentincks. Mrs Bentinck had been a van Tuyll. Belle is struck by the beauty of the countryside: Savoy and Geneva may have more picturesque landscapes but here nature is "smiling and adorned."

The English visit was therapeutic. She had not had to worry about marriage – there were no suitors in England. Back to Utrecht, though, and the worries would return.

CHAPTER SIX

MARIAGE DE CONVENANCE

L IKE A HOUSEBOUND FLY that buzzes round a room looking for a way of escape there now appears the most reluctant suitor of them all – Monsieur de Charrière. Of all the rather improbable candidates who presented themselves to the van Tuylls, Charles-Emmanuel de Charrière de Penthaz was certainly the most improbable. Born in 1735 he was therefore five years Belle's senior; he had been tutor to the children at Zuylen from 1763 so by 1766 she had known him for three years. 25 January 1770 is the first mention Belle makes of Charles (to her brother Ditie):

> "I took occasion to speak to my father about de Charrière: my father is not scornful of this proposal."

They were to be married, as we shall see, 17 February 1771, so Charles had known her eight years of which perhaps five were spent in very hesitant wooing before he was to appear at the altar. But who wooed whom?! His great reluctance to be considered by Belle as her swain was due partly to his observance of the fate of other suitors; partly to his inferiority complex when he compared himself with august personages such as the Count d'Anhalt or the splendid uniforms of such as the Marquis de Bellegarde.

Charles de Charrière, on the other hand, came from a minor though noble family from the Vaud in Switzerland and had been born in the ancestral home at Colombier, three miles from Neuchâtel, where he had spent his entire life so far. He stuttered, he was small, unprepossessing, shy, and preferred not to be noticed. He had, however, that most important characteristic for Belle – he was transparently honest. He had none of the false gallantry she so despised; he was very well educated as befitted the tutor to the family; she knew that if secured as her husband he would never step out of line or seek amorous adventures. Thus she started to ensnare him through her formidable weapon she used against all men who interested her – an exchange of letters, preferably clandestine.

The first recorded letter from Charles to Belle, written from Colombier, is dated 7 July 1766:

> "Mademoiselle, you are amazing! Why do you recall memories that you have forbidden me to retain? How can you say that you are my friend when you disturb me by showing me how much better it would be if you could be something more to me?"

And he goes on to reminisce about a midnight meeting in her bedroom when they talked "tête-à-tête." He pleads that when he returns to Zuylen they should have no more late night meetings "unless she wishes to take things further." These words of course mean "marriage" and not "be my mistress." He tells her that his great admiration of her, his friendship for her will last for all of his life. And, pathetically, he begs that they *should* meet again at midnight! So we can see the housefly buzzing desperately and failing to find any escape. He is confined to the castle of Zuylen and must suffer his years there until he is accepted as a reluctant husband.

It has become the fashion to see Charles de Charrière as a fig-

ure of fun and a poor choice for Belle as a husband; but I believe
him to have been the right choice for her. As we shall see later in
her life in the sleepy little town of Neuchâtel, where the beau
monde was noticeably absent, she accepted her isolation from
most things worldly and concentrated energetically on creative
thinking and writing – of which we are the grateful beneficiaries.
Charles provided the home and the stability which allowed her to
create so tempestuously. He made few demands on her; he wor-
shipped her. I believe she was as happy in these circumstances as
her nervous disposition would allow. None of those degenerate
suitors could have given her the security she enjoyed at Le Pontet. We shall judge more of this later.

Meanwhile poor Charles has to witness the antics of Bellegarde who is still exercising his stop-go movements. Yet another
suitor appears from Germany only to be rejected. Belle is free-
wheeling at this time, not as desperate as in the past to find a solution to her marriage problems. Charles is obviously being held in
reserve. She has her portrait painted at this time by Quentin de la
Tour (see frontispiece and cover). Two further suitors are held up
for examination – a Count Wittgenstein and a Lord Wemyss, the
latter a dissolute fortune-hunter – and rejected. On 13 April 1770
Belle admits to d'Hermenches that another man has caught her
imagination but she does not name Charles. She is obviously
fearful of his response with all his caustic irony and selfish *amour
propre*. We saw earlier that at about this same time she wrote to
her brother Ditie (25 January 1770) that she had broached the
subject of de Charrière to her father who was "not scornful of
this proposal". So Charles is edging to the forefront.

To d'Hermenches she now admits that her anonymous swain
"… has a demeanour that is noble and interesting" and then
spoils it by adding "… but rather awkward." She says that they
are exchanging letters which is increasing their "animation". We
may judge here that their close proximity to each other at Zuylen,

whilst often exchanging letters, is proof again of Belle's preferred method of converse. But this time there is no room for dissimulation as we have seen with d'Hermenches and Boswell. She and Charles are living side by side and know the real truth about each other. Reality is now to the fore.

Belle continues to report to d'Hermenches, amazing though it may seem, and speaks of the responses of the unknown man due to their mutual "animation". Charles, she says, thinks that a marriage between them would be:

> "… the worst thing in the world … I have neither rank nor fortune, I am only a poor gentleman … I have insufficient merit to compensate for the sacrifice you would be making … your attachment is not of the sort that could be sustained … you take as love a passing fancy of your imagination … a few months of marriage will disabuse you of this … you will be unhappy which you will pretend not to be and I will be even more unhappy than you are."

Were there ever words of such crystal clear thinking and such sad expectation? Was the fly not buzzing to increasing little effect?

Charles leaves Zuylen for Neuchâtel in the late summer of 1769. There are still 15 months or so to go before their marriage and the other candidates have still to appear and disappear, namely Wittgenstein and Wemyss. Incredibly, de Charrière is asked to report on the latter who has spent time in Neuchâtel and was known locally to be "debauched, irascible, despotic." Charles advises her to concentrate on Wittgenstein but she replies to d'Hermenches "… it is too late … my mind is made up … all that you say [about other suitors] makes no impression on me." We can see that d'Hermenches is privy to all the intricate goings-on at Zuylen, he is spying all of this from the sidelines and is a *voyeur* with a ringside seat. Predictably, he is very rude to her about de Charrière when his identity is finally revealed. He now presses the suit of Wittgenstein in preference to de Charrière. Charles writes to Belle from Neuchâtel chiefly on the subject of his chickens " … the best cockerel was stolen." In this *opéra bouffe* Charles is assuredly the jester.

Monsieur van Tuyll had been distinctly lukewarm , although accepting of the suit of Charles. Belle's father cannot be blamed for preferring one of her other suitors, however: class, rank, her place in society, the others all offered these advantages even if half of them were dissolute and rakes and the other half fortune-seekers and insensitive. De Charrière was clearly *faute de mieux*. The showdown came when Wittgenstein absented himself to Corsica to fight a war. Wemyss was still a possible suitor but with such a blackened reputation even Monsieur van Tuyll thought twice about him. De Charrière was left on the stage alone and by December 1770 Belle's father had agreed to the match. One last riposte lay with d'Hermenches. He had decided to divorce his wife and offered himself obliquely to Belle. But he was too late. She had decided on the *faute de mieux*. She is 31, rising 32. It is time to settle down – whatever the consequences. Time to leave the Holland she abhors. Time to speak and write in French, her preferred language.

We have a valuable letter from Charles to a cousin in which he speaks of the "novel of his marriage … and that he has known Belle seven years" and that he has tried to dissuade her from this step but that "she persists in believing that she will be happy living peacefully with me in Switzerland." How he has tried – but failed to escape. He writes in the same letter that Belle "… has too much spirit, is too highly born, is too rich …" He will be proved partly right, partly wrong. His admiration for her is manifest and this, with his tolerance, will hold them together – *just!* Both tell the other that they may withdraw from their engagement right up to the altar (shades of *Caliste*). The contract was signed in January. They were married 17 February 1771 in the small church at Zuylen.

The good burghers of Utrecht are speechless with amazement at the incongruity of this marriage. But then it is remembered that Belle had always affronted public opinion and the ladies of the *salons* were not sorry to see this gadfly take to her wings and leave them in peace.

On their wedding day the bride had toothache and the groom was ill from an excess of punch. There is an irony there somewhere – and a presage of things to come?

CHAPTER SEVEN

COLOMBIER

T HEY SPEND THEIR first six months at Zuylen. She is suffering from various ailments which puts rather a damper on their early days of marriage. "I have changed my name and do not always sleep alone, that is the only difference …" she writes to Ditie. Charles is rather too "*ordentlik* [methodical]" and she admits that often he finds her too much to the contrary. But he is attentive and kind and her love is deepening.

Their marriage is really to be a matter of swings and roundabouts. He has exchanged a bachelor's life of small dimensions for a lifetime with a highly strung woman way above him in just about everything. She has escaped from the mists of Utrecht and the chill of the parental home to be with a man she both admires and of whom she is also severely critical. But within these confines the marriage of convenience operates tolerably well – and certainly a great deal better than if she had succumbed to one of those ferocious, worldly aristocrats. For she has always said that she prefers "*les petits gens* [the small people]." As their life together develops for the next 34 years we shall see how they care for each other increasingly; with blimps of course, but with a steady increase in companionable affection. Belle will continue to be the wild one and he her tame worshipper but no one else could have survived Belle except Charles though we shall never know what might have happened if she had married the divorced d'Hermenches. There would have been a quite different plane of priorities: competitiveness one against the other, inhabiting high society where pomp and circumstance reigned and which Belle would have loathed and run away from. The marriage bed with d'Hermenches might have proved to be a disappointment since his reputation for amorous encounters had always been considered to be greater in the telling than in the text.

Monsieur and Madame de Charrière meanwhile still avoided Colombier initially and left for Paris on 19 July 1771. Here Belle complains that there are few people in town, they are all in the country, but she makes do with one or two friends of her husband's. They remain two months. She is sketched afresh by la Tour and Houdon executes her bust (see Plate X, p.53). The theatres are closed, she is bored, it is time to leave for Le Pontet – and make the best of it.

The family house had been built in 1614 and was surrounded by its own vineyards, indeed wine was one important source of income. Two resident spinster sisters awaited her: Louise, the elder, liked by all, including Belle, who looked after the garden. And Henriette, critical of everything and everyone, disliked by all, who acted as housekeeper. Charles's old father lived inconspicuously upstairs, a semi-invalid who survived until 1780. The two spinsters outlived Belle which is perhaps unsurprising given their monotonous lives when compared to the furious intellectual pace to be set by Belle.

Belle gardens and washes garments at the fountain. She retails this to d'Hermenches who retorts that her "*bel esprit*" is being wasted and that her teeth and hair will fall out from sheer boredom. She paints, cooks, cuts out silhouettes. Her writing will come later.

Local friends start to multiply: the brothers Chaillet; Chambrier d'Oleyres; Du Peyrou , who becomes her mentor for her writings and on whose opinion she relies heavily. She even meets d'Hermenches's wife in Lausanne which does not seem to have been acrimonious. She consults the doctors as to her inability to get pregnant and takes the waters in several spas to quieten her nerves, seen by the doctors as a prime reason for her infertility. Dr Tissot says that the two are linked and his word is law amongst the fashionable local gentry. For five years she struggles to have a child, without success, which is a great sadness to them both. In three of our four novels children play an important role, as does pregnancy – as a catharsis? Ill-health continues to plague her (she calls it her "vapours," that reliable eighteenth century term).

Correspondence with d'Hermenches flags and peters out in 1776. They have been writing to each other for sixteen years. Now she is a respectable married woman and all traces of *"libertinage"* have been excised from her own letters for some years though he has references now and again to "what might have been." His divorce had been finalised in 1772 and he berates her now and again for not having waited for him but she, in her wisdom, had really always known him to be only a "letter-lover" and never the real thing. Indeed she asks for her letters back and he prevaricates and holds on to them for which we must be grateful indeed. Significantly, he tells her "... *vos lettres méritent de passer à la postérité* [your letters deserve to remain for posterity]." He remarried (a widow aged 54 who bore him a son and died shortly thereafter). D'Hermenches was to die in Paris aged 63 in 1785.

Belle is adapting both to life within the confines of Le Pontet and Neuchâtel itself. She goes to balls, plays, observes the people and *Lettres Neuchâteloises* will be the outcome later on. She is amused at the democratic way in which the peasants share out the horse droppings that fall on the roads, to put them round their vines. Her beloved brother Ditie dies and she is distraught.

The "young Chaillet" is the younger of the brothers referred to earlier. He is the Suffragen minister at Colombier and lives a quarter of an hour's walk from Le Pontet. A frequent visitor to the de Charrière household, he relishes their good table and company. He also keeps a daily journal and we know from this a great deal of what occurs in the household. From 1775 he visits the family daily. He is the editor of the *Mercure Suisse* which is damned by Rousseau. He is a penetrating journalist whom Belle respects and whose presence she needs in order to sharpen her wits – and vice versa. He also needs the small sums he invariably wins off Charles at piquet. His writing was microscopic and so was his mind. He is allowed the run of the library at Le Pontet.

In 1776 Belle's father dies, severing her last ties with Holland to which she never returned. She visits Voltaire at Ferney but he is disgruntled that day and she does not have the tête-à-tête she had counted on.

Belle and Charles are often on the move. They buy an apartment in Geneva and visit it often, enjoying the beau monde there which is somewhat more sophisticated than in Neuchâtel. Her restless spirit is now held in check and decorum is to the fore. She moves in and out of society in Neuchâtel where she is much feted and admired. By 1784 she tires of all this "dissipation" and the satirical novels start to be written and published. In Chapter 12 we shall discuss the furore caused by *Letters from Neuchâtel*. Visitors to Le Pontet comment on Charles's erudition, especially in science, and Belle's charm as a hostess, but her acerbity is noted

Plate V (a): Top: Le Pontet, Colombier. From a contemporary drawing.
Private collection
Plate V (b): Bottom: Colombier village *circa* 1830 beside the lake of
Neuchâtel. Le Pontet is below the castle on the hill to the left.
Private collection

Plate VI: Four silhouettes by Madomoisel Moula.

(a) Local worthies taking tea.

(b) Louise de Charrière, the gardening sister of Charles.

(c) Benjamin Constant, 1762, aged 25 whe this silhoutte was cut at Le Pontet. Note tl ungainly posture.

(d) Belle aged 48. She sent this likeness to Benjamin de Constant in 1788 when he wa 21. He wrote to her "... *Quand vous sourie il y règne un heureux mélange de douceur et de vivacité* ... [when you smile there is present a happy marriage of gentleness an animation...]

Bibliothèque publique et Universitaire, Neuchâtel

towards local people. A Mademoiselle Moula is a frequent visitor and cuts out skilful silhouettes (see Plate VI, pp. 34–5).

Belle's nerves are giving trouble. She travels hither and thither to take the waters but finds little alleviation. Chaillet considers she needs to be loved passionately – what perceptiveness from a cleric! She rents for three months a château at Chexbres, quite alone. This saddens her husband who visits and writes poignantly that he and his family at Le Pontet are indeed infuriating for her to live with, and apologises for this. It is the first visible crack in their relationship. Her meeting with the young Benjamin Constant widens that fissure as we shall see in the next chapter.

We are now in 1784 and should note that *Lettres Neuchâteloises* and *Mistriss Henley* were both published this year. The novels and her writing generally have now begun. It was inevitable that when the marriage cooled she needed to write in order to find solace and as an antidote to the boredom of the daily round at Le Pontet.

CHAPTER EIGHT

PARIS AND BENJAMIN CONSTANT

I N 1786 MONSIEUR DE CHARRIÈRE decided that, after 15 years of marriage, they needed a change of some magnitude. Paris beckoned and they were to be there for a year and a half. Belle was now 46. Her novel-writing was at its height and her fame spreading. Three of our novels had been written and published, the fourth, *Caliste*, was written in Paris and followed in 1788. This last work caused her the greatest pain to write. "I have never had the courage to re-read *Caliste*; it cost me too many tears to write." An "*inconnu* [unidentified]" young man of Geneva whom she had met there had provided the spark that ignited this second part of *Letters from Lausanne*. Charles de Charrière obviously thought it wise for them to leave Switzerland behind them for a while. They were to be in Paris from February 1786 to August 1787. Colombier with its enclosed daily round and its two fussy spinsters was to be exchanged for the excitement and culture of the enchanted city where Belle would surely flourish and shed her vapours.

But another young man was waiting for them in Paris. Benjamin Constant was the nephew of Belle's first love – d'Hermenches – aged just 20 to her 47 when they met. Benjamin was tall and lanky and his silhouette (Plate VI) shows that his stomach protruded and he hunched his shoulders. Among the foppish gallants at the *salon* where he and Belle first met Benjamin appeared as gauche, awkward and ill-at-ease. His appearance and manner, not to mention his lineage, made an immediate impact on Belle; she remembered her opening remark to his uncle "*Monsieur, vous ne dansez pas?* [Sir, do you not dance?]." She remembered also her words written later to Benjamin's uncle that with their first words they quarreled but with their next they were friends for life. It was ten years since she had corresponded with the uncle but the memory remained. Her new friendship with the nephew was to endure for 18 years until her death in 1805.

During these next 18 years we can follow their relationship through their exchange of letters. This was the most endearing of all her friendships and it has many strands: teacher-pupil; mother-son; lover-*inamorato*; protectress-protected. Benjamin above all needed sympathetic encouragement, a mentor, an admirer, in contrast to his elderly grandmother who had brought him up in Lausanne and a father who lashed him with his military tongue. The stage was set for Belle to pick up the pieces and make a man of Benjamin. He had not experienced such a forceful personality before and they spent long hours talking far into the night with Charles snoring contentedly next door, resigned to his wife's new friendship which has fired her up into the Zélide that he remembered and loved. He must have reflected that he had made the correct decision in coming to Paris.

Benjamin meanwhile is ordered by his father, the Colonel, to think seriously of marriage and to settle down preferably with a rich wife whose dowry and income could cope with the gambling debts that he himself had incurred. There are also rumours that Benjamin has been seeing too much of a married woman from Neuchâtel. A Mlle Pourrat, aged 16, was an heiress and pretty – might Benjamin not secure that refuge for all their troubles? Benjamin is not averse to this idea but learns that the girl is already affianced. Benjamin persists in his approaches, encouraged by Belle and especially by Charles who had good reason to want him married. The relationship between his wife and Benjamin was perhaps gaining too much strength. This confusing situation with Mlle Pourrat became known as "*le dédoublement Constantien* [a two-sided problem]." The word *dédoublement* has passed into the French language and is now a psychological term. In the present scene Benjamin continues his pursuit of Mlle Pourrat whilst knowing full well that she was unprocurable.

Benjamin flees to England to escape the clutches of his father who has sent for him to explain his ineptness in the marriage market. The young man writes to Belle "Love me in spite of my follies; I am a good devil at bottom." In London he hoped to recoup a debt from, we learn, a Mr Edmund Lascelles who said that, regretfully, he had no memory of such a debt. Benjamin finds himself eventually in Boswell's old town of Edinburgh where he makes merry with old student friends. Belle reflects that the two young men in her life whom she really loved – both incongruous and absurd – found themselves in the same town at the same time though they did not meet. Belle has told Benjamin of Boswell's vanity and when Benjamin looks at himself in the glass he exclaims "Oh! Jemmy Boswell!"

Returning from England on his "extremely small white horse, hideously ugly and very old", his only companion is a cur that trots at his heels until, on the Dover road, the cur expires with exhaustion. Benjamin is now obeying a summons by his father to return to him in France. His father, the Colonel, is playing whist on his arrival with three officers of his regiment and greets his son with "Is that you? You must be tired. Go to bed." So much for parental affection. Benjamin stays three days but their converse is strained and sparse. Thankfully, Benjamin leaves for Switzerland and arrives at Colombier on foot. It is 3 October

1787. He had come home, the only home he had ever known, and his friend-mother-teacher-lover awaited him. It was to be the first of many visits. Benjamin's first meeting with Belle and his subsequent adventures in England on his small white horse are told in his *Cahier Rouge*.

His father now commanded that Benjamin should go to Lausanne to be observed and guided by various relatives, following which he should repair to the Court at Brunswick where he had procured for his son the post of Chamberlain. Benjamin, true to form, disobeys his father and returns instead to Colombier where he stays for a couple of months.

Belle and Benjamin worked at opposite ends of the same table. He was engaged in a history of religions, she on her papers and her novels.

But Brunswick now beckoned. The furious father insisted that his son's *liaison* with "that woman" must cease. Benjamin writes to Belle dolefully from Basle: "... *si on ne rend la vie trop dure, j'ai une retraite à Colombier* [... if life becomes too hard, I will always have a retreat at Colombier]." He begs her to thank Charles for his kindnesses towards him. Monsieur de Charrière was in fact extremely fond of the wayward youth in whom he saw something of a son. Belle and he push him on his way to Brunswick assuring him that he will have a full life to lead and will forget all about them. He remonstrates that no *fräulein* can or will replace *her*. Benjamin at this point is undoubtedly panic-stricken at leaving Colombier and clutching at straws he goes so far as to suggest

Plate VII: Benjamin Constant aged 20, when he first met Belle aged 47 in Paris in 1786. From a contemporary miniature on ivory. Their intimacy was to last 8 years. Benjamin was a frequent visitor at Le Pontet until he encountered the redoubtable Madame de Staël and took up the cause of the French Revolution.

elopement to Belle – they can live happily together in Paris or London, and if he should predecease her she can always return to the bosom of her family! He likens her to her own *Caliste*. She reproves him gently and wisely refuses his offer.

In Brunswick Benjamin soon suffers from the stiff etiquette of the Court. The Duke, nephew of Frederick the Great, is a good all-round man and administrator but is surrounded by a coterie of elderly sycophants whom Benjamin finds just as ignorant as the young courtiers and "stiff to boot". He says he only speaks to young women under 30 which causes Belle some misgivings, rightly as it turns out because on 8 September 1788 he writes that he has become engaged to a Wilhelmina von Cramm. Interestingly, Belle writes to Benjamin in English. "You are an odd sort of a man. I talk of your Minna, but not a word in answer …"

Benjamin's family circle had been disrupted by the headstrong Colonel being at odds with his own soldiers. He had brought a legal action against them for mutiny. The Court had found against him but instead of waiting for judgement he had fled and disappeared. He had another dozen law suits extant and the family was now clearly penniless. It behoved Benjamin to find a rich wife and Minna von Cramm was on offer, 8 years older than Benjamin but a favourite at the Court in Brunswick.

Benjamin marries his Minna, Belle receives them both gracefully at Colombier; their correspondence lessens, then ceases, and we shall not take it up again for some time. Meanwhile, such is the coolness now manifested between them that they ask each other to burn their letters. They compromise and each burns only some of them, luckily for us. We are now at September 1789 and the French Revolution approaches. So does Madame de Staël who is to remove Benjamin from Belle's hearth – and heart.

CHAPTER NINE

BELLE AS MUSICIAN AND TEACHER

A S W E L L A S T H E stream of literary work that poured from her pen, music composition remained important to her right to the end of her life.* In Paris in 1786 she took lessons in composition from a certain Florido Tomeoni; she practised many hours a day on her harpsichord, a habit she never lost, and launched into music composition which included minuets and trios not only for the harpsichord but also for the violin. Operas, both librettos and music, were composed by her though there is no record of any of them being performed. Another Italian, Niccolo Zingarelli, well known conductor of the Naples orchestra, helped her to polish and transcribe her pieces and even stayed at Colombier where he was a much-revered guest. One opera which has not survived included a full ballet! This was *Polyprène ou le Cyclope* [Polyphemus or the Cyclop]. Another opera, *Zadig* was based on the *conte* by Voltaire and tremendous efforts were made to have it performed in Turin, alas to no avail.

It is generally considered today that none of her music was any better than the conventional compositions of the period. She was not discouraged at her relative failure in the world of music,

---

*   Cf Caliste's death.

relative that is to her literary fame which was by now an established fact. Certainly her operas caused her greater difficulty and time in their composition than did her novels. *Caliste* was written in six weeks. But music was a life blood to Belle and because it represented more of a challenge to her than her written work, so she gave it more of her indefatigable energy. Her music went unsigned, except a jolly little air which reverberated round the *salons* of the Suisse Romande:

> "*L'amour est un enfant trompeur*
> *me dit un jour ma mère* ...
> [love is a deceitful child
> said my mother to me one day ...]."

And as the composer of that little ditty Belle must have written it from her heart.

After her stay in Paris she returned to Colombier, in 1787, and was not to leave it until her death in 1805. These 18 years were less productive in literary and musical output and were given over largely to the care and teaching of her young student-maids. For Belle to survive in the frowsty atmosphere of Le Pontet, especially now that Benjamin Constant had gone, she had to adapt herself and her life to the other activity she was supremely good at, namely teaching. She now never took a walk outside the walled garden of Le Pontet. She remained her own prisoner and busied herself with giving advice and instruction to a succession of grateful young females.

We saw that in *Lettres Neuchâteloises* Belle used the pregnancy of her most favoured companion-maid, Henriette Monachon, as a central theme and her protection of Henriette against the Neuchâtel authorities was a fight of epic proportions. Henri-

Plate VIII: Henriette L'Hardy. Self-portrait. Belle's favourite pupil
Henri L'Hardy, Colombier

ette's second pregnancy was fought with equal dedication though this time the authorities were determined to expel mother and child from the precincts of Neuchâtel. She duly departed but was allowed back after a spell of exile and in due course married a widower with two children. She had served Belle as companion-maid from 1788 to1800 and had been more friend than servant. It is said that they read Locke together. Belle always said that she deferred frequently to Henriette: when she was in the wrong over something she gave in to the maid – and vice versa. That degree of latitude was rare in a well-ordered eighteenth century household and indeed there were voices raised against the unprecedented freedom of the Charrière domestics. Even Mlle Louise's voice was raised against Henriette's *second* pregnancy which was considered by all Neuchâtel people to be one step too far. Belle's defence of the maid appalled the locals who ostracised both Belle and Charles for their protection of the maid and even his firm support in all things for his wife wavered a little under the social pressure.

Some say that Belle's appetite for teaching "mars her dogmatic little novels" (thus Geoffrey Scott in *Portrait of Zélide*). This seems to me to be quite wide of the mark. It is exactly the propensity of her heroines to instruct which gives Belle's novels their drive and realism. If we reflect on the forcefulness of her teacher-characters we will take the point: Marianne in *Lettres Neuchâteloises* is very much the leader who instructs the males who surround her; *Mistriss Henley* attempts to inculcate some feeling and direction into her husband without success; in *Lettres de Lausanne* Cécile's mother teaches her daughter interminably

Previous two pages: Plate IX (a): Charles-Emmanuel de Charrière.
Plate IX (b) Isabelle de Charrière.
From miniatures attributed to Arlaud.
Bibliothèque publique et Universitaire, Neuchâtel

and those around her; and *Caliste* strives valiantly to put some backbone into William.

Belle's advice to her brother Vincent in Holland was to send his son Willem René to Eton, though aware of its great expense! There he would receive the best instruction from the best teachers but her advice is not followed. Later on she receives her nephew at Le Pontet, in 1799, and he stays with her for a year and benefits from her disciplined course of studies. Even before he arrived she had warned him that she would "*op winderai* [wind him up]," and that she was herself a good "winder-upper." In English she wrote to him that she was a "teaching devil," so he had been warned. He writes home that she is exceedingly amiable and neither pedantic nor severe. She tells him that in a single year she has taught English to three people. He is made to rise at 6 a.m. and after a glass of milk (only, no breakfast) he is called to her bedside to read the paper to her from which he himself presumably benefits. Lunch is at one o'clock sharp, there is an English lesson thereafter and supper is at 9 p.m. His teaching programme is laid out with precision:

(a)   50-100 pages of history read in French (each day).
(b)   Ten to a dozen pages read in Dutch of which one or two
        pages should be translated into French with corrections
        by Belle, the fair copy then to be transcribed by her pupil.
(c)   There are specific instructions as to his reading of poetry
        and literature.

Even when Willem René leaves her to return to Holland via Paris she directs his steps there: one evening at the opera, one at the Comédie Française, and so on. He is to call on Benjamin Constant but on no account to call on Madame de Staël.

A remarkable student was a fourteen-year old Marianne Ustrich, born to a peasant woman but with an Austrian father of noble birth; neglected, penniless, driven to herd goats for her sustenance, but with a remarkable appetite for self-instruction. She read Fénélon's *Télemaque* at the age of 11. The child is brought into the household at Le Pontet to learn sewing and a servant's duties, including that of a pastry cook at which she excels. Belle arranges for her to move to Munich as a cook and remembers her in her will.

Henriette L'Hardy (Plate VIII) was the most important "daughter" to grace Le Pontet other than Henriette von Machon. This Henriette reminds Belle of a van Dyck portrait and she busies herself in trying to find her a husband. There is vague talk of Constant as a swain, but in the meanwhile Belle arranges that she should be lady-companion to the Countess Dönhoff, morganatic wife of Frederick, King of Prussia. Frederick approves this choice and Henriette is a success. She and Belle correspond regularly. Belle advises the girl on etiquette and sends a reading list of worthwhile books to be read. Regrettably, the Countess falls out of favour with the King for having dabbled in politics. She leaves Germany with Henriette and they repair to Switzerland where they visit Le Pontet and are examined with care by Belle. She finds the Countess beautiful but vapid. Henriette is enjoined to write her memoirs, under Belle's guidance of course, which is eventually published under the title *Mes Souvenirs sur Berlin*.

And lastly, the beautiful Isabelle de Gélieu who was also the most interesting and intellectual. She was 19 years of age when she met Belle. Coming from a literary family she sent Belle some verses she had composed at the age of 16 to which Belle retaliates also in verse. The two were to be friends for life. She became a regular visitor to Le Pontet and by October 1795 they were writing to each other in English, so much so that they were to combine in translating an English book *Nature and Art* into French. They then cooperated in *Louise et Albert* which is a variant on *Mistriss Henley*. Belle always said the work was largely by Gélieu: "Albert and Louise are her children but my godchildren." She exhorts the young girl to "read, think, write – and come often to see me."

Getting de Gélieu married proves to be an *embarras de choix* [an excess of choice]. Three men are after her hand at the same time with Belle privy to every move made by each and thoroughly enjoying the confusion. The three suitors vie for Isabelle's hand. Belle favours a parson with a good income to whom de Gélieu is finally married in 1801. Belle was now 61 and was known to be content at the outcome.

CHAPTER TEN

MADAME DE STAËL AND THE
FRENCH REVOLUTION

W E MUST GO BACK TO 1789 when Benjamin Constant married his Minnie and a cloud inevitably passed over the friendship between Benjamin and Belle. Forward to 1794 and Benjamin's divorce from Minna improved their relationship until the fateful date of 18 September that year when Benjamin met Germaine de Staël. And what a meeting! She picks him up when he is walking on the road near her house, Le Coppet near Lausanne; she takes him home and he writes to Belle – rather unwisely? – that he had breakfasted, dined, supped, then breakfasted again at Le Coppet. Belle draws her own conclusions from this and is furious. Benjamin had indeed fallen for Madame de Staël. He writes to Belle that Germaine is the "second woman I have found for whom I would exchange the world – and you know who is the first." This scarcely mollifies Belle. She is 54; Benjamin is 26; Germaine is 28. Belle can hardly compete.

Madame de Staël had in fact called to see Belle a year earlier,

Plate X: Isabelle de Charrière, from a plaster bust by Houdon, 1771, when she
was 31 and had just moved from Utrecht to Neuchâtel.
Musée d'art et histoire, Neuchâtel

curious to see the author of *Lettres Neuchâteloises* and *Caliste* and wanting Belle to intercede with the King of Prussia over an *émigré*. During that visit Germaine proved to Belle that their views and characters were vastly different and Belle reported : "*Elle a entendu une platitude que je ne disais pas et en a répondu une autre* [She thought she heard a platitude that I had not uttered and answered it with another]." It was all the harder for Belle later to bear the infatuation of Benjamin for the woman who would transport him to Paris and the world of politics, out of the eighteenth century and into the nineteenth. Now Benjamin sports "smoothed hair, yellow trousers and perfume ..." Decidedly not to Belle's taste.

To be fair to Benjamin, he had chafed at the confines of Switzerland and was keen to enter the world's stage. He had passed from Reason and Enlightenment to Romanticism and Extremism, holding de Staël's hand on the way. Across the border in France the Revolution was being enacted with commentary and articles emanating from the de Staël-Constant hideout at Le Coppet. Refugees from the *ancien régime* streamed across the frontier and were often helped by Belle. The stream became a flood after the Fall of the Bastille. Jacobins came to the fore in Neuchâtel itself and wore their distinguishing red bonnets. Belle writes tracts in support of moderation; Charles transcribes these "*jusqu'à se donner la crampe au doits* [to the point where this caused him cramp in his fingers]." Her standpoint was counter-revolutionary. Emigrés were being met with increasing controls as they crossed the border and France even threatened to invade the Principality if their nationals were not better treated.

In May 1795 Benjamin and de Staël leave Lausanne for Paris. Belle writes to Henriette l'Hardy "I wish no harm to the golden

Plate XI: Madame de Staël by Firmin Massot
Château de Coppet

tresses of the one, nor to the black mane of the other, but if some small humiliations should overtake the famous daughter of the celebrated Necker I would certainly not grieve." She has nurtured and fashioned the mind of the youth for eight years, has prepared him for his future as an influential politician in Paris. He was her most successful student. He is to hold office under the Consulate, later to be disbanded by Napoleon. Eventually he will be known only as the author of *Adolphe* and the *Cahier Rouge*, a mere footnote in history.

The complexities of the *pré-Revolution* [forerunner of the Revolution] and the Revolution itself and its aftermath lie outside our biography of Belle, especially as she disliked the intricacies of politics and hardly bothered to understand them. Her political opinions were criticised by a friend and Belle remarked "I wish he would tell me what these are."

CHAPTER ELEVEN

THE FINAL CLIMAX

WE ARE IN 1794 at Colombier. Correspondence with Constant has dwindled to nothing but Belle is still writing philosophical, pedagogic novels such as *Trois Femmes* which flood from her pen but are not well received and nowadays are scarcely reprinted in French, let alone in English. Charles continues to sit in his corner in front of the fire faithfully transcribing her work. They draw closer, husband and wife, as the days lengthen and the young people visiting Le Pontet dwindle to nothing. The household is now on its own and the pace of life lessens. "*A quoi bon?* [what use is it all?]" is a sentence Belle repeats nowadays more often than in the past. Disillusion has set in. Belle writes to Benjamin 20 February 1801 that ... she is rising an hour earlier to read Tacitus ... she shares her midday soup with Miss, their dog ...she may sleep a little with Miss in her arms ... she discusses books with Charles ... he prepares a punch if there are visitors ... she prefers nowadays to sleep in his room at night so she can hear if he stirs ... . Little now disturbs the small momentum of their lives. Henriette Monachon (now Madame Degex) is less than happily married and asks to return to Le Pontet but is firmly refused; Isabelle de Gélieu, as we saw in Chapter IX, involves Belle in her tripartite affairs. Benjamin's cousin, Charles, visits Le Pontet and is saddened at the enforced immobility of Belle and her husband. They are evidently both unwell. The cousin considers that if Monsieur de Charrière were to die first it would destroy Belle.

The gloomy household is enlivened by the arrival of Therese Huber, the fifteen year old daughter of Belle's German translator, Ludwig Huber. *"C'est un joli et doux petit remplissage dans la maison* [she is a pretty and sweet little occupant of the house]" writes Belle. Therese is to be schooled for the post of governess so Belle joyfully returns to her mission as teacher. The household take to the young girl except Henriette, the critical spinster, who "looks at Therese sideways."

Correspondence with Benjamin re-opened. His speeches to the Tribunat are criticised favourably; he is involved in the printing of some of her later works; she relays an account of life at Le Pontet. Meanwhile he has replaced Germaine Staël in his affections by an Irish beauty named Anna Lindsay. He was to be ousted from the Tribunat in January 1802 by Napoleon and never regains a political role. Now letters cease between them until 1805, the year of her death. In April he asks whether he may call at Le Pontet but she puts him off pleading ill health. Her last recorded letter from Le Pontet was to him, dictated to Therese Huber.

> *"Je prétends être mourante; mes amis ne veulent pas juger comme cela parce que je n'ai aucune souffrance qui tue, mais l'extinction de vie me paraît être la mort.*
> [Supposedly I am dying, though my friends believe otherwise since I have no mortal symptoms – but the ceasing of active life seems to me to mean death]."

So life is no longer worth living and this means death. She has reached that point of acceptance. If her energies are to be circumscribed then she of all people must welcome death. This duly occurs on 27 December 1805.

Henriette l'Hardy and Therese Huber were at her bedside when she died. She had not suffered at the end. It seems that the cause of death was a malignant tumour which she had had from the age of 16.

A young minister, Charles Lardy, had a month earlier attempted to convert Belle to the Christian faith but she was "always sceptical." Belle's doubts had never lessened from those early childhood days at Utrecht and were not going to do so now.

At the funeral her coffin was carried by those who worked for the de Charrières in their vineyards. Charles was too ill to attend his wife's funeral. The grave was unmarked, it being the law at that time that no inscriptions should be erected. The cemetery has now been converted into tennis courts, a transformation of which Belle would surely have approved.

Her financial affairs proved to be in disarray. She had been overspending for years, mostly in favour of the various incumbents with whom she surrounded herself. Henriette l'Hardy was appointed executrix of Belle's papers "to sort and keep , give or burn as she shall think fit and so that no one else may read them." It is not known how efficiently these instructions were carried out.

Following Belle's death, there was a farcical event whereby Monsieur de Charrière asked Henriette to marry him. He had always had a penchant for her. Understandably, she refused and a year later married a younger man (24 to her 40). Sadly Henriette died in giving birth to a son. Monsieur de Charrière lived on, by now senile, for two years and died in 1808, aged 73. Louise died aged 80, Henriette aged 74. Le Pontet drifted into disrepair.

Two days before Belle died Benjamin wrote to his aunt: "*Si, comme je pense, on se retrouve dans l'autre monde, Madame de Charrière est une des personnes que j'y chercherai avec le plus d'empressement.* [If, as I believe, we meet again in the next world, Madame

de Charrière is one of those for whom I shall seek with the greatest eagerness]."

Belle had written to Ludwig Huber 5 February 1801: "*La mort
interrompte tout, les bonnes et les mauvaises entreprises. C'est une
grande finisseuse.* [Death interrupts all, both good and bad. It is a
great termination]."

CHAPTER TWELVE

THE NOVELS

I T WILL REPAY READERS to read the novels before reading this chapter so that they can follow the conclusions drawn with greater understanding. For those interested only in the novels themselves, not my conclusions, their translations with my prefaces will be sufficient but my attempt below to appraise her four novels may be useful.

We may start with the letter-form known as epistolary, the form by which the four novels are constructed. Letter-writing was of course the accepted means of communication between friends (and sometimes enemies) and fulfilled the role of the telephone today. Letters were delivered by servants locally at once; state postal systems appear to have achieved same-day delivery or next-day at the latest. Between society hostesses letters passed daily. It was accepted that women were the skilled exponents of writing letters (far superior to men) partly because therein women expressed their feelings more readily than face to face where etiquette demanded formality.

An epistolary novel is "a story written in the form of letters, or letters with journals, and usually presented by an anonymous author masquerading as 'editor'." (*The Oxford Companion to English Literature*). It was exceedingly popular as a literary form and

Belle was one of its greatest exponents. Her skill in letter-writing had been honed, after all, by her long exchange of letters with d'Hermenches, James Boswell and many others and it was but a short step to write and publish her anonymous novels using the same technique.

She will have had many popular novels in letter-form to follow: *Les Liaisons Dangereuses* by de Laclos appeared in 1782; Richardson's *Pamela* in 1740; Rousseau's *Julie ou la nouvelle Eloïse* in 1761. Belle's *Lettres Neuchâteloises* appeared in 1784, the first of our novels discussed below.

We have seen that Belle preferred French both to speak and write – and that Sainte-Beuve described her command of the language as "the French of Versailles." Once in Switzerland she does not seem to have written her native Dutch except to members of her family. Her knowledge of English after her six months' sojourn in England, and much reading in the language, was excellent; her letters, especially to Boswell, are interspersed with English sayings and epigrams which are usually accurate and amusing asides. There is in her French an orderliness (as befits a Dutch-born person with *ordentlik* in her language) and accuracy that is a delight to interpret and translate. Humour, irony are never far from her prose and her "*bel-esprit*" invades all she ever wrote.

The span of her writing was quite amazing: eleven novels, 26 plays, both librettos and scores for operas (many lost), chamber music, innumerable pamphlets both political and literary, and of course her ceaseless letter-writing. Her complete works have now been gathered into ten volumes, published in Amsterdam, prepared by seven editors and issued 1979-84. Her fame and importance have grown in consequence of this attention. Critical appraisals of her work are becoming numerous, especially in America. It seemed the right moment to translate into English at least her four better-known novels, for the benefit of English readers not able to enjoy the French originals. Our four novels here have all been in print in France almost without a break since they were first issued. Three of them appeared in an English translation by Sybil Scott (wife of Geoffrey Scott) in 1925 as *Four Tales by Zelide*. These three were *Lettres de Lausanne (I and II)* and *Mistriss Henley*. *Lettres Neuchâteloises* has never been published in an English translation though it recently appeared in Dutch.

Belle's novels are about women, for women, and although initially published anonymously (until the truth leaks out as to their author) are clearly by a woman. Her heroines are conventional but in unconventional roles. Belle exposes the unfairness of the position women are forced to adopt in society, obliged as they are to give in to the prejudices and outright stupidity of the male gender. Yet she does not advocate rebellion; all four heroines in our novels have to toe the line which society dictates. Thus, Marianne, Mistriss Henley, Cécile and Caliste – our four heroines – all suffer at the hands of men who are really anti-heroes in their ordinariness and obtuseness. They are also destructive. In *Mistriss Henley* and *Caliste* the men are hidebound in their obstinacy as is Edouard (unwittingly) in *Lettres de Lausanne (I)*. Only in *Lettres Neuchâteloises* are the men shown to be sensitive and caring (Meyer, his uncle, Max) and it is in this novel that Marianne de la Prise is seen to be a woman in control of the crisis. In the other novels women are mostly subservient.

Belle's protest at the role of women is never loudly expressed. It is always subtle and quietly poignant and I defy any reader to remain unmoved when following the paths of Caliste and Mistriss Henley, subjected as they are to the insensitive prejudices of their opposing males.

Her subtlety carried far more conviction and influenced society more than any rancorous polemic would have done. The novels must speak for themselves.

There was invariably an uproar when one of her novels appeared as they threatened society and its rules. People believed they were being personally characterised. Pamphlets defending themselves issued forth and Belle looked on amused at the accuracy of her portraits – albeit unintended.

> "If you paint out of fantasy, but truthfully, a flock of sheep, each sheep will find its own portrait, or at least that of its neighbour. Which is what happened to the people of Neuchâtel and they were much offended."

Thus her witty letter to a friend after the appearance of *Lettres Neuchâteloises*. Belle and her husband were ostracised by Neuchâtel society when its author was identified and Belle seems to have been genuinely surprised at this. In its second edition she includes a poem addressed to "the good people of Neuchâtel" asking them not to be offended.

Pregnancy is a factor of importance in three of our novels – and something to avoid at all costs in the fourth (Cécile in *Lettres de Lausanne*). Belle's own inability to conceive may have provided the unconscious motive for this. In her own household she had her much-loved maid-companion Henriette Monachon to deal with – twice pregnant by different men – and whom she had to defend against the authorities of Neuchâtel. These wanted to exile mother and child out of Neuchâtel and its precincts. Belle successfully arranged for both to remain, and on the second occasion Henriette luckily chose marriage and thereby avoided the ignominy of exile. These episodes in Henrirette's life are used as a central feature in *Lettres Neuchâteloises* where the little seamstress Julianne becomes pregnant. The pregnancies that occur in three of our novels are either unwanted or at best tolerated and there must be significance in this.

Sexual excess was much feared in the eighteenth century and since women were viewed as sexual beings it followed that men avoided the upper levels of society for their physical needs and concentrated for these on the lower orders. This of course spread diseases. James Boswell during his time in London, before he comes to Utrecht, was much put out at being infected by a third-rate actress (Louisa) whom he upbraids furiously for being unclean. In our four novels *libertinage* is never far away from the action, or plot, but is usually under control – as with Belle herself whom we saw preferred her indiscretions to be in letter-form rather than in fact. D'Hermenches was a most useful surrogate until her marriage.

We might glance at the number of protagonists in each novel. *Lettres Neuchâteloises* has five people writing letters and pushing forward the plot thereby; *Caliste* has four though only one in reality carries the narrative; *Mistriss Henley* and *Lettres de Lausanne (I)* only one each. Readers will decide which they prefer. My own preference is for more voices (polyphonic) since this induces more variety in the characters presented to us although admittedly we lose the intensity of the single voice.

Of course Belle was privileged in that she could finance her publications herself. She is on record as saying that she did not shrink from self-advertisement in the public domain – rather the reverse in fact. So she could write and publish her novels of protest against the authority of men and see these swiftly in print. She relished the pamphlets that attacked her provocative views – and wrote more of the same in answer.

"Closure" (bringing a story to a conclusion) is much discussed in connection with Belle's novels. None of our four novels draws a conclusion. We are introduced to the players in a given situation, we accompany them for a while, then leave them some way down the road with no conclusion drawn as to their future. Admittedly in *Caliste* the heroine dies but William is left hanging by a precarious thread; in *Lettres Neuchâteloises* Meyer has had his guilty burden lifted from his shoulders – but is a penniless office clerk likely to satisfy and sustain a commanding personality such as Marianne who is clearly his superior? In *Lettres de Lausanne (I)* Cécile has been left on the shelf by the young Milord with no happy outcome for her in sight. Mistriss Henley's future is black indeed and the reader is offered two alternative endings: the heroine may subsequently die in childbirth, or continue to live as a mother and virtually a prisoner in a big house with an insensitive man. There is something Joycean in the non-closure of Belle's stories and time and again one thinks of Joyces's *Dubliners* where characters come and go without climax or ending. Belle has no tidy endings either.

At the time of writing her novels Belle infuriated readers by her arbitrary treatment of her plots. Madame de Staël wrote to Belle that "I know of nothing more painful than your way of beginning but not finishing; these are friends from whom you separate us." Readers liked their plots to be nicely rounded off with villains in jail and heroes winning their ladies. Today we greet Belle's realism with a sigh of admiration. She is one of our most modern novelists.

LETTERS FROM NEUCHÂTEL

PREFACE

Letters from Neuchâtel was published in 1784 when Belle was 44, three years before she met Benjamin de Constant but following a mysterious encounter with a young man in Geneva: *"le chagrin et le désir de me distraire me firent écrire les* [the pain and the need to distract myself made me write the] Lettres Neuchâteloises." This satirical little novel infuriated the people of Neuchâtel with its lampooning of their narrow ways and inbreeding. And they assumed Belle was drawing their self-portraits.

> *"Le titre de mon petit livre fit grand peur; on craignit d'y trouver des portraits et des anecdotes. Quand on vit que ce n'était pas cela, on prétendit n'y rien trouver d'interéssant. Mais ne peignant personne, on peint tout le monde. Cela doit être, et je n'y avais pas pensé. Quand on peint de fantaisie, mais avec vérité, un troupeau de moutons, chaque mouton y trouve son portrait, ou du moins le portrait de son voisin. C'est ce qui arriva aux Neuchâtelois, et ils se fâchèrent* [The title of my little book caused great fright; people feared to find themselves in actual portraits. When it was realised that this was not the

case the book was said not to contain anything of interest. But in painting no one, one paints everyone; this must be so and I had not thought of that. If you paint out of fantasy, but truthfully, a flock of sheep, each sheep will find its own portrait, or at least that of its neighbour. Which is what happened to the people of Neuchâtel, and they were much offended]."

Letters from Neuchâtel was her second novel (*Le Noble* was the first) and the first printing in 1784 had several errors which were corrected in a second edition the same year. It has been reprinted spasmodically in French ever since but never translated into English, this being its first appearance.

The *conte*, after more than two centuries, retains a freshness and a realism, due in no small measure to the letter-form that moves the plot forward. The various characters write their letters from Neuchâtel to unseen friends and relations whereby the reader is involved in each twist and turn of the tale. It concerns a German youth who comes to Neuchâtel to learn commerce; he helps a young seamstress with whom he has a casual affair and she becomes pregnant. This results in a drama involving the lady of his heart – Marianne de la Prise.*

We observe dances in assembly rooms, concerts, plays, polite gatherings of society in this little town sitting prettily, if primly beside its lake. Its inhabitants today, heirs to their eighteenth century forebears (Belle called them "*bonnes petites gens* [good, modest people]"), are probably not very different nowadays in their gossipy attitudes to life. Neuchâtel remains a quiet town, "carved out of butter" as described by Alexandre Dumas on account of the buildings largely constructed from yellow stone.

---

*   Belle was a devoted disciple of Marivaux, whose *Marianne* has the same truth of detail and place as she achieves in *Letters from Neuchâtel*. The name is surely not a coincidence.

Belle leaves her little novel without an end. What becomes of the naïve seamstress? Does the young German survive his problems? Does his love of Marianne lead to a happy ending? In a telling remark Philippe Godet in his Preface to a 1908 reprint of the novel writes: "*l'auteur ne tient pas à nous dire comment ses histoires finissent; il lui suffit d'avoir éveillé notre réflexion et mis en activité notre pensée* [the author does not wish to tell us how her stories finish; it suffices her to have evoked our reflection and set our thoughts in motion]." She does not unwrap the plots of her novels – these evolve of themselves. There are no tidy endings. "*Je me suis intéressée vivement aux lettres neufchateloises mais je ne sais rien de plus pénible que votre manière de commencer sans finir, ce sont des amis dont vous nous séparez* [I am much interested in the letters from Neuchâtel but I know of nothing more painful than your way of beginning but not finishing; these are friends from whom you separate us]." Thus Mme de Staël in a letter to Belle.

In answer to the cries of protest on the appearance of the first printing of *Letters from Neuchâtel*, Belle adds some verses addressed to her angry readers (p. 121–2) – in delicious satirical form which would hardly have soothed ruffled feathers. She contemplated a sequel, as we know, but did not pursue the idea. Now that the name of the author is revealed, the "*grande verité qui a fait vraiment un peu illusion* [the realism that created something of an illusion]" would be lost. The little novel is partly autobiographical. Mlle de la Prise is Belle to the letter – bossy, kindly, outspoken beyond permitted eighteenth century acceptance. The young man Meyer is subservient to Marianne which echoes the attitude preferred by Belle in her male admirers. The pregnant little seamstress is the double of Henriette, Belle's own maid who suffered the same fate (twice) and whom Belle defended steadfastly against the Calvinist people of Neuchâtel.

Note from the editor. Letter headings in these Letters vary as to the form of the dates. I believe Belle was inconsistent with these on purpose so as to impart a reality to the letters. I have maintained these and followed the second edition of the French version which Belle corrected and oversaw through the printer.

Some of the language used by the little seamstress is regional and lacks syntax but I have translated this in a straightforward manner.

FIRST LETTER

Julianne C. to her aunt at Boudevilliers

My dear Aunt,

I have received your letter in which you inform me that you and my dear Uncle are well, for which God be praised! As for my cousin Jeanne-Marie, it is said that she will soon marry our cousin Abram; this pleases me greatly as I have always loved her. If the event is not to take place until the spring, then my cousin Jeanne-Aimée and I can join in the dances at the wedding, which will please me mightily.

As for the present, my dear Aunt, I must tell you what happened to me the day before yesterday. We had worked so well on the dress for Mlle de la Prise that my mistresses bade me take it to her right away. There was quite a crowd of people as I went down to the bottom of Neubourg. A young man, who was both pleasant-looking and nicely dressed, passed me and, as I turned to look at him, the dress which was folded over my arm, fell to the ground, as I did also. It had rained and the path was slippery. I managed to keep the dress intact as I fell, but it became slightly dirtied. I did not dare to take it to Mademoiselle, nor did I dare to return with it in this state to my mistresses. Some rough boys were taunting me and I started to cry, when the young man came to my rescue. He helped me up and offered to come with me to tell my mistresses that what had occurred was not my fault. They can be quite nasty and although I was somewhat ashamed to have him do this, I would have been more worried to return alone. The young man duly explained to them that it was not my fault and when leaving he gave me a small écu, to console me – as he said. My mistresses were amazed that such a fine-looking man should accompany me and they could speak of nothing else the entire evening. And yesterday they had another surprise in that the young man returned once more in the evening to enquire whether the dress had been successfully cleaned. I was able to tell him that it had, and that indeed we had nothing to fear from Mademoiselle, who was one of the nicest ladies in Neuchâtel. There, dear Aunt, this is what I wanted to tell you. There is both good and bad in all this; for the young man is so nice but I do not know his name, nor whether he lives in Neuchâtel. I have not seen him before and may never see him again.

Farewell and fond greetings to my Uncle and cousins, Jeanne-Marie and Abram. Our cousin Jeanne-Aimée is well and does her daily round. She greets you also.

Julianne C***

SECOND LETTER

Henri Meyer to Godefroy Dorville in Hamburg

Neuchâtel, .. October 178..

I arrived here three days ago, my dear friend, across a country-side covered in vines and on a poor and narrow road much impeded by those gathering the grapes and their various equipment. It is said that this is a joyous sight and I might have agreed with this, if the weather had not been overcast and cold. The girls were dirty and half frozen. I do not like to see women working in the country except perhaps to gather in the hay. It is so hard on the young and pretty and even more so on those who are neither. It evokes in me a guilty feeling and in my carriage the other day I felt embarrassed to pass through the middle of these poor families who were picking the grapes.

When picked and pressed into open barrels, the grapes hardly offer a very tempting prospect, jolted about as they are on little four-wheeled carts. Neither was I in a good humour. I was leaving studies that amused me, friends whom I love, to enter a society unknown to me and an occupation entirely novel and for which in all probability I had no talent. Leaving you behind is bad enough and I feel my past ties have been broken. I had little fear for the future, however, nor great regrets in leaving, since the friend of my father would be obliged to receive me well, yet I retained a certain sadness and felt out of sorts.

But let me pause to describe my reception and life as it now is. Monsieur M. welcomed me; I am adequately lodged, the apprentices and other clerks neither please me nor displease me. We eat communally except when invited by our employer, which has already happened to me twice. You see how respectable it all is. I am neither bored nor amused. The town would be attractive enough if there were less obstructions and the streets less dirty. There are some beautiful houses, especially in the suburbs, and when the mists allow the sun to shine, there is a good view of the lake and the snow-clad Alps, but it is not like Geneva, Lausanne or Vevey. I have engaged a violin teacher who comes each day from two o'clock until three o'clock, because we do not return to the office before three. It is quite enough to be seated from eight till noon and from three to seven. On days with a lot of post we must remain even later. During other leisure hours I take lessons in music or drawing – I know enough of dancing already – and after supper I read, so as to continue my education. I even seek to extend my Latin. It may be said that none of this is much use to a future businessman, but I believe outside his office a merchant should be as other men.

They are very pleased with my writing and my skill with figures. I get the impression that they wish to persuade my uncle to advance me as much as possible in my chosen career. There is a big difference between me and the other apprentices as to the tasks given us. Not to be too vain, I dare to suggest that it comes down to the different way in which we have been brought up.

There is one whom I pity to be occupied with matters quite beyond his intelligence and who learns nothing. It would be natural if he were jealous of me. I try to show him every attention, so that he is at ease with me. The others are young rascals.

I am grateful to my uncle for the manner in which he has arranged both my spending and receipt of money. Thirty louis are paid on my behalf each month for my board and lodging, and a half louis for my washing. I am given ten louis for my minor pleasures for which I need not account, and I am promised this sum every four months. As for my lessons and clothes, my uncle has promised to pay all of these bills that I may send him during the first year, without questioning them. He writes that by this arrangement I can count myself rich; he can afford the expenditure and has not wanted me to feel hindered, nor to risk running up debts, nor to borrow, nor to conceal any of my expenditures. And has said that in this manner I may pursue my own destiny and not deny myself those pleasures on which I had not reflected too much beforehand. If my mother* and other trustees find fault with my expenses, he will pay these out of money set aside for his own minor pleasures, thereby denying himself such pleasures that might have made him self-indulgent. So you see me as a noble lord, my friend. Ten louis in my pocket, board and lodging paid, and full liberty for my personal expenses.

Farewell, dear Godefroy, I will write to you again in two weeks. Love your friend as he loves you.

H. Meyer

---

*   It is clear that Meyer's father is dead and his uncle is acting as his guardian. His employer in Neuchâtel, M., was a friend of the deceased father. All this is clear from the text – but readers must work it out for themselves!

THIRD LETTER

Henri Meyer to Godefroy Dorville

Neuchâtel, Nov. 178..

I begin to find Neuchâtel somewhat prettier. We have had a frost, the streets have dried up. Gentlemen – I mean those whom one greets respectfully in the streets and whom I hear named Mr Councillor, Mr Mayor, etc. – have lost their anxious manner and are slightly better dressed than during the grape harvest. I don't know why all this gives me pleasure, because nothing has changed. I see little servant or working girls in the streets who are pretty, well dressed and lively. I am under the impression that almost everybody in Neuchâtel is active and industrious. It is true that I do not see such beautiful people as in … but the young girls are pretty enough, if a little thin, and for the most part brunette. I am told I shall see a different crowd at the concert. Events there are due to start the first Monday in December and I shall certainly subscribe. There I shall see comedies performed by women, which strikes me initially as somewhat extraordinary. There are balls also every fortnight, but these are restricted to societies who do not permit counting-house clerks and apprentices to take part; and they are quite right in this, it seems to me, since we would amount to a crowd of scamps. There may be exceptions to this rule, but generally it is correct. If all are barred, then no one can complain. This is what I say to those companions who deeply dislike being excluded, whereas in truth they are not fit to be received in fine company.

It is all the same to me, but I hope they will allow me to take part in a concert. It is already arranged between my friend Monin, who plays the sax-horn, M. Neuss and me, that we will put on a little concert on Sundays; my violin teacher will be there. He will conduct us and will play the tenor violin. He asks no more than a bottle of red wine! He likes to drink and knows it is better to drink one bottle with his pupils than to risk drinking several bottles in a tavern, only to return in a tipsy condition to his wife. These musicians are distasteful people and one must avoid their society and try to learn from them only their art. I read music well and I draw good enough sounds from my violin, but I shall never master great intricacies nor refinements.

One thing strikes me here. There are two or three surnames that I hear spoken of constantly. My shoemaker, my wig-maker, a little errand boy I use for messages, an affluent merchant – all these have the same name, as also two seamstresses whom I met by chance, a very elegant officer who lives opposite my employer, and a minister whom I heard preaching this morning. Yesterday I met an especially well-dressed and beautiful woman of whom I asked her name: the same. There is another name, common to a stonemason, a cooper and a councillor of the State. I asked my employer if all these people are related to each other; he replied that in some manner they are, and this pleases me. Surely it is pleasant to work for one's relatives when one is poor, and then to give others work when one is rich. There is not in these people the same haughtiness, nor that sad humility evident elsewhere.

There are certain families that are not so numerous, but when people from such families are described to me I am usually told: "That is Madame A, daughter of Monsieur B" (one of the numerous families); or "That is Monsieur C, brother-in-law of D" (also one of the numerous families). So much so, that it appears that all Neuchâtelois are related. It is not surprising that they do not stand on ceremony one with the other and that they dress as I saw them at the time of the grape harvest, with their big boots, woollen stockings and silk handkerchiefs round their necks. These strike me most forcibly.

I have heard speak of the nobility but when discussing the

pride in our german nobility with my employer, he said that when he himself was ennobled, he put "de" in front of his name only to please his wife and sisters; to change his signature in this way meant nothing to him, as he said, and was only to please them.

Farewell, my dear Godefroy. My best friend here has just called, asking for some tea. I am going out to find my teacher and M. Neuss and we shall make music. I did not think we would begin until next Sunday, but I am very ready to start this evening. Farewell, I embrace you. Write to me, I beg of you.

H. Meyer

FOURTH LETTER

Henri Meyer to Godefroy Dorville

Neuchâtel, Dec. 178..

Thank you, dear friend, for your long letter. It gave me great pleasure, truly the greatest, and in fact I have had need of it after an event that has just occurred. You may think these words are a little confused, but that is natural since my thoughts are likewise. There are things I would find absurd to recount to you, but in the following episode I tell you the entire truth and without any exaggeration. If one ever lacks truthfulness, and without good cause, one cannot know where such insincerity will end; untruths cost little and each day are rendered more habitual. What would become of humour, trust, in a word – all that one holds dear? Herewith almost a sermon! When one is displeased with oneself in certain matters one wishes, at least, to give pleasure to others.

To return to your letter, it seems that you lead a most agreeable life; excepting the caprices of your sister-in-law, I see nothing I would wish to change. But you must beware in courting the younger sister, rich as she is. She may indeed resemble her sister in her countenance and in the sound of her voice and indeed may come to resemble her in others ways once she dares to show her true self. And you may not be as patient as your brother.

Last Monday I attended a concert and, thanks to M. Neuss, I was permitted to take part. So attentive was I to my playing that I took no notice of what was happening in the hall – until I heard the name of Mlle Marianne de la Prise. By a great coincidence I had heard this person being praised by another some days after I arrived in Neuchâtel. The name alone caused me the greatest pleasure and I looked about me to see who it was that was so named. Whereupon I saw a young person come on to the stage, fairly tall, very slim, well yet simply dressed. I recognised her dress as one I had picked up with care one day from a muddy street. That is a long story which I will recount to you perhaps another time if there is a sequel to it, which in truth I hope will not occur. But to return to Mlle de la Prise mounting the stage. It was natural enough that she should wear a dress with which I was acquainted, yet it was strange indeed that she should be going to sing beside me and that I should accompany her. I saw her walk up, then stop to pick up her music, and I must have regarded her with so much attention as to cause her to blush deeply, or so I was told afterwards. She had let fall her music and I had not had the wit to retrieve it. When it was time for me to take up my instrument a fellow-musician had to tug me by the sleeve. Never have I acted so stupidly nor been so angry with myself for this. I blush when I think of it. I would have written to you immediately afterwards, that same evening, if I had not felt obliged to help the other clerks to get their letters off before the post departed.

Mlle de la Prise sings prettily enough but not with a strong voice. I am certain she could scarcely be heard the other end of the hall, even if there had been no noise. I was affronted that they did not listen to her, but perhaps glad they could hear her so little. I would like to have given her my hand to conduct her back to her seat; and assuredly I would have done this if I had not been so distracted and maladroit. I feared to commit other follies. Perhaps I would have missed my step in descending the short ladder and caused her to fall. I tremble when I think of it. Certainly I did well to stay put. The symphonies that we played restored me a little to myself. I listened to no other singer, though I believe there was one who sang more strongly and was even more beautiful than Mlle de la Prise. I do not know who she is, nor did I look at her.

Farewell, my friend. My violin teacher has just arrived. This evening there will be a big post to get off so I will be unable to add to this letter. When I am allowed to go to the concert on a Monday I must work hard on a Thursday. But this Friday I shall arrange for some sort of recreation, as this is the one day of the week when no post arrives or leaves. I am already fully accustomed to Neuchâtel and the life I lead here.

H. Meyer

FIFTH LETTER

Julianne C... to her aunt at Boudevilliers

178..

My dear Aunt,

You may be a little surprised at what I tell you, but I assure you none of it is my fault. I am certain that if it had not been for that Marie Besson with her wicked tongue, none of this would have happened. You remember I wrote to you about the dress of Mlle Marianne de la Prise, which fell in the mud, and how this Monsieur helped me to pick it up and wished to accompany me to my mistresses? And how he gave me a small écu which that Marie Besson made much of? I told you also that the next day he came to ask if the dress had been able to be cleaned. In fact my mistresses had put a tuck over the part that had been dirtied. Mlle de la Prise thought that this was quite all right, for I recounted to her the whole story, which caused her to laugh. She asked Monsieur's name but I did not know it. I told him all this and how Mlle de la Prise was such a good and great lady. He wanted to know where I was from, how much I earned and whether I liked my profession. When leaving, I went to open the door for him, when he placed a double écu in my hand, which he pressed, and I think he may have kissed me. When I re-entered the room, one of my mistresses and that Marie Besson stared at me, whereupon I asked Marie: "Why are you looking at me like that?" and my mistress said to me: "And you, why are you blushing? And why should we not look at you?" Whereupon I replied: "Take care!" and I began to work, half at ease but half annoyed.

The following morning at the break of day, I ran to see Jeanne-Aimée to tell her all that had happened, and we settled it that with my three small écus I would buy a muslin scarf and a muslin bonnet with a low brim and a red ribbon to go with it. And then on Sunday on our way to church we met Monsieur who did not recognise me at first, because of my hat and scarf, and having seen me only on weekdays. Several of Monsieur's colleagues from his office were with him and said how pretty I was, but said nothing about Marie Besson who was also with us; she was put out of sorts by this and became worse as the day went on. She became very formal with me and called me Mademoiselle.

But last Thursday was even worse. I had been left alone in the house to finish some work and at noon I went to the fair with Jeanne-Aimée; we were admiring some gilded crosses in a shop when who should enter but Monsieur, who saw we liked them and gave us one each. Of course it was because of me that he gave one to Jeanne-Aimée, since he did not know her, but mine was more beautiful. I quickly returned to my work because I saw one of the ladies for whom my mistresses work. I gave my cross to Jeanne-Aimée to put a ribbon in it and asked her to bring it to me that evening.

That same evening I was trying the cross round my neck when my mistresses returned unexpectedly. They upbraided me most terribly and said I was a street-walker who left my work to run after gentlemen who gave me fancy presents. That Marie Besson said the worst things possible, and one of my mistresses said she did not want to have a street-walker in her house, whereupon I said I would leave right away.

I collected my things and went to sleep at Jeanne-Aimée's. The following day I rented a little room with a shoemaker who is the cousin of Jeanne-Aimée's aunt. I look after myself and I know enough, thank goodness, to earn my own living. Already I have two dresses and three cloaks for the maidservants of one of my mistresses' customers who are not offended by my having received presents from a gentleman. I am acquainted also with girls who work in a dress-shop and they will certainly have need of underclothes for themselves – they are pretty girls and I am certain that gentlemen will wish to given them presents. And if I lack money to buy firewood or candles or other necessities, I am sure that my Monsieur will see to my needs. It is, after all, because of him that I was obliged to leave my employment with my mistresses. He could easily come and see me in my new lodging, because he is not proud.

Farewell, my dear aunt, I send you my greetings, and please greet everyone with you on my behalf.

J. C...

SIXTH LETTER

Julianne C... to Henri Meyer

Dear Sir,

I hope Monsieur will excuse the liberty I take in writing him this letter. I have unfortunately not been able to see him in the street to speak to, and indeed Monsieur might not be too pleased at my boldness in speaking to him in front of everyone during the day; and it does not behove a respectable girl to be on the streets at night. But I would have told Monsieur how I had left my mistresses, who called me a street-walker and all because I accepted the gilt cross given me by Monsieur. I ask nothing of Monsieur since I am not in a state of misery, but firewood is dear and in the long winter evenings my hands will freeze as I sit in the window at my sewing. The shoemaker where I lodge is at the bottom of the Rue des Chavannes.

I am honoured, sir, to be your humble and devoted servant,

Julianne C...

SEVENTH LETTER

Henri Meyer to Julianne C.

Mademoiselle,

What happened yesterday will have left you more angry than myself and it is clear it does not suit you to receive my visits. I advise you to try and return to your mistresses whom you can assure they will hear nothing more of me. Yesterday I forgot to give you the louis that I brought with me for you to buy wood and improve your lodging, if you stay there. I am sending you an additional louis herewith, together with the first, and beg you immediately to pay off your lodging and return to your mistresses, for your own self-respect, or go to your parents in your village.

I am, Mademoiselle, your very humble servant.

H. Meyer

EIGHTH LETTER

Henri Meyer to Julianne C.

Mademoiselle,

I regret that you were seen leaving my house; I am truly upset at my love of you and indeed for my own self-indulgence. It is not surprising that I was touched by your tears, but I nevertheless reproach myself bitterly for my ensuing weakness. Nor can I accuse you of showing me such affection as to justify my actions. I beg you not to return here. I have told the servant who saw you leave, not to receive you if you call again – and I am resolved not to visit you myself. You should consider our acquaintance at an end.

H. Meyer

NINTH LETTER

Henri Meyer to Godefroy Dorville

Neuchâtel, 1 January 178..

I am somewhat out of sorts today, my dear friend. My employer had the goodness to invite me to a sumptuous dinner where we ate as I have never eaten before, and tasted and indeed drank 20 different sorts of wine. Several people were half tipsy, but seemed scarcely any happier for this. Three or four young ladies were whispering together in a malicious fashion and seemed surprised when I addressed them and scarcely answered me, their attention being uniquely centred on two young officers; their smiles and outbursts of laughter concerned some secret of which I was ignorant. I wondered in fact whether they were listening the one to the other, since their laughter seemed to be more for effect than gaiety. It seems that true laughter is rare in this town, and even tears are shed only for effect.

You see how vexed I am. In reality this is due to the attitudes arising from the sale of wine. During the last six weeks, Neuchâtel can discuss only the new vintage and its price. Half the population believes the price too high, the other half too low, depending on their own involvement. I heard it discussed again today, even though the price was fixed three weeks ago.

One event occurred at the dinner table which was both interesting and painful for me. One of the young ladies spoke of Mlle de la Prise; she could not understand, she said, how someone with so small a voice could be asked to sing at the concert. "Her pretty face", said a young man, "makes up for that." "Pretty face indeed", replied another of the young ladies, "she certainly needed a pretty face to overcome her strange behaviour."

You can imagine how this affected me – I did not speak after that. When a neighbour asked me some casual question, I replied yes or no coldly. When people rose from the table, I ran home to share with you my bad humour.

May the coming days of this year not resemble those that have past! May your own days be pleasant and smooth! I am filled with foreboding. I question what I have achieved in the past year and compare myself to then and now. I am truly upset and anxious. A new period of my life is opening; I neither know how I will emerge from this, nor how it will finish.

Farewell, my friend.   H. Meyer

TENTH LETTER

Henri Meyer to Godefroy Dorville

Neuchâtel, 20 January 178..

I have things to tell you, my dear Godefroy, that produce a strange bewilderment in me. Three days ago I was given two tickets for the ball, one sent to me in the morning and the other in the evening, but neither identified the sender. I was with my one good friend here, Monin, when the second one arrived, and accordingly I gave it to him. But hardly was that done than I wondered if I had acted rashly. The tickets had been sent to me personally and I doubted I had the right to dispose of them. But how to reverse it? How to tell my overjoyed friend that he should return the ticket until I was better informed as to the sender? I had been remiss, but after all what harm could come from my imprudence. My friend is a good-looking fellow, of integrity, and a better dancer than I am. I resolved, therefore, to be brave and take on myself anything untoward that might arise. Yesterday, Friday, came the desired, anticipated evening and we set out for the ball, as happy as could be, but for myself a little anxious. The matter of the ticket was not the only thing to keep me in suspense; Mlle de la Prise would doubtless be there and I did not know if I should approach her and in what manner. Should I speak to her, could I bring myself to ask her to dance with me? My heart was beating and I had her face and dress in my mind's eye when, lo and behold, there she was, sitting on a sofa near the door. I could scarcely focus on her clearly but I did not hesitate and, unreflectingly and fearlessly, I went straight up to her to speak of the concert, of the melody she had sung and indeed of other things. Taking no notice of the curious looks being given me by one of her companions, I begged her to honour me with the first quadrille.

She said she was engaged for that. Well, the second? Engaged. The third, engaged.

"the fourth, the fifth? I shall not give in," I said, laughing. "Then it must be much later on," she replied. "It is already late and we shall start soon. If Count Max, with whom I have the first dance, does not appear in time, I will dance it with you, if you wish."

I thanked her and in that moment a lady came up to me and said: "Ah! Monsieur Meyer. You have received my ticket?" I answered that I had received it and that I had in fact received two tickets and given one of them to M. Monin.

"How is that?" said the lady. "A ticket that was sent to you? It is not in order for you to pass it on."

"I was wrong, indeed, Madame," I replied. "But it was too late, I had given it to him already. It might have been better for me not to have come at all. He knows nothing of all this and that I have been at fault."

"Well," said the lady, "perhaps there is no harm done this time."

"Yes," I answered. "And if we cause offence by this, then we shall not be invited again. But if one or other of us is re-invited, then I flatter myself that it will not be one without the other."

Whereupon she left me, whilst casting a look of approbation at my friend.

"I will try to dance a quadrille with your friend", said Mlle de la Prise, enchantingly; then, as people were getting ready for the quadrille and the Count Max had still not arrived, she gave me her hand with a grace that charmed me and we took our places. We were about to begin when Mlle de la Prise cried out: "Oh! There is the Count now!"

He it was who approached us, looking vexed and ashamed. I went up to him and said: "Sir, Mademoiselle only agreed to dance with me should you not arrive in time. Now that you have done so, I am sure she would wish me to give up my place to yourself."

"No, Sir," replied the Count, "You are too kind. I am late beyond forgiveness and I deserve my punishment."

Mlle de la Prise seemed equally content with both of us. She promised him the fourth quadrille, the fifth for my friend and the sixth for myself. I was happy enough; never had I danced with such pleasure. Dancing at this moment was a quite new experience with a meaning and wit never enjoyed before. I paid homage to the creator of the dance, who must have been a person of sensibility with a partner the equal of Mlle de la Prise. It must have been ladies of her quality who inspired the Muses.

Mlle de la Prise dances with gaiety and lightness, yet with decorum. I have seen other young girls here who dance with more grace and some with greater perfection, but none who, in the round, dance as agreeably. One may say the same of her face – there may be those more beautiful, more striking, but none pleases as much as hers which is a view shared, it seems, by all the men present. I am amazed at the confidence and indeed gaiety she inspires in me. I sometimes wonder if we had known each other as children, so much do we think the same thoughts and I anticipate what she will say next. If I am happy, I would want her to be able to witness that happiness; but if any of my actions are unhappy, my shame and sadness would be doubled if she were aware of these. There were certain things in my conduct which displeased me before the ball and which have caused me even greater displeasure since then. I hope she remains ignorant of these; I hope above all that her good influence remains with me and prevents any relapse. She could be my guardian angel if I were to be of sufficient interest to her!

The Count Maximillian de R*** is from Alsace and belongs to an illustrious and ancient family. He is here with his older brother who will be immensely rich. They have a tutor with them whom I have not yet seen. They are both far advanced in their military service and are here to finish their education.

The Count Max, as he is known, was telling me at the ball that so far he has not found the solace in literature and the fine arts that he had anticipated. "But, Sir," said a man seated near us, though not, I had thought, within earshot, "How could anyone have sent you to Neuchâtel for those things you wish to learn? There is talent among us, but no luminaries; our womenfolk act in comedies they have not read; no one here understands orthography*; our sermons are ungrammatical; our lawyers speak a dialect; our public buildings are hardly communal; the countryside is absurd; we are more superficial, frivolous, ignorant than …."

At this moment Mlle de la Prise came to warn the Count that their dance was about to begin. I rose to follow them whilst bidding farewell to our caustic informant; his rancour and exaggerations had made me laugh. Whilst Mlle de la Prise and the Count were dancing, I was approached by the lady who had earlier spoken to me. She asked me about myself and I told her I was the son of a merchant from Augsburg.

"Son of a shop-keeper" she replied.

"No, merchant" I answered, and I felt that I blushed. "Of a merchant. I know the difference, since my Uncle is a well-to-do shop-keeper."

Apparently she wished to be polite, but this was hardly evident when she seemed to scorn my father and his occupation. She asked where I had learned French and I replied that this had been in France. When I said I had also spent some time in Geneva in the home of a minister of the cloth, for instruction and preparation for my communion, she started to discuss politics – about which I know nothing. I was glad when the dance finished and we were obliged to cease our discussion.

---

*   The art or practice of spelling words correctly.

I danced the sixth quadrille with Mlle de la Prise with an even greater pleasure than the first; on this occasion I was to dance with her in my own right and not to take the place of another. I now wanted to leave, I was so happy, enough things had happened to me for one day. I hoped to bid farewell to the lady who had invited me. She was in conversation with others and I heard my name and the words *vigour* and *goodwill* whereupon she came up to me with another lady, both grave and affable, and they said I would be welcome at future balls as well as my friend. I went to find him and we thanked the ladies and withdrew. Mlle de la Prise was dancing with Count Max's older brother.

Farewell, my friend. When I call Monin my friend, this does not mean the same as when I say: my friend Godefroy Dorville. Monin is a nice fellow, whom I help along and who helps me to enjoy life; he is less tedious than his companions, who do little else than play pranks on one another and who seek less to advance themselves than to humiliate each other. I have more sympathy for the tricked than the trickster.

H. Meyer

ELEVENTH LETTER

Mlle de la Prise to Mlle de Ville

Neuchâtel, ...

My dear Eugénie,

A second winter begins since you left here, a second winter of giddy dissipation and yet I lack both a friend and probably pleasure. I miss you as much now as a year ago. The world promised me compensations which have not been forthcoming; I have glimpsed them briefly but they have faded away when confronted.

And I have needed some distraction. My father has not recovered from his latest attack of gout. My mother complains of our accommodation, our surroundings, our servants; she quarrels with my father's sister and with my cousins. Little offences accumulate and each day appear more serious when complained of. Sadly, we have had to sell some land at Val de Travers and our vines at Auvernier have produced little, despite cultivation and manure.

My father accepts all this with admirable courage. On the contrary, he has told me to subscribe to the balls; to purchase two new dresses, to take lessons, in fact he orders me to divert myself and be gay and I shall obey him in this so far as I am able. The kindness shown to me by my father and the liberty he allows me are my great compensation. But he is so weak! His legs are always swollen, you would hardly recognise him.

And you, what are you doing? Will you spend the winter in Marseilles or in the country? Do you dream of marriage?! Can you do without me? For myself, I do not know what to do about my heart. When I want to say what I feel, what I want for myself or others, what I desire and think, nobody listens to me. I interest no one. But with you, everything had life; without you all seems dead. Other people have different needs — mine are of the heart. But do not imagine that this sadness and weakness that I exhibit are for always. This morning my mother gave notice to an old servant who had served us for ten years. I wanted to write to you immediately but I would only have saddened you.

Concerts will begin in a month and balls in the New Year. We have two German counts who are singularly amiable. Whilst waiting for these events to take place, I hemstitch napkins and play piquet with my father. He wants me to sing again at the concert. This will neither benefit nor harm anyone, since no one will hear me. But this summer I have managed to become something of a reasonable musician; I can accompany on the harp and harp-sichord, but not play solo pieces, for which I will never have skills enough.

Mlle ... will marry in two weeks time. You saw how her love began; it has continued lukewarm yet constant. I think it will be a successful marriage since they love themselves more than they love each other.

Farewell, my Eugénie. I shall write you later another, less insipid and less sad letter.

Marianne de la Prise

TWELFTH LETTER

Mlle de la Prise to Mlle de Ville

Neuchâtel, .. January 178..

You cried when reading my sad letter, Eugénie? I cried reading yours, from gratitude and affection. Is it not a noble thing when two hearts are similar and can express sympathy? If we lived together we would need little more than ourselves to make us happy. It is egotistical of me, but my wish is that you continue to "belong" to me and do not marry.

There is small chance that I shall escape from you in this man-ner. You know how depleted are our fortunes. My father shows unconcern for himself bur worries about me. He reminds me constantly that after his death, which he implies is not far off, the pension that enables us to live will cease and I shall have practi-cally nothing. My mother will continue to enjoy her revenues from stock given her in trust by my uncle, especially if she chooses to live in his country. But enough of all that. I like to

believe that my father mistakes our situation and I care nothing
for myself. I merely say all this to emphasise the unlikelihood of
marriage when fortune lacks.

The concerts have begun again. I sang in the first of these and
believe I was mocked by some, on account of I know not what.
Some small difficulties assailed me, each of little importance, but
taken together caused me some embarrassment. I will not trouble
to recount them now but I shall write you more fully another
time.

Farewell, dear Eugénie.

Marianne de la Prise

THIRTEENTH LETTER

Mlle de la Prise to Mlle de Ville

Neuchâtel, .. January 178..

I have endeavoured to write to you recently but there seems little
to tell you of any substance. Each day I take up my pen but nothing is written. Events occur that are too unimportant and would
bore me in the telling, events that have confused me and are difficult to recount. Sometimes I think nothing untoward appears to
have occurred to change my life; the winter has started like others
with, as usual, several young strangers living in Neuchâtel, about
whom I know nothing, even their names, and with whom I probably have nothing in common.

As I told you, I went to sing in the first concert; I let fall my
music; I sang badly. I attended the first ball, danced with everybody, including the two counts from Alsace and two young book-
keeping apprentices. What is so extraordinary in all that as to be
worth recounting to you in detail? Formerly I might have regaled

you with a long account, if you had had the patience to hear it. But now I feel differently, my world has changed. Excepting you and my father, things of the past no longer interest me. I have new hopes and fears that make me indifferent to all that used to inspire me and, on the contrary, which inspire in me now an interest in things that I once disregarded.

I perceive that there are those who are protective of me, while others seek to hinder me. There is a certain chaos in my heart and head. Permit me, dear Eugénie, not to say more until matters have unravelled somewhat and until I regain my usual sanity, always supposing that I may do so. To have told you nothing would have been too painful for me; to tell you more is impossible since I know no more myself.

Farewell then. I kiss you tenderly. All that I can deduce about myself, you will know also. Caution will not silence me. Any fears would seem foolish to you and I shall not baulk from risking your bad opinion of me. My only fear is in boring you.

Marianne de la Prise

FOURTEENTH LETTER

Mlle de la Prise to Mlle de Ville

Neuchâtel, .. January 178 ..

You really want to know more? And so you shall in due course. I wrote you one foolish letter, then another to excuse the first. The letter was not sent, I forgot to do so, I scarcely knew what I was doing during those days. Now I send you the second letter without reopening it; I hardly remember what I wrote but you shall be the judge of my thoughts.

Your own letter was charming; you will not love, you will

never love any man betrothed to you; at least you will not love him very much! If you do not marry him, you will marry another. But if you do marry him you will desire to please, which will unite you agreeably – perhaps! You will not demand that all his looks are towards yourself, nor yours towards him. You will not reproach yourself for looking at another, for having thoughts of another, for saying something that might hurt him; you will explain your thinking which will prove you to have been virtuous and all will be well.

You will do more for him than for me, but you love me more than him. We understand each other better, we have always done so, there is between us a sympathy that can never be engendered between you and him. If this is acceptable to you, marry him. But reflect on this, Eugénie. Look around you to see whether another might inspire in you the same sentiment as you have for him. Have you read no novels? Have you not shared the sentiment of some heroines?

And discover if your intended loves you differently than you love him. For example, tell him that you have a friend who loves you dearly and that you love no one as much as you love her. See if he blushes or becomes angry – if so, do not marry him. If he does not care at all – do not marry him either. But if he says he is sorry that he will have caused you to be away from me and that you can both visit me in Neuchâtel, he will be a good husband – and you can marry him.

I do not know where these thoughts come from, since I did not think them a moment ago. Perhaps there is little sense in them. Yet I assure you I have a good opinion of my observations, of my ... how shall I say? ... of that light that shines in my heart and reflects in yours? Put your trust only in yourself; ask; think. No, ask no one since no one will hear you. Ask only yourself.

Farewell.

Marianne de la Prise

FIFTEENTH LETTER

Mlle de la Prise to Mlle de Ville

Neuchâtel ..... 178..

Does my heart seek a lover? And have I found one? Dear Eugénie, how I perceive your delicate nature is concerned for me! I see your big eyes looking at me in some surprise, though I assure you no scandal merits your consideration! I will recount to you exactly what happened, unconcerned for your delicacy and prudence (I nearly said prudery) and you may retort by telling me that I have been undignified. But we must not fall out over this.

Some while ago a little seamstress dropped in the mud a dress she was carrying to me. A young foreigner helped her to recover it, accompanied her back to her mistresses, to whom he explained her predicament, and gave her some money on leaving her. The tale was told me the following day.

The girl was pretty, certainly, she pleased me with her goodness and personality, such that a man about town would not be averse to being seen with her in the street. Her experience with the dress had hardly been her fault. I asked the name of the young man, but she did not know it and we spoke no more on the subject.

The other day I was at the concert and my friends pointed out a young man who was to play the violin. They informed me he was a young gentleman in the firm of M... called Meyer. In passing near him to take my place to sing, I looked at him closely and he me; I saw that he recognised my dress. In turn I recognised him from his description as having rescued the dress, whereupon we were both lost in contemplation one of the other to the point where I dropped my music score and he forgot to take up his violin. We neither of us knew what to do next! He blushed, I likewise, though I knew not why, since I had nothing of which to be ashamed. Later I was teased about the young man's confusion, whereupon I was tempted to remark that mine equalled his. My own confusion was not noticed, however, and it is apparently the role of a young man to be in love for several weeks with a young woman before she is susceptible to him. I cannot boast that I followed this custom. If it turns out that M. Meyer is as taken with me as I believe to be the case, then he will be able to boast in his turn that I was at once and equally taken with him.

You can see how differently I feel now than the last time I wrote to you, and I must say that I could not feel happier. Whatever may happen to me in the future, it seems to me that if one is loved and one loves equally, one cannot be unhappy. My mother has been scolding all about her since this happened, but my joy has been untroubled. My friends no longer appear to me to be sullen – mark that I say *friends* out of the goodness of my heart, for in truth I have no friend but you. I even prefer you to M. Meyer; if you were here and he pleased you, I would yield in your favour. Do not imagine that he and I have spoken; I have not even seen him again since the concert, but I hope he will come to the next assembly and I shall beg the good ladies to be so kind as to invite him. There we shall certainly speak to each other, even if I have to speak to him first.* I shall position myself close to the door when he enters. The question will be swiftly decided whether M. Meyer is to be the soul of my entire life, or whether I have been engaged in a pleasant little dream.

Farewell, dear Eugénie; my father is so nice to me, he says his daughter has no equal in her charm and figure. So you see that my madness may have some justification. Adieu.

Marianne de la Prise

---

*   It is worth recalling that Belle herself was bold enough first to address Constant d'Hermenches: "*Monsieur, vous ne dansez pas?*"

SIXTEENTH LETTER

From the same to the same

Neuchâtcl, .. January 178..

I cannot wait for your reply. I feel I should apologise for my last letter, which was certainly strange and a little mad. Perhaps I write again now to excuse myself rather than to apologise, which has little point to it. My common sense has returned, though this saddens me because the last four or five days have been days of charming gaiety. Everything I experienced had charm. My harpsichord and harp had a life of their own – I talked to them and they replied of themselves.

So my sanity has returned, but there remains in me a natural curiosity as to whether M. Meyer is as good and honest a person as he seems: whether he has good sense and is pleasant; of all this I shall learn and keep you informed. Have no fear that I shall either do or say anything foolish. You know full well that I always have moments of extravagance, but nothing untoward comes of these. I believe it is the great freedom allowed me by my father, as also his freedom of speech, that have removed the reserve and shyness that so well become *you*. Farewell, therefore, and preserve for me your forbearance which I shall not put too much to the test.

Mlle de la Prise

SEVENTEENTH LETTER

Julianne C. to her Aunt at Boudevilliers

Neuchâtel, .. January 178..

My dear Aunt,

I returned to my mistresses since you advised this, as did also Monsieur. I now know his name, M. Meyer, but what good does that do me? It is already five weeks since I last saw him. I wish I had never met him and I expect he feels the same.

I have cried so much. He wrote me two letters, in one of which he led me to think that perhaps Marie Besson was somehow able to tell him I was not a respectable girl, whereas, my dear Aunt, if it had not been for that wicked master clockmaker with whom I lodged (and he was married as well) there would not have been a better girl in the whole of the Val-de-Ruz. I may have played about a little with the boys of the village at their evening gatherings or during haymaking, when the other girls were as bad as I was, and I do not know whether Monsieur would think ill of me for that. But let's not despair too soon; if I have more crying to do, there will be time enough when I am sure.

I certainly had to persuade my mistresses to take me back, although they have plenty of work at the moment; there are balls, meetings, concerts and theatres, and goodness knows what else. These ladies amuse themselves in so many ways. But perhaps they are just as good and kind as a poor young girl who cries over her work and who has not enjoyed their schooling and etiquette, has not learnt in their nice books; they have their bonnets, their ribbons, their dresses with gauze trimmings on which we must work through the night and sometimes on Sundays , all of which they may have when they desire them from their mother or husband – unless given to them by young men. But what of all this?

If my cousins, Jeanne-Marie and Abram, have not been told about Monsieur, then it serves no purpose that they be told. I am, my dear Aunt, your most humble niece.

Julianne C.

EIGHTEENTH LETTER

Henri Meyer to Godefroy Dorville

Neuchâtel, .. January 178..

You say the style of my letters has changed, my dear Godefroy, yet you do not say for good or ill. I believe for good, even if I myself have changed for ill. But life changes and one must change with it, whether one likes it or not. We learn and become responsible for our actions. We are less carefree, less joyful, but if wisdom and a true happiness take their place, we shall have little to regret. Do you remember our reading together? We read that a Mlle de K* – I forget the rest of her name – after two or three days became a different person. This I failed to comprehend at the time, but I now do so. I know now that I must pay for my own mistakes, though I wish that others did not have to do so. It is all so difficult; we do nothing that affects us alone, as indeed nothing is done to us that affects us alone either.

In my last letter I rendered you an account of the ball at which I danced with Mlle de la Prise. For two or three days I scarcely went out of doors, even for a walk. On the Tuesday, however, I was asked to dinner with my employer. There were less people than at the New Year and they were all men, of different ages, among whom were some who seemed to me exceedingly pleasant and of gentle upbringing. We had risen from the table, and were

---

*   Mlle de K. was a character in *l'Ingénu* by Voltaire.

taking coffee, when the caustic Monsieur (from the ball) entered the room. He was reproached for not having come sooner.

"I am obliged to you", he replied, "but I hardly ever eat away from my own house, since by now I know all the wines of your district and the cheeses of your mountains." Thereupon he approached several young men, I being one, and asked us what we had been discussing before he arrived.

"Concerning certain young ladies" answered one of them; "we discussed who was the prettiest and disputed much on this."

"And," he asked, "who did you nominate?" Several were mentioned. "Just so!" he retorted swiftly, "I expected this. You have preferred dolls, marionettes, parrots. Whereas there is one ..."

I was near to the door, hat in hand, and was in the act of leaving, when: "Stay," he cried. "I will not name her." I pretended not to hear and descended the staircase as fast as I could.

The following Friday I had determined to spend the evening quite alone in reading and writing to my uncle. But Count Max arrived, saying that he knew Fridays to be my days of leisure. He stayed with me until seven o'clock. He is so pleasant and well informed; his speech soothes my ear after days of being buffeted by the awful German spoken by those from Basle, Berne and Mulhouse. I begin to lose my own language. The Count is reproachful of me for this and will hand me some German books. He himself spent 18 months in Leipzig.

I am amazed I can tell you so calmly about Friday, when it was the Sunday that was interesting! But perhaps I am hesitant in describing Sunday, which was a strange mixture of happy and unhappy meetings, of pleasure and of pain! I believe I behaved with decorum, indeed I could not do otherwise. Do not expect an account of great happenings; it all took place within a quarter of an hour. And as to the events that preceded it ... for you to understand these I would have to explain everything. Perhaps you can guess those parts of the story I do not reveal; and if you guess only half of it no harm will have been done.

Earlier this week it had rained considerably, followed by freezing weather. Sunday morning it snowed, which brought milder weather, then in the afternoon it froze once more. The water in the streets and the morning snow became a skating rink such as I have never seen, and with the approach of the colder evening air it became increasingly dangerous underfoot. Monin and I were returning from Cret* where we had been walking after church, to profit briefly from the few rays of the sun. We had to take great care not to fall.

Imagine the predicament and danger of Mlle de la Prise and two of her lady friends whom we met near the town gate on the same path as ourselves. I stopped in front of them, barring the way, believing I saw Mlle de la Prise already fallen to the ground, injured, wounded, or something worse. I do not know now what I said to them to accept our help, but the two friends who did not know me started to refuse, when Mlle de la Prise said to them forcefully: "But you are foolish; we shall be happy to accept." So saying, she took Monin's arm and begged me to take care of her friends.

We proceeded in silence, thinking only of not falling. We had covered perhaps a hundred paces when I saw a young girl whom I had met previously by chance, being pelted with snowballs by two small boys who were seeking to cause her to slip and fall. She recognised me and her confusion at seeing me and anger at the boys combined to bring her into some danger to herself; she could have fallen against a milestone which stood against the corner of a house.

She was the first girl to whom I had spoken on coming to Neuchâtel and I helped her on an occasion less serious than this

---

* A walk on a raised hill a quarter of a league from the town. Meyer forgets here that his friend is not familiar with Neuchâtel.

one, at a time when I had not yet known Mlle de la Prise. Should I now ignore her and disdain my acquaintance with her? I begged the two ladies in my charge to hold on to Monin and not to move, whereupon I approached the two boys and gave each a hearty slap. Seeing nearby a man of good appearance, I begged him in as pleasant a manner as I could muster, to accompany the young girl wherever she wished to go. After which I returned to the two ladies and we recommenced our walk.

After a few moments silence, one of the two young ladies said to me: "So you know this young girl, Monsieur? Yes?"

"Yes, Mademoiselle," I replied. "Some days after I arrived in Neuchâtel …"

I did not continue. I could not recount my story in full, the beginning of which was more to my credit than the end, when I played her false. Something else stopped me. As I was speaking, I looked at Mlle de la Prise, so far as the slippery conditions permitted, and I thought I saw her blush deeply and her expression to change. To explain to you all the feelings that chased through me would be impossible; sadness, regret, hope, pleasure. If only I could have absorbed the moment to the full – the two young ladies could have walked on their own!

We all proceeded forward without speaking and when at the door of their destination I bade farewell to my two ladies, who thanked me. Mlle de la Prise did not speak to me, but thanked Monin fulsomely. It was already getting near to dusk but I thought she appeared somewhat distracted. At the same moment, the Count Max arrived and gave her his hand, calling out to me as I left: "Where are you going?"

"To my lodgings," I replied.

"And what will you be doing?"

"Playing music."

I returned home, I would have liked an hour or two to myself, but that was not possible. Neuss and my teacher arrived together,

Monin gave them something to drink, and we started to play our set piece.

Half an hour later, the Count entered, asking to listen to us. He did not care for our piece and will next time bring his flute. At nine o'clock he suggested we dine together, which I agreed to.

So I end a prodigious letter. Monday I was at a concert which Mlle de la Prise did not attend. Tuesday I only went to the office, and today is Wednesday, with my letter leaving on the morrow.

H. Meyer

NINETEENTH LETTER

Henri Meyer to Godefroy Dorville

Neuchâtel, ..January 178...

Yesterday after lunch Count Max called at my office to suggest a walk together since it was pleasant weather. There is little choice in walks here; we went to Cret and there came upon Mlle de la Prise with one of her cousins. We asked whether we might accompany them to which they acceded. After walking a little we returned towards the town, talking of many things, the Count witty, Mademoiselle gay. Her cousin and I remained relatively silent but I was content to listen peacefully. I hoped no further untoward encounter would take place and indeed we met no one. But as we approached Mademoiselle's house a slight rain began which increased and became heavy as we arrived at her door. She asked us gracefully to enter with the assurance that her father and mother would be delighted to receive us. I had little work to finish in the office that afternoon having worked through the previous evening.

Monsieur de la Prise had been an officer in the French army , now retired and aged more by gout than his years. He gives the impression of having lived well and to enjoy society still – though to enjoy that of his daughter above all else. He resembles her. His manner is frank and open, a trifle free in his ideas, kindly and polite in attitude. I have been told that his family was one of the oldest in the country, that he had been born to a fortune but had spent it all. Certainly that was the impression he gave.

I will not speak of the mother. It does not seem possible that she is the wife of her husband, nor the mother of her daughter. She is French, I am not sure from which province. She has been beautiful, and indeed is still. She received us as well as she was able, gave us tea, grapes, small cakes, a little meal which in the past I would have laughed at but which on this occasion I found delightful. I felt as though I was one of the family with father and daughter. I refused nothing offered to me by Mademoiselle Marianne; she chose the bunches of grapes the Count and I should eat, and for the first time I no longer felt a stranger in Neuchâtel.

The rain having ceased and our little meal finished we prepared to leave, whereupon her father suggested we should make a little music with his daughter. I said I would collect the Count's flute and my violin and would verify at my office that I could take the time off. Accordingly I departed and in due course returned with the instruments.

The little concert was the pleasantest you can imagine. Mlle de la Prise accompanies well, she is very musical, and there is no better flautist than the count. The flute touches our hearts more than any other instrument.

The evening was drawing on, nearing nine o'clock, a fact advertised by Madame who was now hovering round us somewhat anxiously. Her husband begged her to let us continue playing, then said to us:

"Messieurs, when I was rich I would not have dreamt of

guests leaving us at nine o'clock. In this I have not changed and accordingly invite you to supper, which would give me the very greatest pleasure."

Madame said: "If only you had said this earlier!", at which she left the room; her husband followed her leaning on his cane and shouted from the door: "do not trouble yourself, Madame, to prepare for us a late supper; we shall be content with an omelette."

We had neither accepted nor refused but it was clear that we were to remain; so we continued our music. Mlle de la Prise seemed glad that we had not taken too much notice of her mother.

A quarter of an hour later we were summoned to the table to partake of a simple but good supper. One can state that Madame was not over-sullen in doing the honours of the table. Her daughter was gay, her father enchanted by her and his guests hardly less so.

At ten o'clock a relative and his wife came to visit. News was exchanged and it was recounted that a young girl of the Pays Vaud was to marry a rich though sullen man, albeit she was loved passionately by a penniless stranger who was full of merit and spirit.

"And does she love *him* ?" asked someone. The reply was yes, in the same degree as he loved her.

"In that case she is quite wrong, " said Monsieur de la Prise.

"But her marriage is an excellent match for her, " said Madame. "This girl has nothing; how could she do better?"

"Make ends meet with the other one," Mlle de la Prise said half through her teeth, who until now had stayed out of the conversation.

"Make ends meet with the other one!," repeated her mother. "That's a fine proposal for a young girl! I do believe you are mad."

"No, no, she is not mad," said her father. "She is quite right and I like what she says. It is what I had in mind when I married you."

"Oh, well, and what a mistake that has been!" she replied.

"Not absolutely," said the father, "since this girl here was born of it."

Mlle de la Prise had been sitting at table with her head bent forward over her plate, her hands over her eyes. Now she slid along a stool which was placed partly under the table between her and her father, and on which his legs were propped, to kneel in front of him and take his hands in hers; her face lay against his hands covering them with tears and kisses. We heard her gently sigh.

It conjures a scene impossible to recapture. Monsieur rose to his feet, said nothing to his daughter, but raised her to sit on the stool in front of him, and in doing so with her back to the table. He held one of her hands, whilst with the other she dried her tears. Nobody spoke. A few moments later she went to the door without turning round and left the room. I rose to close the door she had left open. Everybody rose, the Count had his hat, I had mine.

At the moment when we were approaching Madame de la Prise to bid her farewell, her daughter re-entered the room. She had recaptured her air of serenity.

"You had better ask these gentlemen to be discreet," her mother said to her. "What would the world think of you if it learned of your remark?"

"Well, my dear mother," replied her daughter, "if we speak of it no more we can hope it will be forgotten."

"Do not flatter yourself, Mademoiselle," said the Count. "I fear we shall not forget it for a very long time!"

We left the house, walking for some time without speaking. Finally the Count said: "if I was richer ... but it is impossible ...

I shall try not to think of it again. But you?" he asked, taking my arm. I pressed his, embraced him and we went our different ways.

Good night Godefroy. Last night I did not close an eye. I am off to bed.

Henri Meyer.

TWENTIETH LETTER

Henri Meyer to Godefroy Dorville

Sunday for Monday. February 178 ...

I wrote to you on Wednesday and sent it off on Thursday without adding to it. We worked late that night. Friday I had a bad headache and did not go out, Monin kept me company, he read to me, we made some music. He is a good fellow – and I must recount a tale he told me.

Yesterday he went into the fencing school to speak to someone when he heard my name mentioned by a group of young people nearby. He did not hear what they said, but saw Count Max leaving his teacher with whom he had been fencing, go up to the group.

"I find it distasteful, Messieurs, " he said, "that you should speak in this way of a young man of esteem, particularly since you know him to be a friend of mine."

When Monin told me of this I thought , for the first time in fact, how pleasurable it would be to adopt an autocratic tone if I had to defend someone as did the Count on my behalf.

Saturday – yesterday – the Count came to take me to call on Monsieur and Madame de la Prise, this being the correct etiquette after our supper with them. But Monin had made me promise not to go out yesterday, nor today; I have one of those heavy colds that this year can be of long standing and treacherous if neglect-ed. This good fellow yesterday worked two hours longer on my behalf at the office.

Therefore the Count went alone and recounted to me at my fireside yesterday evening what had taken place. After the usual opening remarks, Monsieur de la Prise spoke of his daughter, saying that after his death she might need the help of someone like himself to place her at the German court.

"I had a misspent youth," he said: "I spent too much of my fortune. But my follies have been compensated by the good nature of my daughter; and her future is more assured than that of many others. Assuredly I cannot complain. And I cannot be reproached for having neglected to present her to the world which, in truth, is not surprising for what father could neglect such a girl? But, sir, to return to what I was saying earlier, I can assure you she is well born enough to hold her own in whatever company she may find herself, be it in that of the grandest princess of Europe. My ancestors came to this country with Philibert de Chalons, then sovereign. Our name then was ****. The younger branch, wishing to differentiate themselves took the name of de la Prise – the older branch owned much property in Burgundy but became extinct. I can prove all this, of course. I tell you it, not to boast, but to inform you in case she should one day need your help. Your own eyes will inform you, nevertheless, that I speak truth. But here she comes now, and since our conversa-tion is not exactly gay, perhaps we can speak of other things."

Both the Count and I have good memories so you can be sure that M. de la Prise's discourse was word for word as I have recounted. It certainly gave me food for thought. Our evening together was pleasant enough though a little sad. Tomorrow I shall be well enough to go to the concert where Mlle de la Prise will assuredly sing to please her father, and I will get as close to her as possible the better to hear and accompany her. Farewell, dear Godefroy.

Henri Meyer

TWENTY-FIRST LETTER

To the same

Neuchâtel, February 178 ..

How to recount all that I have to tell you? Will you blame me? Will you have cause to complain at me? Or will Mlle de la Prise seize your imagination at my expense? But why conjecture when I am hard put to it fully to appreciate my situation and explain it to you. Ah, Godefroy , what events have come my way, what sensations have I felt ! Will I be able to tell you about all this correctly?

Yesterday at three o'clock I was still unaware of these events and went light-heartedly to the assembly rooms. On entering I looked for Mlle de la Prise, at first to no avail, then in she came, looking pale. She looked grave and solemn as I had never before seen her. In greeting her I felt that I also became pale and for some moments could not speak. I came to my senses however and asked her which quadrille she would grace me with, where-upon she replied that she would not dance. Count Max approached us and she said to him: "sir, I must speak with Monsieur Meyer. This may take a little time and you may find it strange that I should need to address him directly: but you are his faithful and discreet friend. I hardly think you will mock me for engaging him on a subject that , but for pity of another, I would be a stranger to. Will you also forego dancing this evening? In a minute we will all three sit on this bench, you in the middle between Monsieur Meyer and myself whereupon I shall give the impression of speaking to both of you. Probably we shall be interrupted but we must not be offended by this. Sometimes one of us may have to leave then to return and take up our conversation anew. I ask your pardon for such a preamble which must appear pedantic. I admit to being very much affected by the need to settle this matter. And it can hardly be surprising that at my age – but let me go now and speak to my friends for a moment and I will return when dancing begins."

It was necessary indeed that she should cease speaking since my trembling legs demanded that I sit down. I felt more dead than alive. She had not looked at me, indeed she had looked away from me at the time she was speaking. I said to the Count that we should sit down.

"Can you guess what she has to speak to you about?" he asked.

"Not exactly, " I replied. " 'For pity of another?'" he asked.

I was silenced as Mlle de la Prise returned to sit at his side.

"But, sir" she said to the Count. "You have not answered me. Will you sacrifice a part of your evening that might otherwise be gay and amusing to hear a tale that is somewhat sad and does not concern you?"

The Count assured her that he was at her command in this, as in all things.

"And you, sir" she said to me. "I have not asked if you accept that I should meddle in your affairs?" I nodded my head in reply which was all I could manage.

"And do you consent to the Count knowing all that has happened to you since arriving in Neuchâtel? I should have asked you this before."

"I consent to all that may please you, Mademoiselle, " I replied.

"Well then, " she replied, "I will tell you that two seamstresses were working yesterday at my mother's and had brought along a young assistant who appeared pale, sad and trembling; she asked me not to go out that evening, as I had intended, and to allow her to speak to me alone on the pretext of trying on clothes in my room."

Here we were interrupted by several ladies, one of whom Mlle de la Prise invited to sit between me and the Count. Imagine, if you can, the state that I was in. The visitor duly left and Mademoiselle took up her story again.

"I agreed to stay on and when we were alone the girl recounted how she had met you, how you had helped her, and the fatal consequence that had transpired. In floods of tears she said she was with child and what was to become of her? And to become of the child with no support?"

Mlle de la Prise ceased speaking and for a long time I could not say a word. Several times I tried and failed to open my mouth, then I heard my voice saying: "did she tell you, Mademoiselle, that I had seduced her?"*

"No, sir."

"Did she tell you when, and how I ceased to see her?"

"Yes, sir, she told me all and had the goodness also to show me your letters."

"Mademoiselle, I have reason to believe I am the child's father, and therefore neither the mother nor the child will ever be abandoned, from shame or unhappiness. The child will be brought up and I shall care for it always. For the moment, just let me draw breath! I am hardly in a fit state to thank you. I must go outside to get some fresh air and will return in a quarter of an hour. It is all

---

* "Seduced". The law distinguished the difference between a carnal affair having its origins in feelings (as here) rather than seduction achieved by "criminal manoeuvres" which was heavily punished. I suppose "criminal manoeuvres" may be taken as rape. And we must bear in mind that pregnancy out of wedlock was punished by exile.

so sudden! I am so young still ... it is only very recently that women have ceased to be strangers to me! Events have overtaken me one after the other. But she did say I had not seduced her and I have not seen her for two months? Certainly she must be saved ..."

I left on that note to walk in the street for about an hour, coming and going like a demented madman. Me, Godefroy, with a pregnant mistress, shortly to be a father! Eventually I returned, according to my promise, to find Mlle more relaxed and laughing. She pressed us to take some tea which she poured out for us. We sat down again with the Count.

"Well, Monsieur Meyer, what would you like me to say to the young girl?"

"Mademoiselle," I replied, "promise her – give her – or I should say cause her to be given – through the auspices of an erstwhile and trusted servant – each month a sum of money which you consider reasonable. I will stand the cost of all this. I am only so glad it is you – though I would not have wished it thus – I am nevertheless so happy that it is you who are caring for this – it is a sort of link between us – may I dare to say that? It is at the very least an obligation that binds me to you. You can never doubt my gratitude, my respect, my duty and devotion to you."

"None of those shall I doubt though I do not merit them," she replied to this.

"You therefore accept this burden? The young girl will not suffer, will not have to work? She will not be insulted or reproached?"

"Have no fear" she replied. "I will account to you each month what I have done and you can thereupon give me both your thanks and the next installment." She smiled with these last words.

"It won't be necessary for him to see her again?" asked the Count.

"Not necessary in the least" she replied hurriedly. I looked at her. She saw this and blushed. I bent down next to her whereupon she asked whether I had dropped something.

"No, nothing. I bent down to kiss your dress. You are an angel, a goddess!"

I got to my feet and stood in front of them, crying but not embarrassed by this. Only they were aware of my predicament. The Count showed his compassion, Mlle was much moved and said: "we have reached a happy solution. The girl was not upset unduly and not wholly unhappy." She and the Count would return home where the young girl was still working. I was told to remain, even to dance if I wished. I gave my purse to the Count and I saw them leave. Thus finished this strange evening.

Saturday evening I met the caustic one in the street. He stopped me in friendly fashion.

"Sir! The stranger in our midst! We are not unkind people in this town but we are sensitive and can take offence. We are quick to anticipate and to be watchful of others. As we are unfamiliar with passion we may not always recognise an intrigue but beware! If it is your intention to cause us to suspect an intrigue between yourself and the most amiable lady in Neuchâtel, I beg you not to give me proof of it ..." and he went on his way.

I am sending you the copy of my letter to my uncle. The Count was able to read it to Mlle who sealed it herself whereupon the count put it in the post.

TWENTY-SECOND LETTER

Monsieur ...at Frankfurt

Neuchâtel, .. February, 178..

My dear Uncle

A young girl, a seamstress, whom I did not seduce, says that I caused her to be pregnant and that I am the father of her child. Circumstances, in particular the person in whom she confided, persuade me that she speaks the truth. I have sufficient funds for the present to support her in her needs; and the child shall certainly not want for food during my lifetime however straitened may be my circumstances. But if I die before reaching an age to make a will, may I entreat you, dear uncle, to regard the child as that of your nephew. You have the assurance that it is the child of myself and a Julianne C. I will elaborate no further.

I have the honour to be, dear Uncle, your humble and obedient servant.

H. Meyer

TWENTY-THIRD LETTER

To Monsieur Meyer

Frankfurt, .. February, 178..

Let the young girl come to me. Ensure she has what she needs to make the journey. I will pay the costs. I wish her to have the child here and I will take care of her in her delivery. All this on one condition; namely that after delivery of the child the mother will depart leaving me the child. I may help the mother financially if I am satisfied with her conduct. I know that in Neuchâtel a child's circumstances are recorded at its baptism and I do not want yours to be brought up in this sad knowledge. If one day the child acquires this knowledge then it will be sufficiently contented in its life so as not to reproach you; providing, of course, you have meanwhile behaved so well that the child would anyway have preferred you as its father – despite the stain that accompanied its birth and the manner of that birth. It is up to you, Henri, through your conduct to remove the stain from your son or daughter.

Charles D.

Herewith a bill of exchange for 50 louis.

TWENTY-FOURTH LETTER

Monsieur Charles D... at Frankfurt

Neuchâtel, .. February, 178..

My dear Uncle

The girl is on her way. What can I say to you? Mere thanks are not enough. May heaven bless you ! As also my child! I cannot say more.

H. Meyer

TWENTY-FIFTH LETTER

H. Meyer to Godefroy Dorville

Neuchâtel, March, 178..

I am sending you a copy of my uncle's letter. I did not see the girl before she left. Mlle de la Prise, the Count and an old servant of hers took care of everything.

TWENTY-SIXTH LETTER

To the same

Neuchâtel, .. March 178..

After the remarks by my caustic protector, whom henceforth I shall call by his name of Z***, Count Max asked Mlle how she wished me to conduct myself. "As before" she replied. "He must go to the assembly, the concerts, and indeed perhaps some of my relatives will invite him."

The day before yesterday the Count and I were at my fireside, thinking of many things. We needed some distraction and I suggested we visit Monsieur Z***. I owed him this courtesy in view of his interest in me, an interest that involved Mlle de la Prise and my conduct towards her. For days I had not walked out, I was sombre at work, I worked harder than ever to distract me from my troubles. I warned the Count that Monsieur Z*** would probably fire at us bitter comments and curious though interesting notions on the country, its commerce, government and customs.

Off we went to find him; and he expressed to us his piquant views which suited my taste. I do not remember all that he said but he intimated that people of this town are: sociable, busybodies, kindly, clever, much talented as artisans but not at all in the arts. Greatness is as foreign to them as simplicity, neither of which they understand nor perceive.

Will you come and see me if you come to Strasbourg? Are your affairs in Frankfurt so pressing? Farewell, dear Godefroy, from your true friend

H. Meyer

TWENTY-SEVENTH LETTER

To the same

Neuchâtel, March, 178..

I was duly invited by Mlle's family and relations when all of Neuchâtel's best company were present. She did the honours and was the flower of the gathering. She seems changed: her manner is less gay yet no less natural; she is as striking as always yet her eyes sometimes appear sad. She is self-assured yet reserved; she seems more serious. Her old carefree and vivacious manner has been replaced by a gentle seriousness that merits her position. She so much deserves my praise! She has saved a young girl from certain misery, from vice, perhaps death, and a child from opprobrium and perhaps also from death, if not a protracted misery. She has also saved a young man hitherto uncorrupted.

On Monday there was no concert – they acted a comedy instead. Suffice it to say that here there is no more talent for acting than for singing. The comedy, as played, showed our local women acting the parts of marquises, soubrettes, villagers, by turn scolding, artless, affected.

Yesterday, at the assembly Mlle danced with everybody and I with as many partners as wished to dance with me. I danced a quadrille with her. My heart felt constricted and palpitated, but what a difference from the first time I danced with her in this same room, when my heart told me the same story.

Monsieur Z*** greeted me with an air of approval and shook me by the hand.

Godefroy, I await with impatience your letter telling me whether or not you will visit me. You would see Mlle de la Prise and the Count Max, and your best friend would embrace you.

Meyer

TWENTY-EIGHTH LETTER

Mlle de la Prise to Mlle de Ville

Neuchâtel, .. March 178..

I was not wrong! He loves me, it is certain that he loves me. He has not said as much but if he had said it a thousand times it would still be the case. All has not been so easy since those first days, Eugénie, when I have known sorrow, distress and something that resembles jealousy. Ah, may I always be preserved from that! I would prefer not to love him any longer than to have to fear this terrible sentiment. Luckily I have not had to put it to the test as I have never had any doubts on that score. I do not wish to remember the past, only the happiness of the present. I am at ease with myself despite the pain I have suffered. I would gladly have paid more dearly still to reach my present contentment, my present role: that of friend, the dearest friend one could imagine. I am at the centre of his affairs, I act for him, I know his thoughts. We understand each other without a word spoken. We could be surrounded by a thousand strangers: only I would exist for him, and he for me. Each would ask the other for advice or assistance; to give and receive would be equally pleasing between us. In addition we would share difficulties, pleasures, needs. We were certainly born one for the other, not necessarily to live together, that I cannot yet know, but to love one another. You may find this letter foolish but you would be wrong. It is not at all foolish and I know what I am saying. Adieu, dear Eugénie. I will not let you have him after all!

Mlle de la Prise

TWENTY-NINTH LETTER

Henri Meyer to Mlle de la Prise

Do I dare to write to you. Is it really to you that I am writing?
Am I writing for you or rather for myself – to open my heart in
order to relieve it?

You love me! Is it not true that you love me? If you do not
love me I shall accuse Heaven of cruelty and even injustice. I
would then be the plaything of a deceiver. The affinity I feel, the
sympathy for you that gripped me at our first meeting would not
be real. Yet these feelings are real – and I believe real to you as
well! Your blushing at the concert when you sang next to me
showed that you felt this too. I believe I merit your love, that I
should not have to persevere to gain the prize of your heart, but
that it should be given to me just as mine is given to you.

If you do not love me, do not say so. Deceive me I beseech
you, and for your own sake also, because you will reproach yourself for my despair. Forgive me, Mademoiselle, my delirium. If
you find me presumptive, then your heart does not understand
me, will never do so and my heart is then lost. It can never be
given to another, nor could I ask it of another.

I am so young still, even the hope of happiness might be
denied me. Do not pronounce sentence! What is it to you if I am
deceived? Spare me, do not undeceive me!

Perhaps I would not have told you all this if I had not been
obliged to leave you. Content just to see you or even to hope to
see you; each day having my esteem for you yet my fear also of
displeasing you; the uncertainty of all this would no doubt have
prevented me for a long time from asking or saying anything. But
I cannot depart from you without saying that I love you. Can you
doubt this?

My oldest friend, Dorville, friend of my childhood and my

youth is ill at Strasbourg. He asks me to go in a written request. I leave tomorrow before dawn. Will I be able to send you this letter? Can I expect a reply? Count Max has promised to come this evening but he is late. Ah, here he is now, I hear him outside. He may read what I have written, scarcely legible though it is, and has undertaken to carry my letter to you or to find a way for you to read it.

H. Meyer

THIRTIETH LETTER

Count Max to Henri Meyer

I called at xxx's where I knew she was to be found. They had finished their games and she was sitting alone. I asked her to read a letter from one of my friends. She read it, took a card and asked me for a pencil. First she drew a flower, then she wrote. Read the card – but you have already read it! Happy Meyer! How do you endear yourself to us? How charm us? I am invited for supper but thereafter I will call on you and stay until you leave. I might even come with you!

M. de R***

Reply from Mlle de la Prise

If you had been deceived, Monsieur, I would be much troubled – but in that case I would now undeceive you.

Note to the First Edition.

The publisher of these letters knows neither whether they have a sequel nor where he might obtain such a sequel should it exist.*

---

* Belle certainly contemplated a sequel but rejected the idea for the best of reasons. The realism that infused the first *Letters* would be lost now that their authorship had been exposed.

Vers ajoutés à la deuxième édition des
Lettres neuchâteloises

Peuple aimiable de Neuchâtel,
Pourquoi vous offenser d'une faible satire?
De tout auteur e'est le droit immortel
Que de fronder peuple, royaume, empire.
S'il dit bien, il est écouté,
On le lit, il amuse, et parfois il corrige;
S'il a tort, bientôt rejeté,
Il est le seul que son ouvrage afflige.
Mais, dites-moi, prétendiez-vous
N'avoir pas vos défauts aussi bien que les autres?
Ou vouliez-vous qu'éclairant ceux de tous,
On s'aveuglât seulement sur les vôtres?
On reproche aux Français la folle vanité
Aux Hollandais la pesante indolence,
Aux Espagnols l'ignorante fierté,
Au peuple anglais la farouche insolence.
Charmant peuple neuchâtelois,
Soyez content de la nature:
Elle pouvait, sans vous faire d'injure,
Ne pas vous accorder tous les dons à la fois.

Verses added by Belle to the second edition of
Letters from Neuchâtel

[Good people of Neuchâtel,
Why be offended by a slight satire?
Surely an author has the right to propel
Sling shots at people, kingdoms, empire.

If he speaks truth he will be certainly heard;
He will be read, will amuse, may bring about change.
But should he speak falsely then his every word
Will be rejected and denied in des_er_ved exchange.
So tell me, are you then of a mind
Not to have faults as others inspire?
Or do you prefer to stay rigidly blind
To those faults to which you must surely aspire?
The French we reproach for being so vain;
The Dutch for their layabout ways;
The Spanish treat us all with a lofty disdain
And the English with insolent gaze.

So, charming people of Neuchâtel,
Accept with good grace nature's way
Of according you talents that sadly may
Not please you always so well].

LETTERS FROM MISTRISS HENLEY

LETTERS TO AN UNKNOWN LADY IN FRANCE
BY WHOM THEY WERE PUBLISHED IN GENEVA,
MARCH 1784

PREFACE

T HE TITLE OF Mistriss rather than "Mistress" was used by Belle purposely to convey its pronunciation in the English manner. This is the form used for the title of this novel.

The two opening pages of the original book have been eliminated here. These dealt with the narrator's views on a recent rather scandalous book by Samuel de Constant. Entitled *Le Mari Sentimental* (published 1783), the author was the uncle of Benjamin and the younger brother of the redoubtable Constant d'Hermenches. Samuel published his work anonymously but Belle knew of it and had read it avidly. It told of a good-natured ex-army officer, aged 46; he marries a woman of 35 who proceeds to turn upside down his comfortable, orderly home. He commits suicide. The people of Geneva were in uproar, believing the book to have been set in their town and to have described actual people. Constant's work emphasises that the wife is all to blame and the husband wholly wronged.

Belle's married couple on the other hand are fairly evenly balanced in their mutual incomprehension. Her *Mistriss Henley* was clearly written in some sense as an answer to Constant's novel and is indeed far more subtle. It also caused the same brouhaha in Geneva.

"*J'écrivis* Mrs Henley, *qui causa un schisme dans la société de Genève. Tous les maris étaient pour Monsieur Henley; beaucoup de femmes pour Madame; et les jeunes filles n'osaient dire ce qu'elles en pensaient* [I wrote Mrs Henley which caused a schism in the society of Geneva. All the husbands were for Monsieur Henley; many of the wives for Madame; and the young girls did not dare to say what they thought]."

She wrote the above some years later in 1804 in a letter to a friend. There had been much discussion as to the participants in Belle's little novel and there was much denying of identities as there had been in de Constant's work. The truth as to the true participants in *Mistriss Henley* lay rather closer to home - in Neuchâtel in fact. Mr Henley was Monsieur de Charrière very much to the life; Mistriss Henley was largely Belle herself. The marriage described was *their* marriage. The pain in the intractability of the novel's man and wife must have been reflected in their own lives. In the book Mistriss Henley says:

> "You did me too much honour in marrying me. You believed - and who would not - that, in finding in her husband everything good and admirable, her situation to be of some opulence, given every enjoyment and consideration, any reasonable woman could hardly avoid being happy. But I am not a reasonable woman! And we have both discovered it too late."

These poignant words say it all and poor Monsieur de Charrière had to copy out the book for his wife and send it to the printer! What he can have thought as he transcribed "He [the husband] would not be recognised as Mr Henley and he would be unlikely in any case to read my words."

Mistriss Henley was written and published in the same year as *Lettres Neuchâteloises* was issued – 1784 – so she must have worked very fast indeed. It was probably written within a month. Her sudden burst of literary energy was caused (or so believed Benjamin de Constant) by her unhappy love affair with the young man in Geneva "of very mediocre parts" but handsome, as well no doubt as a reply to *Le Mari Sentimental*. The young man of Geneva never had his identity firmly revealed (though there were rumours) and he remains the *inconnu de Genève*.

Mistriss Henley is both a feminist and psychological novel with implications for modern day readers. The anguish expressed in the six letters rises in tempo as the young wife-to-be-mother realises her desperate plight.

FIRST LETTER

Would you care, my dear friend, for me to describe the history of my marriage from its inception and as it exists today? I will recount events to you that you know already so that you have a complete understanding of the background.

I have an idea! If my letters seem to you to have any validity and might be of sufficient interest to be read by others, why not transcribe the letters but change the names and omit what seems to be of little use or even to be boring! I am sure that many wives are in the same situation as I am. I would like, if not to change them, at least to warn husbands and put things in their place – and for justice to prevail! I have a slight scruple over my idea – in that I have no serious complaint against my husband. He would not be recognised as Mr Henley and he would be unlikely to read my words.

Let us begin.

I was orphaned at a young age, devoid of fortune, yet brought up wanting for little and with a kindness that maternal love could hardly have surpassed. My aunt Lady Aylesford had lost her only daughter and I occupied her place; I was cherished and loved as though I had been her daughter. Her husband had a nephew of my age who would inherit his fortune and title. The nephew was amiable and we were brought up in the belief that we were destined for each other – an idea that pleased us both and inspired a confident love between us. He was sent off to travel: Venice, Florence; where his faithfulness to me was challenged by one with greater seductive charms; Naples; and the year following he died in Paris.

I will not describe my subsequent suffering for several months – you saw how I was in Montpelier when we met there later on my travels. I still bore the marks of my chagrin and my health was affected. My aunt was scarcely less afflicted than I was.

Fifteen years of expectation and care for a favourite project – all vanished, forfeited. I had lost all that a girl can lose.

But at twenty years of age the heart can glimpse other avenues and I returned to England rather less unhappy than I had left it. My travels had improved and emboldened me: I spoke French more readily; I sang better; I was admired. I received compliments but discovered that these caused enviousness in others. Critical comment pursued the least of my actions and other women censured me.

I did not like those who fell in love with me: I refused a man who was rich but ill bred and without education; I refused a nobleman the worse for wear and in debt; I refused a young man whose fortune was exceeded by his stupidity. I was thought to be disdainful; my previous friends mocked me; the world found me to be odious. My aunt did not exactly reproach me but warned repeatedly that the £3000 she received would cease at her death and that her own capital did not exceed this amount.

Such was my situation when, a year ago, we went to spend Christmas with Lady Waltham. I was already twenty-five; my heart was sad yet wide open. I despised those tastes and talents which had given me vain hopes and an unfortunate fastidiousness which threatened any happiness that I might achieve.

There were two men in the house. One, aged forty, had come from India with a considerable fortune: nothing was considered suspicious as to his means of achieving his fortune, but neither was his reputation altogether untarnished; when one questioned how fortunes were made in India he tended to avoid details.

He was handsome, well mannered, free in spending and liked good living, the arts, and the pleasures of life. He spoke to my aunt. The dowry he offered was considerable: ownership of a beautiful house in London which he had just bought, and 300 guineas a year for pin money.

The other man, available also for marriage, was the second son

of the Earl of Reading, aged thirty-five years, a widower for four
of these. His wife had left him very well off and had bequeathed
him an angelically beautiful little girl of five years. He himself
had a good figure and was tall and of noble mien. He had blue
eyes as gentle as his smile.

There you have it, my dear friend: as he was, and as he
appeared to be. I found all that he had to say to be a reflection of
his agreeable person. He recounted to me the delights of his life
in the country, and of the pleasure he would take in sharing his
elegant solitude with a kindly companion of taste, of good spirits
and talented. He explained that for his daughter he wanted, not a
governess nor a stepmother, but a mother. Towards the end he
spoke out even more clearly and on the eve of our departure he
made the most generous offers to my aunt on my behalf. If not
impassioned I was certainly moved and touched by this.

Returning to London my aunt discovered all she was able to
learn about my suitors. Nothing derogatory attached to the first
and only the most advantageous to the second. Upright, cultivated, just, all spoke of Mr Henley as having a perfect equanimity. I
was of course obliged to choose between them and, dear friend,
you will realise that I scarcely hesitated in my choice.

The base side of my nature may have had a preference for the
riches of the Orient, for London, for a freedom of movement and
great opulence – but the nobler side of my nature was disdainful
of all this and preferred the *douceurs* of a more reasonable, more
sublime happiness such as the angels themselves would have
applauded. If a commanding father had been there to oblige me
to marry the nabob, no doubt my duty would have been to obey
him; whilst forgetting the origin of my fortune I would have used
the riches of India in favour of the poor of Europe. In a word, I
would have accepted a happiness born of a dubious origin,
unashamedly and even with pleasure. But to give myself of my
own free will in exchange for diamonds, pearls, carpets, per-

fumes, intricate muslins – and for grand supper parties and feast-
ings – for all these I could not make the nabob my choice. I gave
my hand to Mr Henley.

Our wedding was charming. Witty, elegant, becoming affectionate, Mr Henley charmed everyone; this was a husband that
one only read about, too perfect perhaps sometimes. My every
fancy, my caprices, my impatience – all were met with his reasonableness and moderation. Only did he seem to lack understanding
for my longed-for presentation at Court.

I flatter myself that the companionship of a man I admired so
much could only cause me to resemble him. We left for his estate
at the beginning of spring. I was full of good intentions. I was to
be the best of wives, the most tender stepmother, the most worthy mistress of a house that one had ever seen. Sometimes I mod-
elled myself on the most respectable roman matrons; at other
times as the wife of a feudal baron; or I saw myself roaming the
countryside as simple as a shepherdess, as gentle as the lambs and
as joyous as the birds that sang all around us. This, therefore, my
dear friend, is a fairly long letter, yet I will take up my pen again
very soon.

SECOND LETTER

We arrived at Hollow Park. It is an ancient, beautiful and noble
house bequeathed to Mr Henley by his mother, herself the heiress
of the Astley family. I was delighted by everything. I was
touched by the white-haired servants running to greet their kindly master and their new mistress. The child was brought to me –
how I caressed her! I promised myself to care for her assiduously,
in an attachment of great tenderness. I spent the remainder of
that first day in a sort of delirium. The day following I dressed
the child in the fineries I had brought her from London and pre-

sented her to her father, whom I counted on pleasing agreeably.

"Your intention is charming" he told me. "But it is not in a taste I would wish to inspire in her; I fear that those shoes, however pretty, might prevent her running properly, and the artificial flowers do not go well with the simplicity of the countryside."

"You are indeed right, sir" I replied. "I was wrong to adorn her in such things. Yet now I do not know how to deprive her of them. I wished to attach her to me by childish means and I have only managed to cause her sadness and myself to be mortified."

Happily the shoes were soon spoiled, a locket lost, the flowers caught up in the brambles where they remain, and I amused the child so successfully that she had no time to regret her lost baubles.

She could read in French as well as in English. I wished her to learn the fables of La Fontaine and one day she recited to her father the Oak and the Reed with such charm that my heart missed a beat and I blushed with pleasure. I spoke the words for her under my breath.

"She recites wonderfully well," said Mr Henley, "but does she understand what she is saying? It would be better perhaps that she absorbs truth before fiction; history, geography ..."

"You are right, sir" I said. "But the maid could just as well teach her that Paris is on the Seine and Lisbon on the Tagus."

"Why this impatience?" replied Mr Henley gently. "Teach her La Fontaine's fables, if that amuses you. After all it cannot do any harm."

"No," I replied quickly. "She is not my child, she is yours."

"But, my dearest, I had hoped ..."

I did not reply and went away crying. I was wrong, I know this. It was I who was in the wrong. I returned after a little time, and Mr Henley seemed not even to remember my impatience. The child dawdled and yawned near him without his appearing to notice her. Some days later I attempted to begin a history and geography lesson but both teacher and pupil were soon bored. Her father thought she was too young to learn music and doubted whether such a talent might not anyway encourage pretentiousness rather than pleasure. The little girl chattered frivolously around me and followed my every movement in such a stupid manner; she began to pester me and finally I banned her from my room. She was estranged from her maid. The poor child was certainly less happy and less well behaved than before I arrived. If she had not developed the measles, which I caught in my turn through nursing her night and day, I am not sure that she would have interested me any more than the child of a stranger.

As for the servants, none had anything to complain of in me, although my elegant personal maid had turned the head of a neighbouring farmer; he had previously spoken for the daughter of our old and excellent housekeeper – whose sister had been wetnurse to my husband's mother. Peggy, the daughter, and her mother, respectively desolated and affronted, had both left the house despite all my entreaties. I make up for the loss as best I can, helped by my maid who is and always has been of good character – if not, I should have dismissed her long ago but the entire household regrets the absence of the old housekeeper, as I do, and the excellent jams she used to make.

I had brought with me from London a superb white angora cat which Mr Henley found no more beautiful than any other cat. He often joked at the imperiousness exhibited by cats which attract our admiration or our disdain. Nevertheless he caressed my Angora since he is kindly and will always make a gesture towards any creature of sensibility akin to himself.

But it is not the history of the cat that I wish to impart to you. My room had its walls hung with bands of sombre green velvet alternating with lengths of tapestry stitched by Mr Henley's grandmother. Large armchairs too heavy to move though excellent for a nap, embroidered by the same hand and clad in the same velvet, together with an uncomfortable sofa – these made up the furnishings of my room. My cat slept, lacking all respect, on the armchairs and caught its claws in the embroidery. Mr Henley had removed the cat gently several times. Six months or so ago, prior to going out hunting, he came to my room to bid me farewell when he saw my cat asleep on the armchair.

"Ah!" said Mr Henley, "what would my grandmother, what would my mother, say if they could see this?"

"They would undoubtedly say," I replied forcefully, "that I must indulge myself in my furnishings in the same manner as they did, namely that I should not be a stranger in my own room; and that during the time I have been complaining of these heavy chairs and sombre tapestries, they would have asked you to give me alternative chairs and hangings."

"To give, my dearest life!" replied Mr Henley. "To give to oneself? To give half of oneself to the other half? Are you not mistress here? Formerly all this was thought beautiful ..."

"Yes, formerly" I replied. "But I live in the present."

"My first wife liked these furnishings," said Mr Henley.

"Oh! Would that she were still alive!" I cried.

"And all this because of a cat that I have in no way harmed," said Mr Henley resignedly with his manner both gentle and sad. And he went out.

"No," I cried. "It is *not* the cat ..!" But he was already far away. A moment after I heard him in the courtyard giving his orders tranquilly whilst mounting his horse.

His unresponsiveness put me beside myself. He had said I was the mistress here. I rang. I ordered the armchairs to be put in the drawing room, the sofa in a storeroom. I told the lackey to take down the portrait of the previous Mrs Henley which faced my bed.

"But, Madame," protested the lackey.

"Do as I say or leave" I replied.

He believed, as no doubt you will also, that I was disposed against the portrait but in truth I do not think so; it was hung on the tapestry which had to come down, and so therefore did the portrait. I had the tapestry cleaned and carefully rolled up. I had basketwork chairs put in my room, and myself put out a cushion for my cat which, however, did not profit from my attentions. Upset by all the hubub it fled into the park and was not seen again.

Mr Henley, returning from hunting, was surprised to see the portrait of his wife in the dining room. He entered my room and, without speaking, wrote at once to London to have me sent the most beautiful Indian wallpapers, the most elegant armchairs and embroidered muslins for curtains.

Was I wrong, dear friend, other than in my manner? Do ancient things have greater merit than new ones? Do those who appear reasonable sometimes oppose their own prejudices and tastes, in favour of others more vital?

The story of the dog hardly bears telling; I was obliged so often to expel it from the dining room during meals that it may not return and stays in the kitchen.

The matter of relatives is more serious. There are those I will receive with my best welcome because they are ill at ease; yet such as they cause me to yawn and I never visit these folk of my own volition since they are the most boring in all the world. When Mr Henley says to me "let us go and visit cousin so-and-so" I go, for it is not disagreeable to travel with him either on horseback or in his carriage. But if he says to me "my cousin is a good woman" I will reply "she is not. She finds fault, is envious and captious." .

If he says that a male cousin of his is a gentleman whom he esteems, I will reply that he is an ill-mannered drunkard.

So I speak the truth, but I am wrong for I cause him pain. My father-in-law I get on with very well; he lacks spirit, perhaps, but he is good natured. I have embroidered some waistcoats for him and I play the harpsichord which he enjoys. But my sister-in-law Lady Sarah Melville who lives with him throughout the summer treats me with such a disdain that visiting the chateau becomes impossible and I go there rarely.

If Mr Henley said: "Put up with her haughtiness for love of me, and my love for you can only increase. I love my father and brother. Your coldness can only distance them from me; and you will yourself be aggrieved at the loss of the happiness and gentle feelings that you could have inspired." In which case I would undoubtedly answer: "You are right, Mr Henley, I do feel the loss you describe; this will undoubtedly afflict me increasingly and more than I can say. Let us go and visit your father. An affectionate look from you will compensate me far more than any disdain by Lady Sarah can cause me pain." But in fact Mr Henley sees nothing of all this and nor would remember it even if he had. He would probably say: "Now that you mention it, my dear, I do perhaps remember something of the sort but – had it been so – what does it matter? How could any reasonable person be affected? And cannot Lady Sarah be excused? She is, after all, the daughter of a duke and the wife of the future head of the family."*

My dear friend, blows of the fist would make me less angry than all his reasonableness. I am unhappy and I am bored; I have not become settled in myself. I deplore my wrongs but I am given no means to correct them; I am alone, no one feels for me; I am even more unhappy because there is nowhere I can lay the blame; there are no changes I want to request, no reproaches to make – and I blame and scorn myself for my chagrin.

Everyone admires Mr Henley and congratulates me on my

---

*   Belle is telling the reader here that Mr Henley's brother will be heir to the title, and is therefore his senior.

happiness, whereupon I reply: "Yes, you are right! What a difference between him and other men of his rank, of his age! And what a difference between *me* and Madame This and Lady That." I say it, I think it, but my heart does not feel it. Often I withdraw so that I can cry in solitude. Even now my tears blur the ink on the paper on which I write – I know not their source. Dear friend, adieu, I shall write to you again soon.

P.S. On re-reading my letter, I discover that I have committed more misdemeanours than I had thought. I shall return the portrait of the first Mrs Henley to its rightful place, in my bedroom. If Mr Henley finds it to be better in the dining room , where it hangs in natural light, then let it remain there. I am about to call the same lackey as moved it before. I shall order the horses and carriage and will go to visit my father-in-law. Should he repeat to me some of those things I had wished to hear from Mr Henley, I could even put up with Lady Sarah!

THIRD LETTER

You are quite right, my dear friend, it is not for me to complain of any injustices occasioned by *Le Mari Sentimental*.* I wrote my last letter to you in good faith but my ideas are still somewhat unresolved. I don't believe that Mr Henley has been unhappy – whether through his patience, indifference, virtuousness, or temperament. He feels, I have no doubt, each of my misdemeanours. But because he has never shown me any bitterness, because he has never attempted to prevent any of my mistakes, I have to conclude that he was quite unaware of them and he has not attempted to harmonise our two souls in a happiness that could be shared. He lives and judges me, so to speak, on a daily basis.

---

*   See Preface on p. 123.

An event has caused me some discontent since my last letter. One day when I was feeling particularly depressed at my qualities as a housekeeper, at my slow progress, at my zeal which fluctuates either up or down, Mr Henley enumerated, in the most restrained manner whilst smiling all the time, the things that had gone less smoothly since the departure of Mrs Grace.

"Let us try to get her back" I said at once. "I have heard that her daughter Peggy has a place in London and that her mother is only moderately contented living with her cousin where she now resides."

"You can try. There is no harm in trying, though I doubt you will succeed," said Mr Henley.

"Would you speak to her?" I suggested. "Coming from her old master, such an earnest request will make her forget her resentments ."

"I would not know how … I have business to do … but if you wish it I will send someone …" was his reply.

"No! – I will go myself " I said.

I ordered the carriage and travelled the four miles to where she was living. She was alone and very surprised to see me. Beneath the coldness with which she greeted me at first, I sensed tears and confusion. I explained how lost we felt at her leaving, how much we missed her.

"Might you return?" I asked. "You would be received with open arms. You would be respected and cherished. Why blame us all on account of a young man who does not deserve Peggy, since he chose to abandon her? Perhaps she has not forgotten him? I have learned that she has a place in London …"

"A place?" cried Mrs Grace, clasping her hands and looking up distractedly, "have you come here to insult me?"

"God forbid" I cried in my turn. "I don't know what you mean."

"Ah, Madame" she said after a long silence. "Wrongs cannot

be righted as quickly as they are caused. Your Fanny , with her laces, her ribbons and her town airs, has brought my Peggy and her poor mother an anguish that can only end in our deaths."

She wept bitterly. Persuaded by my caresses and entreaties, she recounted the reasons for her unhappiness. Peggy, distraught at the loss of her lover, and bored with living with her mother and cousin, took off without even a goodbye. They searched for her high and low; she was believed drowned; finally she was traced to London in a house of ill repute where her youth and freshness made her welcome. You can imagine all the asides from her mother in this sad account, all that I felt and contributed whilst she spoke.

Finally, I repeated my first proposal. Despite a thousand objections, all entirely natural and just with which I agreed, I was able to persuade the poor woman to return with me to Hollow Park.

"No one," I said "will speak to you about your daughter. You will not have to see Fanny unless it is your wish to do so. Come, my good Mrs Grace, find some consolation and finish your days in a house where you did such good work in your youth and which I should never have let you leave!"

I put her in the carriage right away, not giving her time to pack or to reflect about leaving. On the way she cried unceasingly as I did. At a hundred paces from the house, I got down from the carriage and instructed the coachman not to advance until I gave him the order. I returned to the house alone: I spoke to Mr Henley, to the child, to Fanny and the other servants. Thereupon I retrieved Mrs Grace, and giving her my keys, I begged her to take up her duties at once.

Five or six days elapsed. Fanny obeyed me by working and eating in her own room. One day I went there to see her work; Mrs Grace came by and, having thanked me for my goodness to her, asked that Fanny be allowed to eat with the others and live in the house as before. Fanny pitied the fate of Peggy and cried on her behalf.

Poor Fanny! Her turn was to come! Mr Henley asked me to come down with Fanny to his study. There we found him with the father of the young farmer and he addressed us.

"Madame, I have come to plead with you and Monsieur to give my son references to take with him to India. There one may grow rich quickly as we are told. He may take your Fanny with him or return to marry her here once he has made his fortune. They must do as they think fit, but I will never receive such an idle coquette from the town in *my* house. Were I to do so I would be calling down on my head all the curses of heaven for permitting entry to my family of one who has caused, by her wretched tricks, the inconstancy of my son and the ruin of poor Peggy. My son will do as he chooses, Madame. But I declare before God that if my son ever sees Fanny again he will no longer have a father or my roof over his head."

Fanny, pale as death, wanted to leave the room but, her legs giving under her, she was forced to lean up against the door. I ran to her at once and helped her to her room, meeting Mrs Grace on the staircase.

"Your daughter is revenged" Fanny told her.

"Lord, what is amiss?" cried Mrs Grace. She followed us and I explained all that had happened. She swore that she had nothing to do with all this and had not in fact seen either the father or his son since her departure from the house.

I left them both and went to shut myself in my room. There I reflected bitterly on the misfortune I had caused both girls. I then wrote to my aunt begging her to take in Fanny and find her a good place, either with a lady or in a shop. After telling the coachman to harness the carriage as quickly as possible, I returned to Fanny and gave her my letter to read. The poor girl broke down in tears.

"But what have I done?" she asked.

"Nothing, my poor child – nothing that you can be blamed for" I replied. "But part we must. I will pay your wages up to the end of the year and will add extra money and wearing apparel that you may rightfully require from a mistress whom you find unjust. I shall write to your parents to send me your younger sister. But we must hurry and I will bring you to the place where the mail coach passes in an hour. Mrs Grace and I will take care of all your possessions which we will send on to you within a couple of days."

The carriage was ready; we went together to meet the mail coach and spoke not a word during the journey. When the mail coach stopped I begged the occupants to take care of Fanny, then returned more sad than I can say.

"Look what I have done!" I told myself. "I have caused the ruin of a poor innocent girl; I have made another unhappy; I have alienated a father against his son; I have caused a mother bitterness and shame."

Crossing the park I cried for my cat and on entering my room I cried for Fanny. Meanwhile Mrs Grace will serve me as a lady's maid. Her sadness which she tries hard to conceal is a continual reproach. Mr Henley appears surprised at all these major activities. He has not quite understood why I got rid of my maid so quickly. He finds the farmer correct in opposing the marriage of his son.

"These women accustomed to the town," he said "never take root in the country and are no good here." He believes we might have reasoned with the son, and that I could have kept Fanny. He considers that by continuing to see each other they might in fact have become estranged.

What will happen only God will decide; but I have done what I conceived it right to do and spared myself further scenes which would have affected my health and depressed me. Fanny has been gone two weeks; Lady Aylesford will care for her until she can find her a place. Her sister arrives this evening. She was in London only time enough to learn how to dress hair, after which she has been a year in her village. She is not at all pretty and I shall ensure she does not become elegant. Farewell, dear friend.

PS. My letter could not leave the other day; on sealing it I was warned that I had missed the mail.

Fanny's sister is slovenly, clumsy, idle and impertinent – I cannot keep her. Mr Henley never ceases to say I was wrong to send away the girl I liked, who served me well and who was irreproachable. I should not have taken literally the farmer's outburst; witness the foolish idea of sending to India a boy who cannot even write. He is amazed, he says, at the passionate extremes that people adopt. We should realise that it is better to minimise these passionate outbursts. I had, for instance, adopted a course out of a generous impulse without reflecting on the disadvantages inherent within it. It would have been better not to have brought the girl here in the first place. He believed he had hinted at this at the time, but since she had come here, after all, she had not been guilty of anything. I ought to have kept her.

Was he right, dear friend? Was I wrong, in this as in everything? It seemed quite natural that on my marriage I should keep my Fanny with me. I had not understood any such hint from Mr Henley. I did not know then that it might be difficult to accustom ourselves to the country – for both Fanny and myself. Why should Fanny not please a countryman and marry him – she is gentle and kind. How could I have known that the outcome was to be a sadness for the family and ill luck for him? I was not at fault to send her away; I could be neither her jailer nor her accomplice in either refusing his visits or encouraging them. I could not be held responsible for either their unhappiness or their errors. Given time, if she forgets the young man, or if he marries whilst on his travels abroad, then I can take her back. I do not intend to forsake her.

It is certain that I was too hasty. I should have waited a day or two, consulted Mr Henley, consulted her, tested her strength of will and that of the young man to his father. I was too quick off the mark.

FOURTH LETTER

I involve you, dear friend, in matters of only small interest, long in the telling and the detail! But these matters crowd together in my head and I prefer to recount them all as they arise. Such small events affect and distress me and put me in the wrong.

Three weeks ago a ball was given in Guildford and Mr Henley had subscribed to it. A relative of his, who has a house there, had invited us to spend the previous day with her and to bring the child. We duly went and I took the clothes I wanted to wear for the ball; a dress that I had worn eighteen months earlier in London; a hat; and feathers and flowers that my aunt and Fanny had chosen expressly for this ball and which I had received two days before. I only saw them at the moment of enrobing, not having opened the boxes beforehand. I was wholly contented with my appearance and put on a little rouge as most women do nowadays. Mr Henley arrived from Hollow Park one hour before the ball began.

"You look very well, Madame" he said "because you could not do otherwise. But I find you a hundred times better in clothes of the simplest rather than in all this finery. Besides, it seems to me that a woman of twenty-six should not be dressed like a girl of fifteen, or a woman of standing like an actress …"

My eyes filled with tears. "Lady Aylesford," I replied, "did not think to adorn a girl of fifteen , nor an actress, but her niece, your wife, whose age she knows full well. But, sir, you have only to say that my attire annoys or displeases you, that I would in fact please you by not appearing in this manner, then I will withdraw from the ball with, I trust, a good grace."

"Could you not," he asked, "send a man on horseback to fetch another dress, a different hat?"

"No," I replied, "certainly not. My maid is here so nothing could be found, I have nothing otherwise that might be suitable, and my hair would become disarranged ..."

"Does that really matter?" Mr Henley said, smiling.

"It matters to *me*," I replied. "But should you prefer me not to attend the ball you have only to say so – and I will be happy to oblige you."

And, both angry and moved, I began to sob in earnest.

"I am vexed, Madame," said Mr Henley "that this affects you so strongly. I will not prevent you going to the ball. You have not so far seen me as a despotic husband. I hope merely that reason and decency will govern you, not that you should give in to my prejudices. Since your aunt has judged that your costume is acceptable you must remain as you are. But you should retouch your rouge which your tears have disturbed."

I smiled, and kissed his hand in a transport of joy.

"I see with pleasure, " he said, "that my dear wife is as young as her hairstyle and as light as her feathers."

I went to repair the rouge. The hour of the ball was approaching, and we departed. In the carriage I affected a gaiety for my sake and Mr Henley's but to no avail. I did not know if I had done rightly or wrongly; I felt very ill at ease.

We had not been in the ballroom above a quarter of an hour when all eyes turned to the entrance to behold a figure both elegant and splendid. Beautifully, yet simply dressed, there was much whispering as to this lady's identity. It transpired that she was Lady Bridgewater, wife of the ex-Governor of India who had recently been made a baronet.

How weak I am, you will say, when I admit that I was envious of her. Luckily a distraction presented itself in the person of my sister-in-law. She was plastered in rouge and sported feathers that put mine in the shade.

"You see," I said to Mr Henley.

"But she is not my wife," he replied. He went to take her by the hand and lead her to her chair. Other men, I thought, may wish to do the same for me! A flirtatiousness came over me and I pushed away my sadness to remain pleasant for the rest of the evening. I had my reasons for not dancing that I will declare to you later.

After the first quadrille, Lady Bridgewater came to sit beside me.

"I have asked who you are, Madame," she said in the most graceful manner possible. "Your name alone allows me to know you and to make of you a friend. Your face, also, inspires me because my husband has spoken of you and says that I resemble you!"

Such gentleness and forthrightness quite won me over and my earlier jealousy disappeared. Lady Bridgewater may resemble me but she is younger than I am, taller and exceeds me in slimness; her hair is more beautiful; in a word, she excels me in those things that brook no illusion. I come nowhere near her in gracefulness and her voice goes straight to the heart.

Mr Henley was assiduous in attending Miss Clairville , a local girl, fresh and spirited although modest and not at all pretty. I spent the evening talking to Lady Bridgewater and Mr Mead, her brother to whom she had presented me. I was contented indeed with them and myself.

I invited them to visit me. Lady Bridgwater expressed regret but was obliged to leave the next day for London and afterwards to rejoin her husband in Yorkshire where he was standing for election. Mr Mead, however, accepted for the day after tomorrow. We stayed talking as late as possible.

We withdrew to the house of Mr Henley's relative to rest up and then, after breakfast, Mr Henley, I and the child returned home in the carriage. My head was full of Lady Bridgewater, of her lovely face and voice. "Admit that she is charming" I said. "Who?" he questioned.

"Do you really not know who I mean?" I asked.

"Probably you mean Lady Bridgewater? Yes, she looks well, she is a beautiful woman. I particularly found her to be well dressed – but I cannot say she made a great impression on me."

"Ah!" I replied. "If little blue eyes, red hair, and a rustic manner constitute beauty then Miss Clairville certainly has the advantage over Lady Bridgewater, as well as over all ladies of her quality. For my part, after Lady Bridgewater the most agreeable person at the ball was her brother. He reminded me of my Lord Aylesford, my first *beau*, and I have invited him to dine with us tomorrow."

"Luckily I am not jealous!" said Mr Henley, smiling.

"Luckily for *you*" I returned, "but not for me. If you *were* jealous at least I would know that you felt something; I should be flattered; I would believe I was precious to you; that you feared losing me; that I still pleased you; that, at least, you thought me still capable of pleasing others ... yes," I added, excited both by my own vivacity and his unchanging calm, "the injustice of a jealous man, or the passion of a brutal one would be, to me, less vexatious than the calm and dryness of a sage."

"You put me in mind," said Mr Henley "of those Russian women who like to be beaten. But, my dear, suspend your agitation on account of the child, and do not let us set her a bad example."

"You are right," I cried. "Forgive me, sir, forgive me, dear child" and I took her on my knee and kissed her, her face wet with my tears.

"I set you a bad example," I told her. "I should be taking the place of your mother, I promised you this, yet I have not cared for you and I say such things in front of you that you certainly do not wish to hear!"

Mr Henley said nothing but was evidently touched. The little girl stayed on my knee and her few caresses I returned a hundred-fold, though with more pain than tenderness. I repented bitterly and planned to be more of a mother to her. But in truth I saw into her deepest soul the impossibility of this. She is beautiful, not at all badly behaved, not untruthful – but not lively or sensitive. She can be my pupil but not my child, nor will she desire to be.

We arrived home. I had asked that the Henley father's household should also be invited to dine the following day. Miss Clairville was staying there so she came as well. At table I placed her between Mr Mead and Lady Sara Melville. Before they arrived, and during a day when nothing in particular occurred, I wrote a letter to Mr Henley of which I send you the original with all its alterations. There are almost more words crossed out than those remaining and you will have difficulty reading it.

"Sir, the day before yesterday, in the carriage, you saw how truly ashamed I was of my excessive vivacity*. Do not imagine that, neither on this occasion nor on others has the merit of your patience and forbearance escaped me. I can assure you that my intentions have always been of the best, but of what use are these good intentions when they produce no good effect? You yourself are exemplary though I

---

*   It is worth recalling that James Boswell wrote to Belle in his letter 9 July 1765: "Own, Zélide, that your ungoverned vivacity may be of disservice to you." Belle is now writing this twenty years later.

wish sometimes you could be blamed for something, in order to justify my own conduct. You have made one mistake, however.

"You did me too much honour in marrying me. You believed – and who would not – that, in finding in her husband everything good and admirable, her situation to be of some opulence, given every enjoyment and consideration, any reasonable woman could hardly avoid being happy. But I am not a reasonable woman! And we have both discovered it too late. I do not combine those qualities that would have made us happy with those that you find agreeable. You could have found these in a thousand other women. You do not look for exceptional talents – proof that you contented yourself with me – and certainly there is no one who demands less of the unusual virtues.

"I spoke bitterly of Miss Clairville because I realised with chagrin how greatly a girl like her would have suited you more than myself. She is accustomed to the country and its ways, is active, hardworking, appreciative, simple in her tastes, happy and gay, and you would have been unaware of any talents that she might be lacking. Miss Clairville would have continued as she had been brought up, namely in the milieu of her friends and relatives. She would have lost nothing … she would only have gained.

"But this is idle fancy and the past cannot be recaptured. Let us speak of the future, and above all of your daughter. Let me try to alter my conduct so as to rectify the worst of my faults. In opposing my ideas for her at the outset, you spoke justly and with reason. But in doing so you appeared to criticise all that I stood for, all that I had learned; you were disdainful of all that I was.

"I felt humiliated and discouraged; I was inflexible, I lacked a wish to please. In the future I want to do my duty, not following my own fancies but rather your guidance. I do not ask that you make plans for me, rather I will endeavour to follow your ideas and submit myself to them. But if I am mistaken in any such ideas, do me the honour of not simply blaming me but rather tell me what you prefer me to do instead of what I am, in fact, doing at the moment.

"In this, as in all other things, I wish most sincerely to merit your approval, to win or win back your affection and to lessen in your heart the regret of having made an unhappy choice."

S. Henley

I had taken my letter to Mr Henley in his study and withdrew. A quarter of an hour later he came to join me in the drawing room.

"Have I ever made any complaints, Madame?" he asked, embracing me. "Have I spoken of Miss Clairville? Have I spoken of any Miss Clairvilles?"

At this moment his father and brother entered the room and I concealed my emotion. It seemed to me that Mr Henley paid me more attention than usual – I could not have asked for a better response.

We never spoke of this again.

From that day on I rise early and have Miss Henley to breakfast with me. In my room I give her a writing lesson, then geograpny, history, some ideas on religion. If I could only learn whilst teaching her! Would that my faults would disappear, my vanity also! I cannot yet speak of my success with the child. Only time will tell.

Nor can I tell you all I do to make the countryside more interesting. This estate is too perfect already – like its master – there is nothing that needs changing, nothing that invites my care and attention. An old lime tree blocks my windows from a fine view. I thought of having it cut down, then thought again what a pity that would be. I admire how the leaves bud, then expand and open to reveal a myriad of insects flying, walking, running about. I understand little of all this, and learn little yet I observe and revere this animated world I see before me. I lose myself in its amazing complexity. I am too ignorant to know why a voracious spider needs to eat so many small flies, but I watch, and the hours pass without my having dwelt on my own thoughts or my childish disappointments.

FIFTH LETTER

I can no longer doubt, my dearest friend, that I am going to have a child. I have just written to my aunt and asked her to tell Mr Henley who is in London for a few days. I am overjoyed. I shall try even harder with Miss Henley. For a year I did nothing for her; for the last two months I have been a rather poor mother; I must not become a mother-in-law. Farewell. That is all for today.

SIXTH LETTER

I am not very well, dear friend. I cannot tell you all at once what I wish to recount – the task is long and hardly agreeable. I will rest when I am tired. It is immaterial whether you receive this letter later or earlier; I do not wish to write in the same vein again. After this you will receive only short notes at infrequent intervals telling you whether your friend is still living – or has succumbed.

Either my situation is really a sad one, or I am being unreasonable and am without virtue. The alternatives are, firstly that which I cannot alter, and secondly that for which I must blame and scorn myself. Whichever way I turn, images present themselves to my imagination that are painful and undermine my courage, rendering my existence sombre and painful. What use is it for me to revive, in the telling, those hurtful scenes that cannot be too quickly forgotten? This is the last letter in which I will reveal my heart; henceforth, no more complaints. I must change or be silent.

When I knew I was with child I asked my aunt to tell Mr Henley since he was not to return from London for some eight days or so. During those days I wondered unceasingly whether I should, or should not feed my child naturally. On the one hand I was frightened of the fatigue, the constant care, the sacrifices this would impose and – shall I declare it? – I was concerned also for the distortion to my figure this would bring about. Then again, I was fearful of being considered incapable or unworthy of fulfilling my duty.

But, you will ask, am I motivated only by pride? Should I not anticipate the extreme pleasure in being all things to my child, to attach him or her to me in every way possible? Yes, of course, that is my most constant reaction; but when one is left alone to think, does one not return to the same thing?

I resolved to speak of all this with Mr Henley but I was fearful of opening the subject. He will either approve my ideas as necessary and a foregone conclusion, or he will reject it as absurd and humiliating to myself. In fact he spared me on neither of these counts. In his opinion nothing in the world should except a mother from the first and most sacred of her duties, unless harm might come to the child due to some temperamental defect in the mother. He told me he intended that I should consult his friend Dr M-, to discover whether my excessive vivacity and impatience might indicate a preference for a wetnurse. For myself, my health, my happiness – not a word. His only concern was for the as yet unborn child.

I did not argue the point, I was too upset and saddened – to such an extent that my health suffered.

"What!" I said to myself. "So none of my views are to be considered! None of my feelings shared! No pain soothed! All that I am feeling is to be considered as absurd. Or Mr Henley is hard and insensitive. I am to spend my life with a husband in whom I inspire only a complete indifference and whose heart is closed to me."

Farewell any joy in my being pregnant! Farewell any joy at all!

And I fell into decline. Mrs Grace was the first to notice this and spoke of it to Mr Henley, who could not imagine the cause of it. He believed that my condition had made me apprehensive and suggested my aunt should be asked to come and visit us. I was indeed grateful for the idea; she has been written to and comes soon. I will write again tomorrow, if I am able.

*****

I said nothing of all this to my aunt. I sought from her not so much her sympathy as to be distracted by her company. Sympathy plunges me into a renewed chagrin, whereas I sought only to forget my grief. I heard from her the intrigues at Court, all the news of the City, the liaisons, marriages, appointments, all the frivolities and vanities of the *beau monde*. All this restored my own frivolity and a sort of gaiety – a dangerous transformation whose usefulness was transitory and which would only prepare me for further unhappiness.

Soon I was to think of my son or daughter as prodigies of beauty, talented, cultivated by virtue of an exceptional education, and admired not only by our own country but throughout Europe. My daughter would exceed Lady Bridgewater in beauty and would choose a husband from among the highest in the kingdom. My son, if he was a solider, would be heroic and command armies. If he entered the law, he would be the equal of Lord Mansfield or the Chancellor, but a permanent Chancellor because no king or people could afford that he should leave his post.

Having my head filled with such extravagances, I was unable to conceal something of these from Mr Henley. I laughed at my own folly when I unfolded some of my dreams to him. But it distresses me to think of it anew, and I must lay down my pen.

*****

We were alone. Mr Henley said: "Our ideas are indeed different. I wish that my daughters are brought up simply, that they should attract little attention and certainly not think to attract it. They should be modest, gentle, reasonable, affable women who would make careful mothers; they should enjoy opulence but could do without it. Their position should assure them of virtues rather than renown. And if all of this cannot be achieved, then" – he said, whilst kissing my hand –" I shall be contented with but half the grace, talents and good manners of Mistriss Henley. As to my son, strongly made, a healthy mind, devoid of vices and weakness, of a strict probity which implies an extreme moderation – that is what I ask of God for him.

"But, my dear," he continues, "since you rate so highly matters of ostentation, I do not want to risk your hearing from others something that occurred to me a few days ago. Such a chance hearing might upset you and show to others that we might not think alike. I have been offered a seat in Parliament and a place at Court. It was suggested that a title might be forthcoming, and an appointment for you. I refused it all."

"I could find nothing more natural, sir, if others have wanted to buy your vote, yet against your principles …" I was overcome with emotion and hid my face in my hands so as not to show it. I spoke slowly and tried to speak naturally. "But you approve of the measures being taken by the present administration?" I asked.

"Certainly," he replied. "I favour the King and I approve the policies of present day ministers – but shall I approve those of tomorrow? Will those ministers remain in office? Might I be removed by a cabal of my equals which would be altogether unpolitical? Following which I would return to my estate here which has always been so agreeable to me. I might find it changed, spoiled, as indeed I might be myself, harbouring a hurt *amour-propre*, a frustrated ambition, feelings quite strange to me?"

"Sir," I said to him. "I admire you and have never admired you more than at this moment." The more it cost me, the more I admired him. Never had I been so sure of his superior nature. "I admire you … but to serve the public, one's duty to work for one's country …"

"These are the reasonings of the ambitious" he interrupted me. "But the good one can do in one's own house and estate, amongst neighbours, friends, relations is more certain and indispensable; if I fail to carry out those things I should do, that is my own fault and not that of my situation. I have lived too long in London and big cities in Europe; I have lost touch with the life and interests of the country people. I no longer know how to converse or to learn from them. Whereas I would have carried my faults into a public life with the wrong of having placed myself in such a position – instead of accepting that providence had placed me here."

"I have nothing to say to you further, sir," I said, "but why did you keep this a secret from me?"

"I was in London," he replied. "I could hardly put all this into a letter. And if you had challenged my arguments you would not, in fact, have altered my resolve and I would have pained you when I could avoid doing so. Even now I am sorry that I have to reveal it to you. I do so only because I believe the matter has become somewhat public already. Otherwise I would have informed you neither of its substance nor of my refusal."

There was a moment when Mr Henley ceased speaking. I had wanted to say something, but because of my attentiveness to his every word I could not bring myself to speak. I was torn between the high esteem he evoked in me for his moderation, reasoning, uprightness – and the horror with which I recognised my apartness from his sentiments; I felt so useless, so alone. Exhausted by all this, my head began to swim and I fainted. The care that was taken of me prevented any mishap, but I am not yet back to health. Neither my mind nor body are in a normal condition.

I am only a woman. I shall not take my own life for I do not have the courage to do so. If I am to be a mother I hope not to have such a wish. But pain kills also. In a year, or two years, you will learn, I hope, that I am rational and contented – or that I am no longer ...

LETTERS FROM LAUSANNE
(PART 1)

PREFACE

THIS NOVEL IS REALLY in two parts. They interlock but can be read separately. The first *Letters* were published in 1785; *Caliste*, the second part, in 1788. Belle at this time was 45 and 48.

The first part of these *Letters* was written in eight to ten days partly in answer to a challenge. Her *Letters from Neuchâtel* (1784) had resulted in the announcement of a subscription for an intended *Lettres Lausannoises*, proposed by an innkeeper (*sic*) of Yverdon. Belle took this to be an idea stolen from her earlier novel: "*J'ai été fort aise de me voir imitée, même par un sot* [I have been well content to see myself imitated, even by a blockhead]." Nothing further is known of the innkeeper-publisher but we must be grateful that he sparked Belle to begin work: "*Je préviendrai ce pédant audacieux* [I shall forestall this impudent pedant]." And quickly. The manuscript was copied for the printer as usual by the patient M. de Charrière.

In many ways this novella of Belle's is her best. It is perhaps also her simplest. The plot is virtually stationary, set in the small gossipy town of Lausanne, concerned only with a mother and daughter and their small social rounds. But so also is it the densest - the concern of the mother to protect her daughter of seventeen from the pitfalls of life (which means getting her married off safely) is told and retold in letters to a sympathetic friend over the border in France. The suitors for Cécile come on to the stage one by one, are considered, analysed, then rejected in this tiny world where the rakes are always lurking in the wings and the marriageable men never quite come up to the mark.

Thus we have a young English Milord (? shades of the young Boswell) whose intentions towards Cécile are never quite clear. There is an incautious military cousin who embraces the girl-child surreptitiously and is branded as a bounder in consequence. There is a shadowy minister with a mountain parish, impoverished but lovelorn and rejected because the mother "fears the sly character of the mountain people." And of course because he is impecunious.

The mother dominates the daughter and in reality is a picture of Belle herself in control of the daughter she never had. By the same token her daughter also resembles the young Belle, especially in the physical description. And her husband had to suffer the anguish of transcribing the book for the printer, in the certain knowledge that the mother and daughter in the book are in reality a shadowy Belle, and the child they never had.

Lausanne's citizens took great exception to passages that describe the influx of a hotchpotch of foreign young men and women to Lausanne, as part of their Grand Tour: "*Qui sait si, en secret, toutes les filles ne voient pas un mari, toutes les mères un gendre dans chaque carosse qui arrive?* [Who knows whether, secretly, all the girls do not see a husband, and their mothers a son-in-law, in each carriage which arrives?]." She goes on to say that the young men of the town are dazzled by the foreign girls, the young women similarly by the handsome swains and that, *hélas*, the marriages that might have been made between solid local folk were often put off on account of the flighty imports from abroad. Belle writes to Benjamin Constant: "*Les Lausannois ne m'ont pas pardonné mes lettres* [The people of Lausanne have not forgiven me my letters]."

We are privy to the eighteenth century drawing rooms and the gossip therein, and the good housewives of the town were most indignant at such inuendoes. Belle does not write so much about the *beau monde* as the *monde moyen*, the middle class, and she is on record as preferring to describe the "*petits gens* [humble people]" rather than the aristocrats. This is her preferred scene. She tells us nevertheless of the ways necessary to achieve the higher planes of society - the required etiquette is carefully described so that in a sense this, and her other novels, are important for the *nouveau riche*.

Pamphlet replies attacking the author followed thick and fast.

The reviews were mostly good. *The Journal général de France* said on 16 September 1786: "*Beacoup de petites circonstances, des riens, du bavardage par-ci, par-là mais des vues assez judicieuses, des réflexions assez justes, voilà ce qu'on trouve dans ces lettres* [Many little events of small account, gossiping here, there and everywhere, but wise judgements, valid reflections – these are what one finds in the letters]."

Belle says herself of the *Letters*: "*un roman sans intrigue, sans but surtout* [a novel without intrigue and no ending]." Of course this describes it precisely. There may be little intrigue, and certainly no ending, but that is the way of this author who was surely writing before her time.

To a female relative in Languedoc

30 November 1784

FIRST LETTER

How wrong you are to complain! A son-in-law of perhaps no great merit but whom your daughter has married without reluctance! An establishment that even you consider advantageous but upon which you were not consulted! What of it? What does that matter to you? Your husband and his relatives made suitable financial arrangements and saw to the whole matter. So much the better! If your daughter is happy are you any the less so? If she is unhappy, is that not one chagrin the less for which you are to blame? How truly romantic you are! Your son-in-law may indeed be mediocre but, truthfully, is your daughter so remarkable in her character and esprit? She is to live in Paris, willingly it appears. Would you really have preferred her to live with you? Despite your protestations as to the infamy of Paris - its dangers, seduction, illusion, vanities - would you be so averse to living there? You are still beautiful, and always amiable. Unless I am much mistaken, you would be willing to put on the "chains of the Court" if such were offered to you, as I believe they may well be.

On the occasion of the marriage you will be spoken of, and it would surely be asked if the Princess would not gain from having in her service a lady of your merit - wise but no prude, sincere and polite in equal measure, modest but with many talents. So let us examine this! It is my experience that such diverse merits can exist only on paper, where the words do not contradict themselves as they do in the world of reality. Wise but not prudish! Certainly you are no prude, and I have always seen you as wis-

dom itself – but have I always seen you? Have you told me all
that has made up your life? A woman of absolute wisdom must
also be a prude, or so I believe. Let us go further: sincere *and*
polite? You are not so sincere as it is possible to be, just because
you are polite; nor perfectly polite because you are also sincere;
and you can be both together only because you are but moderately enamoured of each. But enough of that! I do not wish to find
fault with *you* – I am only giving vent to my own feelings.

My daughter's tutors torment me as to her education. They tell
me that a young girl should acquire talents that please the world
but which she may not necessarily herself enjoy. Why the deuce
should she apply her patience and assiduity to the harpsichord
when she is herself indifferent to it. They wish her to be frank,
yet reserved. What does it all mean? They wish her to fear
reproach and eschew praise. I am applauded for my tenderness
towards her, yet they wish me to be less continuously concerned
to protect her from pain and provide her with pleasure. There!
That is how words are put side by side to fabricate character and
create false domestic situations. Thus are we women and mothers
tormented by those who like to moralise.

But to return to ourselves: you are just as sincere and polite as
may be required, and charming, which is why I love you tenderly.
The Marquis X said to me the other day that it is almost certain
that you will be drawn away from the country to Court; whereupon you should not complain at your removal from family
duties. Let yourself be governed by circumstance, by relatives
who impose, and a father who has arranged a marriage for his
daughter – a daughter who is limited in both acuteness of feelings and reflectiveness concerning marriage.

Would that I were in your place! Observing your situation, I
am tempted to blame the lack of religious zeal on the part of my
grandfather. If, like his brother, he had seen fit to go to mass I am

not certain whether he would not have found better in the next world, but certainly I would be better off in this world.

I have the right to complain of my lot. My poor Cécile, what will become of her? She was seventeen last spring. I have had to take her out into society, to show her the world, and let the world observe *her* in the persons of young men who might *consider* her... *consider* her? What a ridiculous expression to use on her behalf! Who would *consider* a girl whose mother is still young, a girl who after the death of her mother would enjoy a mere thirty-eight thousand French Francs. My daughter and I have a joint income of fifteen hundred French Francs. You can see that if she is to be wed it will not be that she has been *considered*, but *seen*. She must therefore be shown around, diverted, allowed to dance – but not seen too much for fear that people might tire of her; and for fear of her guardians* who would scold me, and for fear of the other mothers who will say: "How unwise! Her fortune is so limited! So much time wasted in dressing up and doing the rounds."

And her finery, modest though it be, costs a lot with muslins, ribbons and the rest. Nothing is so exacting as the detailed criticism of women.

Nor must she be allowed to dance to excess, it heightens her colour. Her hair is arranged rather indifferently by both of us and on becoming disarranged it gives her an uncouth look. She reddens up, and the following day has a headache or nose bleed. But she loves dancing passionately. Though tall, she is well made, lively and has a good ear. To prevent her from dancing would be to stop a deer from running.

---

* This is the first reference in these *Letters* to their being no husband-father. We will see that he had died and Cécile , as a minor, has had guardians appointed to supervise her upbringing. These prove to be her mother's brothers-in-law.

I have now described to you her figure and will account to you for the rest. Imagine a good brow, a pretty nose, black eyes deepset and though not large, these are shining and soft; lips somewhat full and rosy, teeth even, a lovely skin, good complexion, a neck inclined to thicken, against which I struggle with all my might; a throat which would be beautiful if it were whiter; feet and hands passable.

There you have my Cécile. If you knew Madame R*, or the handsome peasant girls of the Vaud I could give you a better idea of her. Shall I describe her overall impression? It is one of health, goodness, gaiety, susceptible to love and friendship, simple hearted, direct in manner and whilst not of extreme elegance, delicacy or finesse is both good and beautiful; she is not of high rank.

Farewell! You will now be putting to me a thousand questions about her and ask me why I said "My poor Cécile, what will become of her?" Well, do put your questions. I need to speak about her and there is no one here in whom I can confide.

SECOND LETTER

Well, all right: a pretty young Savoyard youth dressed as a girl. That says it correctly. And don't forget, to conjure up her true beauty one must observe her satiny complexion, lustrous unless she overheats herself! Her satiny look is then reminiscent of the red sweet pea! There you have my Cécile, and if you don't recognise her whilst walking in the street, then that it is your fault!

Why, you ask, the big neck? This is a malady of these parts, a thickening of the lymph gland which causes a swelling of the

---

* A Mlle Roëll is thought to have been the prototype for Cécile. Like Belle, she had been born in Holland but settled in Switzrland (in fact, in Lausanne).

neck. No one knows the reason or has the solution. Those who live in the valleys suffer more than those who inhabit the mountains. I wish a lasting remedy could be found.

You ask how it was that we married with only thirty-eight thousand francs as our fortune, and express surprise that with an only daughter I should not have been richer. Your question is a strange one. A man and a woman marry because they please each other. *Voila*! But I will tell you more of my pecuniary affairs. My father was a captain in the Dutch army. He lived on his pay and my mother's dowry of six thousand francs. She, incidentally, was from a bourgeois family of this town – but so beautiful and amiable that my father never thought of himself as poor or ill-matched. And she loved him so dearly that she died of despair at his death. Cécile takes after her rather than after me or her father. May my daughter have as happy a life though longer!

The six thousand francs from my mother was my total fortune. My father had twenty thousand francs from his father. Our total of twenty-six thousand gives us an income which is just sufficient to live on but you can see that Cécile will hardly be married for her fortune. Yet I could have arranged a marriage for her, but ... I could not have .... since she did not wish it. Her suitor was a young minister, her second cousin on my mother's side, a little man both pale and thin, much cosseted and praised by his entire family. One was led to believe that, on the strength of some bad verses and a few high-flown utterances he was a literary lion and the foremost genius and orator of Europe. We were visiting his parents some six weeks ago, my daughter and I, when a young lord and his tutor* who are *en pension* in that house, also spent the evening with us. After supper games were played including blind man's buff and lotto. The young Englishman is the counterpart of

---

*   The tutor is to become the central figure in *Celiste*.

Cécile – a ruddy country lad to my daughter's handsome peasant girl from the Vaud. He did not shine at the games but Cécile had more time for his bad French than the insipid speeches of her cousin's. Or rather, she had no time whatsoever for her cousin and acted as the tutor and interpreter of the Englishman. You can imagine that there was no comparison between the two men: one was tentative and cautious in playing the games, the other splendidly incautious.

When it came time to leave the cousin's mother warned: "Jeannot, you will accompany Cécile home, but it is cold outside and you must wear your overcoat and button it up well." His aunt brought him his galoshes, and whilst he was buttoning himself up like a suitcase, seemingly about to depart on a long arduous journey, the young Englishman leapt up the stairs four at a time to offer his arm to Cécile. I could only laugh at this and told Jeannot to unbutton himself. If her cousin's chances with her had been still in doubt, that decided it. Although he has rich parents and five or six aunts from whom he will inherit, Cécile assuredly will not marry her cousin the minister.

On the other hand this mummified cousin does have a friend who is extremely alive, a minister also, who fell in love with Cécile after seeing her two or three times at his friend's house. He is a young man from the valley of the Lac du Joux: handsome, blond, strong, who walks ten leagues a day. He shoots more than he studies, and goes to preach at his chapel a league away, in summer without hat and in winter without overcoat or galoshes. He could carry his little friend, if necessary, on one arm. If this "husband" suited my daughter, with all my heart I would go to live with them in a mountain parish. But he has only his minister's pay to live on, no other fortune, and this is not the only difficulty. I fear the sly character of the mountain people, which is one that my Cécile could accept less than all other women. Besides which, my brothers-in-law, her guardians, would never accept such an alliance, and indeed I could accept it only with the greatest reluctance.

THIRD LETTER

Apart from the two men I have already discussed Cécile has an admirer from the *bourgeoisie* but he would likely pull her down to his level rather than rise to hers. He fights, drinks and mixes with women of the town as do German noblemen and young English gentlemen with whom he consorts. Otherwise he is handsome enough and quite amiable but his manners are frightening and his idleness affronts Cécile. Alhough he has some fortune he apes others who have more than he and risks therefore to lose all he has.

There is yet another. This is a young man who is wise, gentle, pleasant, talented and dedicated to business. Elsewhere he might well advance but here is too limited. Should my daughter favour him, and her uncles put no obstacles in their way, I would gladly consent to live with them in Geneva, Lyons or Paris, indeed wherever they wish. But the young man does not perhaps love Cécile enough to leave his native soil – the most agreeable that one could wish for with our beautiful lake and its smiling shores.

You will see, dear friend, that there is no husband among these four suitors. There is a fifth that I could hardly propose to Cécile, a noble yet limited cousin who lives in a sad château where he and his father read only the bible and the Gazette. And the young lord, you will ask? I would have many things to recount to you on his behalf but they must await another letter. My daughter presses me to go for a walk with her. Adieu.

FOURTH LETTER

A week ago my cousin (mother of the little minister) was unwell and we went to keep her company. The young lord, hearing of this declined to take part in a picnic planned that day for all the English at Lausanne and asked to join in receiving us. He had not been seen there since the evening of the galoshes, except at meal-times so at the outset my cousin treated him rather tersely. But Milord tiptoed round so discreetly and spoke so softly and acted generally with such grace that my cousin and her sisters were quite softened towards him. He brought his French grammar to Cécile so that she could teach him to pronounce the words correctly. But although all this pleased the company mightily, the son of the house was as much displeased by it; he harboured such rancour that afterwards he begged his kind but silly mother to ask the lord and his tutor to find other lodgings. He said his studies, indeed his sleep, had been disturbed by the noise they made.

The lord and his tutor came to tell me of this and to ask whether I would take them *en pension*. I refused at once without consulting Cécile or asking her opinion. Whereupon they changed tack and asked about a floor of my house which they knew to be empty. I refused once more.

"But only for two months," said the young man. "One month, two weeks, to give us time to find somewhere else. You might even find us so discreet that you would wish to keep us on! I am not as noisy as Mr S... says of me. I am certain that neither you nor your daughter will hear our smallest step. Except perhaps to come occasionally to you to learn French I will ask nothing of you."

I looked at Cécile. Her eyes were fixed on me. I knew I had to refuse but, in truth I felt as much suffering myself as I caused her. The tutor discerned my reasons and put a stop to any more pleading by the young man who, this morning has been to tell me that they have found lodgings very near by. He asked only that he might call from time to time. I agreed and he went away, having been ushered to the door by Cécile. She then came to kiss me. "You are thanking me" I told her. She blushed, I kissed her tenderly, tears running down my face. I am sure she interpreted this as my beseeching her to be wise and restrained, more effective than the most eloquent exhortation. But here is my brother-in-law and his wife come to call and I must interrupt this letter.

Well, all is known, all is repeated locally, and it is already put about that I have refused to let advantageously an apartment I am not using. My brother-in-law is one of Cécile's guardians and himself lets apartment to strangers, often his entire house when he moves to the country. He therefore finds my actions strange and blames me. I give as my reason that I have not considered letting, a reply that he finds haughty beyond belief. He remained cross when Cécile said I no doubt had my reasons that I did not wish to impart, and that no doubt they were good reasons and he should cease to press me. I kissed her for thanks and tears welled up in turn in her eyes. My brother-in-law and his wife went off not knowing what to make of mother and daughter. The whole town will criticise me. On my side will be only Cécile and perhaps the lord's tutor. You will certainly fail to understand all this concerning letting to strangers and the crossness exhibited by my brother-in-law.

The beauty of our countryside, our academy, and M. Tissot* bring us strangers from all countries, of all ages and characters, but all with a certain fortune. Only the rich can afford to live away from home. We have therefore, in the main, English gentlemen, French financiers, and German princes – all of whom bring

---

* A doctor of Lausanne, famous for his cures.

money to our innkeepers, to the local peasantry, shopkeepers and artisans. Enriched also are those with houses to let in the town or in the country; others are impoverished by the resultant increase in the prices of food and labour, and in absorbing a taste for the luxurious that is beyond our own fortunes and resources. We often live with these invaders, our own society being often the equal of theirs; we can please and influence them, and sometimes they spoil us in their turn. They turn the heads of our young girls; our young men with their simple ways are shown to be gauche and uninspiring, and those who attempt to copy our richer visitors lose their money and often their health.

Households and marriages are not improved by these intruders in our midst; elegant French and beautiful English girls, handsome English men and pleasant but dissipated Frenchmen; even if few marriages are spoilt they prevent many such from fruition. Our young girls find their compatriots inelegant; our young men find the local girls coquettish.

For a long time I have found it to be unjust that we judge more severely the morals of the wife of a small merchant or impecunious lawyer than those of the wife of a well-to-do farmer or duke. The former corrupts and causes greater upset to her husband than the latter. The former makes her husband appear more ridiculous because if she has deceived him only moderately their house becomes nevertheless alien to him – whereas if she has deceived him immoderately she will banish him from the home. If banished, he appears as a fool; if he has allowed himself to be deceived he is taken for a blockhead. One way or the other he loses all respect and starts to fail at his work. People complain about him, then of she who has caused the complaint. She is considered odious.

With rich people, on the other hand, living in a grand and vast house no one has need to complain. The husband has his mistresses, if such he desires, and in fact it is usually because of him (and them) that an upset begins. He is too respected to be thought ridiculous and the wife is *not* considered to be odious. Add to this that she treats her servants well, she raises her children with kindness, and that we dance and eat at her house. What is there to complain of? Are we not all susceptible to being invited?

Truthfully, in this world money opens all doors. It buys out of trouble and preserves what is worth preserving. It allows a person to be vicious with the least inconvenience. A time is coming, I swear it, when money will no longer buy all that we desire. Men and women who have long been spoilt by their intoxicating possession of money will discover certain things concerning it. They will find it an affront that it cannot procure a better health, longer life, beauty, youthfulness, pleasure, vigour. And how many will die without realising its insufficiency?

I realise I have mostly written about unfaithful women both rich and poor. Of men I say much the same. If not rich they give to their mistress that which is needed by the wife; if rich, they give what is only the surplus leaving themselves still a thousand amusements, resources, consolations.

To let my daughter marry a man without fortune I would make sure they loved each other passionately. If, on the other hand, it was a question of a very rich gentleman I would look at him a trifle less closely.

Adieu, dear friend.

FIFTH LETTER

Cécile enchants you and it is right that she should. You ask how I have contrived to keep her fresh and healthy and strong. I have always kept her close to me; she always sleeps in my room and, when it is cold, in my bed. I love her above all else – my perception of her increases all the time. You asked if she has ever been ill. She has had smallpox, as I think you know. I wanted to innoculate her against it but the disease overtook her. It was long and violent. She suffers from very bad headaches; and every winter she has had chilblains on her feet which sometimes keep her in bed. I find this preferable to preventing her running in the snow and warming herself afterwards. My fear that her hands would become ugly has caused me to prevent this through special treatments.

You ask how I have brought her up. My only servant has been a girl reared at my grandmother's and who had then served my mother. It had been at her niece's house that I had left Cécile when visiting you at Lyons. I taught Cécile to read and write the moment she could speak and use her fingers believing that we only absorb fully what we have learned instinctively. From the age of eight to sixteen she has each day had a lesson in Latin and religion from her cousin (the father of the lovelorn minister-pedant); and one in music from a clever old organist. I have taught her as much mathematics as a woman needs to know*. I have shown her how to sew, knit and make lace. All the rest I have left to chance.

She has learnt a little Geography through looking at the maps that hang in my antechamber. She has read whatever has come her way and which appealed to her; she has listened when she has been interested and not found the subject tiresome. I am no bluestocking, my daughter even less so. I have not wanted to guide her in all ways; if she is bored, I leave her to be so. She has had no expensive teachers, she does not play the harp, has learnt only a little Italian and some English. She has learned dancing only for

---

* Belle was an excellent mathematician.

three months. You see that she is no paragon; but, in truth, she is so pretty, so good, so natural that I do not think anyone would wish to change her. Why, you ask, have I had her learn Latin? To enable her to understand French correctly and that I may not have to explain it; to keep her occupied and give me time to myself. And it costs nothing! My cousin the professor had more character than his son and the integrity that he lacked. He was a really excellent man who loved Cécile dearly, and until his death gave her lessons that were as enjoyable to him as beneficial to her. She nursed him during his last illness(as she might have nursed her own father) and the example he set at this time of patience and resignation was the last lesson he could impart to her and the most valuable of all. When she has a headache or her chilblains hinder her, when an epidemic threatens Lausanne (we are prone to these here) she remembers her cousin the professor, and allows herself neither complaint, impatience, nor excessive alarm.

You are kind to thank me for my letters. It is I who thank you for having given me the pleasure of writing them.

SIXTH LETTER

Were there no drawbacks, you ask, in letting her read, and listen, at will – rather than have her learn by rote? Some of your remarks have caused me pain. Perhaps, indeed, it might have been better to have her learn more of one thing, less of another, but consider that my daughter and I are not subjects of a novel! I love my daughter absolutely. Nothing, or so it seems to me, has divided my attention or outweighed my heartfelt interest in, and for, my Cécile.

After receiving your letter I sat opposite to her at her studies; your words of criticism had brought tears to my eyes, and to cheer me up she played on the harpsichord. Some visitors arrived including the young lord who begged her to accept a ticket to a concert. This clearly gave her pleasure but, at a look from me, she refused with good grace. I go to my bed with an easy mind. I do not reproach myself since I do not think I have brought her up badly – the criticism in your letter is forgotten.

If my daughter is unhappy, so am I. And I would not wish to criticise the tenderness of a mother for her child. My daughter is beyond reproach; any reproach lies at the door of society in general. I do not complain of this; I accept it with resignation. Do not apologise for your letter, I know you did not wish to cause me pain. Let us forget about it. You may have thought you were reviewing a book or its author! Tomorrow I will return to this with a tranquil spirit.

Your husband says (in a note to me sent in your last envelope) that I should not complain of the strangers who are in Lausanne for, he says, they do more good than harm. Probably so, therefore I will not complain. We are used to this galaxy of foreigners. We like it. It enlivens us. The world pays homage to our landscape and we welcome this with pride. And who knows that privately our young girls envisage a husband, and mothers a son-in-law in every carriage that arrives?

Cecile has a new admirer who is neither from Paris nor London. He is the son of our bailiff, a young man from Bern, his complexion pink and white and the best young boy in the world. After having met us here and there he has now approached us assiduously , though letting me know that this was to be in secret; his parents from Bern would look askance at their son becoming attached to a young lady from the Vaud. Whether the poor young man comes secretly or otherwise, he will cause no harm to Cécile, nor indeed to his own reputation. Monsieur the bailiff and his wife cannot complain of any seduction on our part. He is coming now, with the young Milord and I leave you in order to receive them. Also with them are the dead-and-alive minister and the more animated one. I am expecting also the young swell and the young merchant, and many others for Cécile is holding a reception; some young girls are to come but more numerous will be the young men. Cécile has begged me to stay at her side to receive her guests, both because she is more at ease when I am there and because the air is too cold for me to leave the house.

SEVENTH LETTER

You say, along with your enchantment of Cécile, that I should banish the young son of the bailiff. You are wrong in this for I wish there could be more marriages between the Vaud and Bern. At present the richest and best born from the Vaud is a poor partner for a Bernois who does better to marry a girl from Bern, gaining more than a fortune thereby, namely support for his career and prestige. I wish that Bernese girls would marry young men from the Vaud. All this would help to equalise more fairly the present imbalance; and we should cease our criticism of Bernese pride.

All here is as it seems – though I greatly fear my daughter's heart is daily more wounded. The young Englishman does not speak to her of love; he may feel it, and she has his undivided attention. She receives a fine bouquet on the days of the balls. He has taken her sleighing. It is always with her that he wishes to dance; it is to her or to me that he offers his arm leaving an assembly. She says nothing of this to me but I see her happy or abstracted, depending on whether she has seen him or not and on his attentiveness to her being more or less marked.

Our old organist has died. Cécile has asked me whether she

can use this hour to improve her English. I have agreed and she learns it fast. Milord is amazed at her progress and seems unaware that he is the cause. They are put together as partners in cards, when they are of the same gathering. I have not wanted her to play cards and have said that any girl who plays as badly as my Cécile is wrong to play at all – and that if she improves in her play I shall be suitably vexed. Whereupon he has had made the smallest draughtsboard and draughts which he keeps in his pocket. How does one stop these young people from playing games? He says that when Cécile is bored of draughts he will procure a small chessboard. Little does he have to fear that she will become bored.

The young lord's tutor is his relative through an older, though untitled, branch of the family. He is scarcely older than his charge and has in his countenance and exterior such charm as I have seldom seen in any man.

Goodness! How involved I am in all of this taking place and how uneasy in the role I should play! I do not name Milord for the same reason that I do not sign my letters or name *anyone*. I have too much concern as to the fate of my letters and what may befall them.*

The tutor is sadness itself; whether this is his natural disposition or due to mishappenings I am not sure. He comes to us each day, living only a step or two away, and sits quietly in the chimney inglenook, strokes my dog, reads his paper and lets me carry on with the housework, write my letters or direct Cécile's homework. He will correct essays when she writes them, he says, and help her to read the English newspaper to accustom her to idiomatic language. Should I send him away? Should I not be

---

*   Belle's own letters were a source of great worry to her. Luckily for us, her entreaties to D'Hermenches and Boswell to burn her letters were ignored.

permitted to let him see how mother and daughter occupy themselves from morning to night, to enable him to judge our amiable and radiant domestic scene, thence to persuade the lord's parents of our excellence? Should I hide things that may displease her young man, whom she likes though I do not yet wish to say "whom she loves." She will shortly be eighteen. Will nature override her heart? Can one say of woman's first love that she is truly *loved*?

You would like me to have Cécile learn some chemistry because all French girls are learning this; that is no conclusive reason to do so, it seems to me. Cécile hears talk of this quite often and will no doubt read whatever she wishes in the subject. Personally I dislike chemistry*. I recognise that we owe chemists many discoveries of useful things, even pleasant things on occasion. But their activities give me no joy. I observe nature as a lover – they study her anatomically.

EIGHTH LETTER

Something happened the other day which caused me much anguish and alarm. I was working with my Englishman sitting silently regarding the fire when Cécile returned from a visit looking as pale as death. I was truly frightened. I asked her what was wrong and what had happened; the Englishman, equally disturbed, and almost as pale as Cécile implored her to speak. She replied not a word, whereupon he offered to leave since it must be his presence that prevented her from speaking. She caught hold of his coat and began to cry or rather to sob. I embraced her and

---

*   Belle is on record as having disliked chemistry.

gave her something to drink but the tears still flowed. Our mutual silence continued for a good half hour. To leave her to herself I took up whatever work I was doing, and the Englishman returned to stroking the dog. Finally she spoke.

"It is difficult for me to explain what has affected me so much, and my own distress gives me more pain than the event itself. Why I am so affected I do not know and I am annoyed with myself for being so. Mamma, what does it all mean, can you understand it if I cannot? I am sufficiently composed now to recount all, and by all means in front of Monsieur. He has shown such care and concern for me that I trust him absolutely. You may mock me if you wish, and I shall probably join you in mocking myself. But, sir, will you please promise not to repeat what I have to say to anyone?"

"I promise you, Mademoiselle," he said.

"I repeat, to *anyone*."

"To no one," he replied.

"And you, Mamma, I beg you not to speak of this to me unless I speak first."

"I have just seen Milord in a shop opposite here. He was speaking to Madame X's lady's maid." She spoke no further and we made no reply. An instant later Milord entered the house to ask her to come for a sleigh ride. She replied that she would not accompany him today but perhaps tomorrow if there was still some snow. Then, approaching her, he remarked that she looked pale and her eyes were swollen. He asked her gently what was the matter. His relative answered that she could not divulge it. He did not insist and looked thoughtful. A quarter of an hour later several ladies entered and the two men withdrew. Cécile composed herself and we did not speak of it again except that, on going to bed, she said she was not sure whether she wished the snow to remain or melt. It melted but they met as usual. She seems now to be more reserved. The lady's maid is pretty, but then so is the lady herself. I do not know which of these has intrigued him but from now on I see matters becoming more serious.

I have no more time now but will write again soon.

NINTH LETTER

You continue to be worried about her Latin. Do *I* know Latin, you ask. No, but my father often said he regretted that he did not have me learn it. He and his father spoke French excellently and never permitted me to speak it badly, a reason why I am so particular in this. One sees that Cécile writes French well; she knows her language but she speaks it ill. I do not correct her. I am amused by her mistakes, they are part of her, they are charming. She is critical of *me* and corrects any faults in spelling. Her written style is more orthodox than mine, though she writes as little as possible saying that it bores her. So much the better; it will be hard to persuade a love letter out of her.

You ask whether her Latin does not make her proud. Gracious, no! What one learns in one's youth is no more strange than breathing or walking. You ask how I came to speak English. Do you not recall that you and I had an aunt who retired to England on account of her faith? Her daughter came to stay with us for three years. She was a person of wit and many talents. I owe her practically everything I know including the ability to think and to read.

But to return to our daily happenings. Last week we attended an assembly at which Monsieur Tissot was accompanied by a striking Frenchwoman with the most beautiful eyes you could hope to see, and an assurance such as is born out of a knowledge of the world. In her dress she exceeded to some extent the height

of fashion but not absurdly so. An immense cadogan* fell lower
than her shoulders and heavy curls masked her bosom. The
young Milord and the Bernois circled round her ceaselessly, from
astonishment rather than admiration – at least that was so with
the Englishman whom I observed closely. Many people crowded
round Cécile also so she had little time to notice his desertion.
But when he wanted to play a game of draughts with her she
explained that she had a slight headache and preferred not to. All
evening she stayed at my side making cut-outs for the child of the
house. I don't know if the young lord guessed the reason for her
turmoil but, not knowing how to communicate with the Parisi-
enne he moved away entirely. As we were later leaving the salon
we saw him at the door among the servants – I doubt whether
Cécile will have a more agreeable moment during the rest of her
life!

Two days later he passed the evening with us with his tutor,
the Bernois and two or three of Cécile's young relatives, and
they all sat about discussing the Frenchwoman. The two young
men lavished unlimited praise on her eyes, figure, deportment,
dress. Cécile said nothing, I said little. Then they praised her for-
est of hair.

"False," said Cécile.

"Ha! Mlle Cécile" said the Bernois, "young ladies are always
jealous of others. Admit it! Is it not true that you are envious?" It
appeared to me that Milord smiled which angered me.

"My daughter does not know what envy means," I said. "Yesterday, she was praising, as you have been, the hair of the
Frenchwoman to a female friend of mine who had earlier been at
the hairdressers; he, who had just finished dressing the hair of the
Frenchwoman, told my friend that the cadogan and heavy curls

---

*   A knot of hair at the back of the head.

were false. If my daughter were older she would no doubt have kept silence over this, but at her age it is natural to speak the truth as she sees it. Were you" – to the Bernois – "not maintaining yesterday with great animation that you possess the largest dog in the country? And you, Milord, did you not remove any doubt that your horse was the better of Monsieur X's and Milord Y's?"

Cécile in her embarrassment both cried and smiled at the same time. "You are too good, Mamma" she said, "to take my part so fully. But, in truth I was wrong, I should better have kept silent."

"Sir," I said to the Bernois, "whenever a lady appears to be jealous of the praises you bestow on another, far from reproaching her, thank her gratefully and consider yourself flattered."

"I am not sure" said Milord's relative, "whether one should be so flattered. Women wish to please men, men to please women – nature has so ordained it. That we wish to profit from any talents bequeathed to us is only natural, and cannot be adversely criticised. If another man were to be praised by these ladies for something I myself had done, I would say 'that was me.' Truthfulness will have its say. If Mlle Cécile had had false hair, which had been admired, I am sure she would have said 'It is false.'"

"Undoubtedly, sir" said Cécile, "but I see now that it ill became me to say this of another."

Then by happy chance we were visited by a young woman, her husband and brother, and Cécile went to play on the harpsichord, giving us *allemandes* and quadrilles to which we danced.

"Good night my Mamma and protectress," said Cécile as we went up to bed. "Good night my Don Quixotte" I replied, laughing. Cécile is developing into a truly amiable young lady. May she not pay too dearly for her charms!

TENTH LETTER

I greatly fear that Cécile has made another conquest and, if so, I console myself with her supposed preference for her lord. Her preference for him may not be a sufficient protection for her; the young man in question is very amiable, a captain in the French service, and recently married. Or who allowed himself recently to be married! He had no fortune when a distant relative of the same name, heiress to an estate which had been in the family for a long time, had said that she would be willing to marry him in preference to others, were it to be so proposed. His parents thought this to be an admirable idea, and found the girl charming on account of her vivacity, boldness, and her quick speech which had given her the reputation of being a rouguish wit. He was garrisoned here and was written to. He replied that he had not so far considered marriage but that he would do what was required of him. Everything was so arranged that on his arrival here on the first of October he found himself married on the twentieth – and by the thirtieth wished he were not. The lady is a coquette, jealous, and haughty. Her wit consists only of foolish chatter and pretentiousness. I went, without Cécile, two months ago to congratulate the pair when they had been here for only two weeks. She wishes to dazzle and please and she has money and beauty enough to play such a part. Her husband, ashamed and upset, flees from his house, and as we are slightly related it is in our house that he seeks refuge. On his first visit he was very struck by Cécile, whom he had not seen since she was a child. Finding us usually alone, or with only the older Englishman here, he has become accustomed to visit us each day.

The two men understand each other very well. Both are cultivated with discernment and taste. The young man is indolent and is no longer so unhappy at being married because he has forgotten that he is so. The tutor is his usual, sad, reflective self. From the first day they have been friends as though of long standing. Daily, though, the young man is more and more occupied by Cécile.

Yesterday whilst they were speaking of America and the war there, Cécile said to me in a low voice, "Mamma! One of these gentlemen is in love with you!" "And the other with you!" I replied. Thereupon Cécile observed the young man more attentively. He is noble in appearance and elegant – he and his wife must emerge from their troubles as they may.

The young lord came here two days ago looking for his tutor, "our" Englishman, and enquired whether we were visiting my cousin with whom they had lodged on first coming to Lausanne. He thought a bad feeling might still exist between them and begged us to take them along. I agreed and the two pillars of my fireplace came as well. My cousin, convinced as always that her minister son would shine more brightly than anyone else, set us to word games, thence to writing questions upon cards. The cards were shuffled, then picked by each of us at random and we then wrote our replies under the questions. The cards were then reshuffled, and written on until quite filled. I was charged with reading them out. Some were banal, others neat. Our handwriting had been disguised by each of us.

On one of the cards was the question: "To whom does one owe one's first education?" "One's nurse" was the answer. Under that had been written: "and the second?" Reply: "To chance." "And the third?" "To love." "It was you who wrote that last reply" someone said to me. "I would like to admit to it" I replied "because it is very neat." The young married man looked at Cécile and said: "It must have been you who owes much already to her third education."

Cécile coloured, more so than I had ever seen before.

"I would like to know who it was" said Milord. "Was it not yourself?" I asked him. "Why does it have to be a woman? Men have as much need of this third education as we do. Perhaps it was my cousin's son, the minister?" "Well," said my cousin, "Jeannot, I believe it must have been you because it was so clever." "No," he replied "for I finished my education in Basle."

Everybody laughed and the evening broke up. On entering our house, Cécile said to me "It was not I who wrote that reply." "Then why did you redden so?" I asked. "Because, I thought … because, Mamma, I thought …" She did not disclose what she had thought and said no more to me.

ELEVENTH LETTER

Yesterday we attended a large assembly at the castle. A nephew of our bailiff had arrived the previous day and was to be presented by him to ladies of distinction. I have scarcely seen a young man of such perfection. He serves in the same regiment as our young married man, they are in fact friends, and seeing our relative chatting to Cécile and myself, came up to join us in conversation. I was delighted at this. No one could have spoken more agreeably than he; his politeness rivalled only his noble manner.

Our little lord was, it is true to say, somewhat put out of countenance. By comparison he appeared as a pretty young man of little consequence. He was ill at ease and stayed close to us, pretending to know only us. Since the two most impressive men in the room appeared occupied with my daughter, he seemed in turn delighted at his own intimacy with her. He plied her with his favours even more than usual; this impressed her though she could have derided him. Very much at her ease, she was happy only at his attentiveness, whatever had been its cause.

You seem astonished that Cécile is permitted to go out alone, and may receive young men and women without me. You blame me for this but you are wrong. We permit such liberties here; why should she not enjoy these when she is so little inclined to abuse them? Circumstances* have contrived to separate Cécile from her childhood companions and she has only her mother as her intimate friend – which is why she leaves me as little as possible.

There are indeed mothers who bring up their daughters as they do in Paris. This may be due to prudence or vanity but what do they gain? I hate restrictions and pride and avoid them where I can. Cécile is just as much related to my family on my mother's side as to those on my husband's side, and she has cousins therefore in all parts of the town. I find it good that she knows all her relatives, whatever their circumstances and wherever they may live – and to be loved by all.

In France I should do as they do in France. Here you would do as we do. Goodness gracious! I find ridiculous those who measure their pride and disdain according to the person they have encountered! Odious and ridiculous! Such vanity has as its cause a fear of compromising one's rank and station in life, not uncommon in our small towns.**.

---

*   What circumstances? These are never explained. A few lines further on there is a reference to her husband – but no explanation as to how he came and went. Such mysteries are a part of Belle's stamp as an author. She likes to keep readers on their toes!

**   Footnote by Belle: "*Several people have found these* Letters *to lack descriptions of '*le beau monde*' of Lausanne. But, although the recipient of these letters may be interested in our customs, others are not. People of the first class resemble each other everywhere. If I as the author put in something special about our high society in Lausanne, would I be forgiven for publishing it? If one praises (or appraises) people only according to their due, one flatters but little though one may cause offence.*"

     This is Belle at her most sardonic! And she is predicting the adverse response of the good people of Lausanne which is duly forthcoming. Belle is also on record as saying: "*J'ai toujours eu de la préférence pour cette classe inférieure à la bonne compagnie.*" [I have always preferred the middle classes to the best company]

TWELFTH LETTER

Were you not to press me with such kindness and insistence to continue these letters I would hesitate today to do so. Until now I have found writing to be pleasant and restful but not today. To narrate to you exactly I must find a letter .... Ah! Here it is in a corner of my desk. Cécile, who has just gone out, may have been fearful of dropping it. I must copy it out for I dare not send you the original – she may need to re-read it some day. On this occasion you can thank me for I undertake a less than pleasant task.

Ever since the moment of jealousy that I have described to you – concerning Madame X's lady's maid and Milord – Cécile has not wished to partner him in draughts in public. Whether this is due to her moodiness, suspicions still harboured or that she sees into her heart more clearly, I know not. She prefers to watch me though she does play cards with him at home. The other evening he started to teach her chess whilst his tutor and my young relative played piquet together. Seated between their two tables I could observe both the men and the children – they were indeed childlike that evening. My daughter continually mistook the moves and names of the pieces giving rise to joking that was gay if not witty. Once the lord became impatient at her lack of attention; this annoyed her and, observing them, I saw they were both in a sulk. A moment or two later, in a continuing silence, I looked again. Cécile's hand was motionless above the chess board. Her head was lowered towards him as was his towards her. The young man appeared to devour her with his eyes. It was mutual oblivion, ecstasy, abandon.

"Cécile!" I spoke quietly so as not to startle her, "what are you thinking of?"

"Nothing," she replied, holding her head in her hands and

pushing back her chair abruptly. "I find these wretched chessmen are tiring me. In the last few minutes, my lord, I have understood them less well than before and increasingly you will have to complain of your pupil. So it is better I leave." Whereupon she rose, left the room and did not return until I was alone.

She fell to her knees and laid her head on my lap. Taking my two hands she burst into tears.

"What is it?" I asked her.

"What is it indeed?" she returned. "What is happening to me? Why do I feel ashamed and why am I crying?"

"Has he noticed your distress?" I asked, and she replied that she thought not. "Annoyed perhaps at his own impatience he seized the hand with which I had retrieved a pawn and kissed it. I withdrew my hand – but I felt so happy that our ill-humour was forgotten! His expression was so tender that I was much moved. Then you said 'Cécile!' to me , and he may have thought I was continuing to sulk because I did not lift my eyes to regard him."

Whereupon she went to bed and I sat down to write to her the letter I mentioned to you earlier.

"My dearest Cécile, I promise you that only this once will you be troubled by the anxiety of a mother who loves you more than life itself; thereafter you can judge for yourself, after I have disclosed to you all that I have learned during my own life. I may remind you of this letter from time to time but I will not repeat it – so take note of what I say.

"I will not say to you what I would say to many other young girls – that if you are imprudent* you will renounce

---

*   The original says "… *si vous manquez de sagesse*" but I feel "imprudent" carries
      the stronger warning by the mother to the daughter. Of course no one dares to
      say *exactly* what is meant! But "lacking wisdom" is too understated and Belle does
      spell it out a few lines later with "the loss of that one virtue that is paramount."

all the virtues. You will become jealous, deceitful, a flirt, fickle; soon you will like only yourself as you will have no friends – and no faithful lover. To you I say the contrary: that those precious qualities that you possess (and will never lose) would be even more greatly harmed by the loss of that one virtue that is paramount.

"Be wise, my Cécile, so that you can enjoy and fulfil your admirable qualities. If not, you will be unhappy. Profit, if you can, from my advice. But if you fail to do so, hide nothing from the mother who adores you. You would have nothing to fear.

Reproaches? I would make none for they would cause me more pain than you. Loss of my love? I should probably love you even more if you were to be pitied and rejected by the world. Die from grief? No, I would live if only to soften your difficulties and to persuade you that, despite any weakness, you still have a thousand virtues and in my eyes a thousand charms."

Cécile, on waking, read my letter. I had asked some sewing girls to come to us and supervising their work in the morning distracted and occupied us, so it was not until the afternoon that she asked me: "if husbands are as you paint them, if marriage is worth so little, would the loss of marriage be so great?"*

"Yes" I replied, "because you can see how rewarding it is to be a mother. Besides, a young girl will regret it if she is not to be married and loved as others are."

Milord came to see us earlier than usual. Cecile hardly lifted her eyes from her work; she excused herself for her inattention of

---

*　Marriage as an institution is here called into doubt. Belle is sailing quite close to the wind as regards convention, but then corrects herself in the mother's next response.

the day before, found it to be quite natural that he had been impatient with her and blamed herself for her ill-humour. After asking me, she begged him to return the following day to give her another lesson from which she would surely benefit more than before.

"What! Is it only that that you recall?" He approached her closely pretending to look at her work. "Yes," she said. "It is that." "I am flattered that you were not angry with me," he said. "Not angry at all" she replied. Whereupon he left, undeceived – or perhaps deceived.

"I have misled him, which is unpleasant" she said to me. "True", I replied "but it was necessary and you had to do it. You have done well. I wish that it fell to you to decide this marriage," I said. "His parents would not take kindly to it, but that is of no account because they would be wrong."

"Mamma," rejoined Cécile, "say what you will to me. But as to my forgetting what you have written, there is no need. I could not forget. I may not have understood it all but the words are imprinted in my mind. Those things you have told me will become clear from my own reading and observation."

Milord came the next day as he had promised; the game of chess went exceedingly well. He said to me during the course of the evening: "You may find me strange, Madame. When I was last here I complained that Cécile was not attentive enough, yet this evening I find her too much so." In his turn, he seemed distracted and dreamy though Cécile did not appear to notice this.

There, farewell. I repeat what I said at the beginning of this letter. You owe me thanks for my transcribing my letter to Cécile and find that I remembered it word for word.

THIRTEENTH LETTER

All proceeds here well enough. Cécile behaves cautiously whilst Milord regards her as though to ask: "Have I been wrong? Is she in fact indifferent to me?" Each day he is more attentive and anxious to please. The young ill-favoured minister comes no more, nor his friend from the mountains. The Bernois maybe feels eclipsed and keeps away. The two men whom I call my fireside supports continue to attend.

I am glad that you are pleased with Cécile but you ask why I indulge her so extremely. Truthfully, I don't know why, although I could see neither justice nor common sense in imposing a stricter regime. How can a young girl guard herself against feelings she can neither know nor comprehend, cannot foresee nor even fear? Is there any law, natural or man-made which says: "the first time your lover kisses your hand you should show no emotion?" Should I have threatened her with boiling cauldrons which await the women who have transgressed?

FOURTEENTH LETTER

What would you say of an event which upset us both yesterday? It has certainly silenced us today. Cécile is still distressed, she slept badly last night which is unheard of and is pale today.

Yesterday Milord and his tutor were dining with the bailiff in the castle. With us was only my young relative, the married officer. My daughter asked him to sharpen the point of her pencil. He took a penknife with a sharp blade with which he attacked the pencil; the knife slipped and he cut his hand so severely that the blood flowed freely. This frightened me and I went to find plasters, a bandage, and water. He went very pale and sat down. I called to Cécile to use her eau de cologne; she moistened her handkerchief and held it against his forehead whilst trying to staunch the flow of blood with her apron. She thought he was near to fainting when suddenly she felt him drawing her towards him. Bent forward as she was she could not resist him and her thoughts were totally confused. She imagined he had made some involuntary movement when he kissed her passionately on her forehead and hair. At that moment I re-entered the room. I heard him say "Dear Cécile! Charming Cécile!" He rose and gave me his chair.

His blood continued to flow. I called Fanchon, my maid, gave her the remedies I had brought and showed her what to do, then left the room with Cécile. More dead than alive she recounted to me what had happened.

"But Mamma," she asked "why did I not move to one side and turn my head away? He had only one hand, I had two. I seemed to make no effort to disengage myself from his arm round my waist. I still held my apron round his hand that was bleeding. I did not resist him; what can he have thought of me? Is it not awful that I lost my judgement just at the moment when I needed it most?"

I did not reply. I did not wish to engrave on her mind such a painful episode; rather, I preferred to treat it as a relatively unimportant event to which she should attach little importance. I did not even wish to express my indignation to my relative. I said nothing. I told Fanchon at the door to let my relative know that Cécile was indisposed and she went into another room to learn English. Suddenly the young officer entered the room unannounced, fearing no doubt that he would be sent away. I did not know what to say to him or wish even to look at him. So I started to write letters. Cécile curtsied to him. He appeared as pale as she. I threw down my pen whereupon the young officer approached me.

"Do you intend to banish me from your house, Madame?" he asked. "I do not know whether I have merited such a cruel punishment. I am to blame, certainly, for having lost my head; it was unpardonable, yes, but I had no ill design in my action, in fact no design at all. I knew you would be re-entering the room."

"I love Cécile. I say it now to excuse my action, but I would have spoken of it before if it were not unacceptable. I love her so that on feeling her hand on my face, my hand in hers, there was a moment when I lost my reason. Tell me, I beg of you, Madame, do you banish me from your house? And you, Mademoiselle? Will not both of you generously forgive me? If not, I must leave Lausanne this very day. I shall say that a friend asked me to take his place in his regiment. I could not live here if I may not visit you, or indeed to visit you if I were to be received in a manner which I deserve."

I did not reply. Cécile asked me how we should decide and I said that anything she might say would have my full support. "I forgive you, sir" she said "and I ask my mother to forgive you also. I am chiefly to blame. I should have been more circumspect, to have given you the handkerchief to tend yourself, to have detached my apron having wrapped it round your hand. I could not have guessed the consequences of all that although it has certainly enlightened me for the rest of my life!"

"But since you have made me a confession, I will make you one also which may help to explain why I do not fear seeing you again. I have a preference for someone else."

"What!" he cried. "You are in love?" Cécile did not reply. In my entire life I have never been so moved. I suspected it, but to *know* it! To know she loves sufficiently to speak out and in this manner; to use her confession to protect herself and to show other men they would have nothing to fear from her. I was sorry indeed at this moment for the young officer and forgave him everything.

"The man you love," he said in an altered voice, "does he know of his good fortune?"

"I flatter myself that he has not guessed my sentiments," she replied in the gentlest of voices. "But how can this be?" he asked. "Because, loving you, he must hang on your every word, your slightest movement – surely he must have guessed?"

"I do not know whether he loves me, " she said. "He has not told me so, and I think I would divine it for the very reasons you have stated."

"I would like to know," he said, "who this man is who is lucky enough to please you yet so blind as not to perceive it?"

"And why would you wish to know this?" she asked.

"Because," he said, "I wish him no harm but also because I believe my love for you to be greater than his. I would speak to him incessantly about you, passionately, so that he would pay greater attention to you, would appreciate you more, and would put his fate into your hands. I cannot believe he is so unhappily placed as I. I should have the joy of serving you and I would find some consolation in thinking that there is another who could never be as happy as I could have been in his place."

"You are truly generous and kind," I said, "and I forgive you with all my heart." He cried* and so did I. Cecile bent her head to her work.

"Had you told your mother?" he asked.

"No," I replied, "she had not told me."

"But you know who it is?"

"Yes, I can guess."

"And if you cease to love him, Mademoiselle?"

---

*   It must be rare for a man to cry in 18th century literature?

"Do not wish it," Cécile replied. "You are too amiable for me to want to ask you not to visit me."

People came to the door and he escaped. I asked for coffee to be brought in and Cécile to serve it, so that her pallor would not receive attention from those visiting us. Only "my" Englishman noticed her disarray when he came in.

"I just met your young officer" he said quietly. "He would have avoided me if he could. Ten days of illness could not have changed his appearance more greatly."

"'You find me pale' he said. 'Look,' showing me his hand, 'what appears as a mere prick (though deep in truth) has so changed my destiny.' I asked him how he had received the wound and he told me it was at your house using a knife to sharpen a pencil. I found this surprising. I could see he was telling the truth, but only part of the truth. In visiting you now I discover you upset and Cécile pale and disheartened. Please allow me to ask what it was that occurred?"

"I have treated you as my *confidant* once, and no doubt will again, but there are some things that cannot be repeated," I said.

Our guests that evening included Milord who said to Cécile: "You have refused all winter that I should give you a purse or wallet; when I go away I would like to carry away a souvenir, and I hope you would give me one also in return."

"Not so," replied Cécile. "If we are not to see each other again it were better that we should forget one another."

"That is firmness indeed for an answer" he retorted, "and you spoke the words 'not to see each other again' as though it meant nothing."

I approached and said to him: "There is indeed firmness in Cécile's reply but in your own response you seemed to mean something even more striking."

"I, Madame?" he questioned.

"Yes, when you spoke of your departure or separation you implied a parting for always."

"That is clear," said Cécile , whilst forcing herself for the first time in her life to assume an air both proud and detached. If detachment was an act, pride was truly in her heart. His tone of voice in uttering "when I go away" had wounded her. He was now worried in his turn.

Is it not strange that one does not care about being loved if one believes one is not?! That one feels so much love's absence and so little its presence? That one enjoys what one has and regrets what one has no longer? That we wound others and take on the pain ourselves of that wound? That one pushes away that which later one would have wished to retain?

"What a day," said Cécile when we were alone. "What has struck you the most?"

"Your words 'I have a preference for someone else'."

She embraced me and said: "There is nothing to fear, Mamma. As he says, I feel firm and want so much not to give you cause for worry or pain. I have been thinking; there may be a way to avoid any more misunderstandings. We should, I suggest, change our mode of life for a while. This may be somewhat inconvenient to you, and perhaps a little to me also."

"How should we live, then?" I asked her.

"I feel we should stay at home less than we do, and these three or four men would find us less often alone. The life we lead is so good for me and so agreeable for them; you are sweetness itself, Mamma, we are too spoiled. There is no restraint on us all, we say what we wish, we suffer no restriction. I believe we should go out more into society. I will leave chess and draughts alone and learn better how to play cards. We shall all become less indispensable to each other. If there is to be any question of love it can easily be shown and eventually confessed. If love is not to be shown that will be even more evident and I shall deceive myself no longer."

I took her in my arms. "How sweet and sensible you are" I cried. "I am so happy and proud of you! Yes, my daughter, we will do what you suggest. At least I cannot be reproached for my weakness or blindness. Would you be as you are if I had implanted my own reasoning in you, if instead of your own soul you had had only mine? You are better than I am. I see in you what I believed it impossible to unite – namely firmness and gentleness, discernment and simplicity, prudence and integrity."

"May this affection, which has conjured up in you such rare qualities not make you pay too dearly for the good it has done you! May it flicker and go out – or make you gloriously happy!"

Cécile was tired indeed after such a day. She asked me to undress her and that I should sup beside her in bed. In the midst of supper she fell soundly asleep. It is now eleven o'clock the next morning and she sleeps still. From this evening I shall begin to execute her plan, and thereafter will inform you how it has succeeded.

FIFTEENTH LETTER

We have changed our mode of living as Cécile requested and we have been much welcomed into the society we had previously neglected. We are treated as novelties. Cécile's bearing and grace have certainly provided a welcome novelty, as has our releasing back into society the four young men that are much requested. The first time that Cécile played at whist the Bernois asked her if he might be her teacher; the keenness he displayed towards her kept Milord at a distance. People have not lost the habit of Milord always partnering Cécile as had been the case before.

We have had in the one day several diverting scenes. Cécile had gone to dine with a sick relative. I was alone at three o'clock when Milord and his tutor-relative were announced.

"Nowadays one must call on you early to find you in," said Milord. "Before the change there were weeks that were far more agreeable than the last week or so has been. Might I ask, Madame, whether it were you or Cécile who wished to go out all the time?"

"It was my daughter," I replied.

"Had she been bored, then?" he asked.

"I don't believe so," I said.

"Then why," he answered, "leave a way of life so convenient and pleasant for one that is frequently insipid and tiresome? It seems to me ..." "It seems to me," interrupted his relative, "she may have had one of three reasons, each of which would do her credit."

"Which are?" queried Milord.

"Firstly, there may have been gossip as to their previous way of living, and envy on the part of the ladies who were jealous of the young men's attentions. A mother, and daughter, must guard against malicious talk."

"And your second reason?" asked Milord. "Wait and I will see whether I find it a better one than the first!"

"Mademoiselle Cécile may have inspired in one of her visitors a sentiment to which she felt unable to respond and which, therefore, she did not wish to encourage."

"And the third reason?"

"It is not impossible that she had herself developed a preference for someone – one that she did not wish to encourage."

"The men would thank you for the first and third reasons, but as to the second, it is a pity we have so little real effect on their propensity to love."

"But, Milord" replied her tutor "since you prefer modesty in yourself as in others, allow me to say that there come to this house two other men who are undoubtedly more agreeable than we are!"

Cécile now returned and Milord asked his relative: "Might you feel uncomfortable if I were to recount to Mademoiselle your conjectures – however honourable you may think them?"

"As you please" he replied. Cécile's eyes sparkled with pleasure.

"Shall we at least play a game of chess without interference from anyone?" asked Milord.

"I would, willingly" replied Cécile, "but that cannot be. I have to prepare myself for a gathering at Madame X [the wife of my relative who had hurt his hand]. I prefer to chat a while" and in fact she chatted so naturally and serenely that I had never seen her so relaxed. The two Englishmen waited while she dressed. We then all left together. At the door of the house to which we were invited, Milord's tutor said it would not be fitting for them to enter with us, and anyway he had another call to make beforehand.

"Would not these ladies be envied for our accompanying them?" said Milord.

"No" replied his relative. "Though we might be envied for accompanying *them*."

Cécile and I went in. The assembly was large. Madame X was dressed in a casual manner. Her husband greeted us but did not stay long in the salon, and was no longer there when we had presented to us two young Frenchmen – the one very lively, the other silent beyond belief. The first moved around freely, the second remained sitting in the place allotted to him. Our two Englishmen now arrived. They asked Madame X where her husband was.

"Ask Mademoiselle Cécile" she replied, teasingly. "He spoke

only to her. His need assuaged, he left soon afterwards."

The Englishmen therefore approached Cécile who informed them quite composedly that the husband had complained of a bad headache and he preferred to be quiet and play piquet with General A in the study. I then left Cécile to her own devices and went in search of the husband. I asked him if his headache was as severe as he had intimated to Cécile, or whether he had felt embarrassed.

"Are you laughing at me?" he asked. "You should know that the General is a little deaf, so I can tell you all. I did have a headache, I have been affected by the deep cut in my hand and yes, I did leave the salon because I felt ill at ease. And in fact I dislike making polite conversation from table to table. The mistress of the house should be the centre of attention and I certainly have no wish to put her in a bad humour."

We were chatting in this fashion when the lively Frenchman put his head round the corner of the study. Seeing us he said: "I would wager, Madame, that you are the sister , the aunt or possibly the mother of the pretty young girl I have just seen in the salon." Which one?" I queried.

"Madame," he replied, "you must surely know which one!"

"Very well!" I said. "I am her mother – but how did you guess this?"

"Not so much her features as by her bearing," he replied. "But how can you leave her to the mercy of our vengeful hostess? Your daughter was offered a cup of tea which I begged her not to accept, and to say a spider had fallen in it. But she merely shrugged her shoulders and drank it down. What courage! But I suspect she has transferred to herself the affection of Madame X's husband. I would like to meet him for I am sure he is very amiable. In the town here where his regiment is garrisoned I am told that he is a noble and brave fellow. But, Madame, this is not the only spectacle in the salon occurring around your daughter. She is surrounded by two Bernois, a German, and an English lord to whom she speaks little and who seems in consequence to be quite out of countenance. He does not strike me as being of fine mettle. In his place I should try harder."

"You paint pretty pictures, Monsieur," I said, smiling though in truth I was rather upset. We left together and I closed the study door. "Did you realise," I asked him outside "that you were speaking in the presence of the owner of the house, who was there playing piquet?"

"Oh! No! I am disgraced," he said and re-opening the study door, approached the two men playing piquet and said: "How can you forgive a young hare-brain whose idiocies you have pretended not to hear?"

"It is just as you have said, sir" replied the husband, rising and shaking the youth by the hand. He drew up chairs for us and plied the youth for news of various officers known to both of them. Whereupon we re-entered the salon where my daughter was seated playing whist. My host drew me aside and said: "Can it be that all has been revealed thanks to that young prattler? That he saw the truth that I had missed?" I left him to ponder his misfortunes.

Our two Englishmen escorted us home and Milord begged with so much urgency to sup with us that I had not the heart to refuse. They recalled the nasty looks and cutting remarks of our hostess. Cécile said little but drew me aside and said: "Let us not complain, Mamma. Let us not laugh at her. In her place, I should probably have done the same!"

"But not from *amour-propre*" I replied.

Supper was joyful. The young lord appeared to be very much at his ease through having no Bernois or other competitors with which to contend.

Farewell! I am sending you a silhouette of Cécile.

SIXTEENTH LETTER

I will copy for you a letter from Cécile's young Bernese suitor
sent to my officer relative which he passed on to me. It stated:

"Your relative, Cécile de XXX is the first woman I would
have liked to call my own. She and her mother are the first
women with whom I feel I could spend the rest of my life. Tell
me, good friend, you who know them well, if I am mistaken in
my good judgement? Secondly, and without asking you to give
your reasons would you advise me to attach myself to Cécile and
therefore to ask her mother for her hand?"

My relative had written at the bottom of the letter: "To the
first question I reply without hesitation, yes; to the second however I reply no. If the reasons governing my *no* should change, I
will inform you at once." And a note to me in the same envelope
said: "You will oblige me by confirming that my replies meet
with the approval of you both. If not, I will hold my reply back
and alter it according to the words you may dictate me to use."

Cécile had gone out. I awaited her return for our response. She
duly returned and approved my relative's reply.

"Think well, my dear child" I enjoined her.

"I *have* thought well" she replied.

"Do not be angry when I ask whether you find your English
Milord more agreeable?"

"No," she replied.

"Do you find him more personable?" I questioned.

"No."

"Do you find him more honest, tender, gentle?"

"No."

"You would be living, at least in summer, in the Vaud. Would
you prefer to live in an unknown country?"

"I would prefer a hundredfold to live here; and I would prefer to live in Bern than in London."

"Would it not affect you to enter a family who might not welcome you?"

"Yes, that would seem most unpleasant."

"Have you some sort of secret understanding with the Englishman?"

"No, Mamma. He is aware of me only when he sees me, and I do not believe he prefers me to his horse, his new riding boots, or his English riding whip." She smiled sadly, and tears glistened in her eyes.

"Do you not think you could forget such a lover as he is?"

"I think it might be possible but I do not know whether that will happen."

"Are you sure you could put up with being single?"

"I am not sure; that is one of those things we cannot judge in advance."

"And the reply to the letter?"

"The reply is correct, Mamma, and I ask you to write to our relative to send it."

"Why don't you write it?" I asked her. Whereupon she took the envelope and wrote inside: "The reply is correct, sir, and I thank you for it. Cécile."

The letter gone, Cécile handed me my work and took hers up also.

"Mamma," she said, "you asked whether I could accept being single. It seems to me that that would depend on the life I was to lead. I have often thought that if I were single amidst those with husbands and wives, children, I would feel sad, certainly; I might even covet the love or husband of my neighbour; but if you saw fit to move to Holland or England to open a shop or a *pension* and, with you, I had little time for wordly things or romantic novels, then I think I would neither covet nor regret anything –

and that life might be very sweet. What we might lack in reality I would make up for in enthusiasm. I would aim to become rich enough to buy a house surrounded by a field, an orchard, a garden, situated somewhere between Lausanne and Rolle, or between Vevey and Villeneuve, and to live there with you for the rest of my life."

"That would be fine" I said, "if we were twin sisters. Thank you, Cécile, for your plan which pleases and touches me. If the plan were more practical it would touch me even less."

"We all die at different ages," she replied, "and perhaps you will have the annoyance of surviving me. "

"Yes, but there comes a time when one can live no longer, and that time will come for me nineteen years earlier than for you."

There we finished speaking, but not our thoughts. Six o'clock sounded and we went out since we no longer pass our evenings at home unless we have true company here – that is to say a mixed throng. Last month we scarcely emerged – this month we go out all the time. Staying at home is a matter of chance and inclination; dissipation is a task painful enough! I pass half my time being uneasy in society and this vexes me mortally. Sometimes I seize these moments of uneasiness and go for a walk with my daughter. Or, as today, I sit opposite an open window which gives on to the lake. Thank you – mountains, snow, sun – for all the pleasure you afford me. Beauteous and friendly nature, I admire you daily and daily you make yourself felt in my heart.

SEVENTEENTH LETTER

My dear friend, you have given me greater pleasure than you can imagine by saying that the silhouette of Cécile pleases you so much. Also that my account of the lively young French officer inclines you to meet up again with his mother and sister, whom you know.

Cécile is less gay given the restraints she imposes upon herself. Were that to continue too long I should be afraid she might lose her freshness, even her health. I have been wondering how to prevent this. If I am congratulated on her manners or education, I can scarcely suppress my tears. I wonder all the time how to distract her, render her some happiness. My fears know no bounds, and no plan has suggested itself. It is too early to decamp to the countryside. If I rented a house at this time it would give vent to prattling gossip and even if later on we took a house near to Lausanne, apart from being very dear we would scarcely have changed the scene. Further afield in the mountains or in the valley of the Lake of Joux and my daughter, no longer present in society, would be the subject of much conjecture both unjust and distressful.

Your letter has just arrived. All uncertainty has now ceased. We will visit you if that is still your wish. Cécile accepts the idea readily. We shall immediately announce our departure and rent out our house to foreigners who require it. Our army officer relative will be pleased that his regiment is stationed close to where you live and he will be relieved at our departure.

Our Bernese friend is now of no account. If the young Milord lets us depart without a word or, at the very least, after we have left does not chase after us – then he must not trouble to ask his parents to accept Cécile as their daughter-in-law! I believe then that she will forget this youth so unworthy of her tenderness, and will come one day to do justice to a man who will be his superior in all respects.

Note from the Editor. The second part of *Letters from Lausanne* – entitled *Caliste* – now begins. It is preceded by a notice from Belle's original publishers:

[Supposing that this second part of the *Letters* is received by the public as well as the first part, we will try to locate further letters that may have been written subsequently by those personages introduced to the public herein.]

LETTERS FROM LAUSANNE
(II–CALISTE)

PREFACE

We have seen in Part I of the *Letters* that *Caliste*, the second part, was published three years later than the first, namely in 1788. The two parts interlock but can be read separately. *Caliste* was written in Paris where Belle had just met the young Benjamin de Constant, in 1787. He was aged 20, she was aged 47. Belle was in fact passing the proofs of the first part at the time of meeting him.

    Caliste caused her much pain to write: "*Je n'ai pas eu le courage de relire Caliste: j'avais trop pleuré en l'écrivant* [I have not had the courage to re-read *Caliste:* I cried too much in its writing]." Belle had had a painful love affair lasting some two or three years with a young man in Geneva and she must have written *Caliste* on the rebound. Constant said of the man in Geneva, in his *Cahier Rouge*: "*Un homme beacoup plus jeune qu'elle, d'un ésprit très médiocre, mais d'une belle figure* [A man much younger than her, of only very middling spirit but with a handsome countenance]." We can be grateful to the young man for having inspired Belle to write *Caliste*. It was published in Paris together with a new edition of the first part of the *Letters*, in 1788, and became the most successful and celebrated of all her novels. It is also the longest.

The ingredients of the plot of *Caliste* are best told by Geoffrey Scott (from his *Portrait of Zélide*, p. 94):

> "The story is put together with all the romantic machinery so dear to the eighteenth century. We have infants confused at birth, fraternal devotion and bereavement, consolation from a woman virtuous and talented but unjustly disgraced, paternal severity, filial submission, feminine meekness, tragic and final separation."

William D., tutor to Milord in Part I, writes to Cécile's mother (in whose chimney corner he sits sadly contemplating his wasted life) to tell her the story of his anguished love affair with Caliste. Caliste herself is not, according to worldly opinion, of the sort to marry. She is a demi-mondaine and William (more of an anti-hero than anything else) is unable to go against his father's wishes that he should not marry her. The father has other plans for his son: a seat in parliament, civil service, some career where the family name and connections will secure a high post – and probably a title. Caliste does not fit into this picture. She had been, after all, an actress, and sold by her mother into being a kept woman by Lord L. The elite of Bath and London *salons* look very firmly askance at Caliste, and the lovelorn William is hard put to it to decide what he should do. He is the most indecisive anti-hero of all time. The fact that she is a saintly person, talented, of good family (originally, before her disgrace) and beautiful counts little in her favour against the prejudices of the age.

In many ways *Caliste* can be read as a novel of suspense. Will William, can he, should he, marry her? Or at least make her his mistress? The tension over this indecision runs right through the novel and does not flag. Or *Caliste* can be read as a feminist novel set in a male-dominated society; all the men in the tale are bigoted and purblind with prejudice.

Benjamin de Constant writes to Belle and praises her for her "rehabilitation of poor mistaken" Caliste. He thinks Belle should have "explained a little more explicitly what *l'auteur a laissé dans le vague.* [the author has left rather vague]" "Le vague" probably refers to the secret affair Belle had had in Geneva., and in some sense *Caliste* is all about a secret affair that cannot be resolved. And, perhaps, as rather a long shot, the affair has parallels with Belle's own clandestine exchange of letters over many years with d'Hermenches, and again, of no possible resolution.

Technically, the novel does "close". Belle's others novels are often criticised for having neither a beginning nor an end - they do not "close". *Letters from Lausanne* in its two parts is beautifully constructed to give a conclusion to both parts. Cécile and Caliste as heroines are both "closed" by the end, albeit sadly.

The combined novel has had enormous success and has scarcely been out of print, in French, since 1788. Its only translation into English was in 1925. On its original publication, the reviews were excellent, viz. the *Correspondence Littéraire*, January 1788: "*Nous connaissons peu d'ouvrages où la passion de l'amour soit exprimée avec une sensibilité plus vive , plus profonde, et dont l'intérêt soit tout à la fois plus délicat et plus attachant* [We know few works in which the passion of love is expressed with a more ardent sensibility or a greater depth, and where the interest is more delicate or engaging]."

EIGHTEENTH LETTER

We await your reply to my last letter, in a pretty little apartment loaned to us in the meantime at a distance of three-quarters of a

---

*   Two miles.

league* from Lausanne. The people who have rented my house were in a hurry to take up residence. I left all our furniture in place so suffered no difficulties or distress.

If the snow refuses to melt, or melts too quickly, we may be delayed in leaving but, in fact, I do not really mind. I would have preferred to put a greater distance between us and Lausanne if only to put fresh perspectives in front of my daughter. However great the love that a daughter may bear her mother, it may be a little sad for them both to be alone together in these gloomy days of March. I was somewhat fearful of seeing her bored in which case it would have been the first time that she resented our close proximity. Thus I have made sure that a portfolio of prints, as well as a pianoforte and some needlework have preceded us. Other matters not under my control may have exercised her rather more … Milord, his tutor-relative, a wretched dog, a poor negro … but let me go back to the beginning.

After I wrote to you last, I determined to attend a large social gathering when I would announce our departure and the letting of our house; I advised Cécile to follow me there half an hour later, thereby saving her those first disconcerting questions and embarrassments.

"No, Maman," she answered; "let me experience it all by your side – both the pleasure and the pain. Besides, protected at your side, I can accept any loss or unpleasantness. *You* know the extent of your love for *me*, but you may not know the extent of my love for *you*. So do not be timid, Maman, and take me along with you. I am not as weak as you think!"

Do I need to tell you, dear friend, that I embraced Cécile, crying as I pressed her close? That I hung on her arm in the street with even greater pleasure and tenderness than before; that I always made sure she should have a chair placed close behind mine in company? No doubt you can imagine all this – but not the arrival of my poor cousin Monsieur X and his friend the

English tutor, visibly out of countenance at the changes about to take place in all our lives. My cousin especially seemed to fear, yet craved to know, our reasons for leaving whilst his friend, Milord's tutor sensed his agitation and sought to comfort him by putting an arm round his shoulders. The tutor seemed to be saying to Monsieur X: "I am your friend, albeit a foreigner, able to help if things go amiss, and not just a sympathetic listener."

I had been thinking so much about your letter, and my daughter's needs, that now faced with these two men to whom we had to bid *adieu* – the one with his passion, the other with his compassion, for her – I burst into tears.

Imagine the surprise this invoked! The silence that ensued was somewhat uncomfortable; uncertainty amongst us all, my cousin pale, Cécile squeezing my arm and asking: "What is it, Maman? What is the matter?" "I am being stupid," I replied. "What does it amount to, anyway? A journey hardly out of this world. The Languedoc is not exactly far. You, Monsieur, you who are travelling anyway may come to visit us; and you, my cousin, you will be attending your regiment nearby, whilst we will be visiting a dear and kind relative who calls for us to visit her. So we are all set and resolved soon to leave. Go therefore, my cousin, and tell Monsieur and Madame Y that they may rent our house for six months."

He went to tell them. The Englishman sat with us. There arrived at this moment my daughter's guardians and their wives and with them Milord, who remained in the background whilst we conversed with them. The Bernois entered and expressed his joy at being nearer to us than he had anticipated. Then the prospective tenants for our house arrived and accepted it, but with immediate possession. There remained only the difficulty of finding temporary lodgings whilst awaiting your reply. We were offered this country apartment, vacated since the autumn by some English people, which I accepted eagerly. Thus was every-thing arranged in the twinkling of an eye and in fifteen minutes securely fixed. But the questions, the exclamations, the brouhaha continued all evening!

Those most interested in our departure asked the least. Milord contented himself by asking the distance to our temporary lodg-ing and assured us that the road for Lyons would be impassable to women for a long while ahead. He then asked his tutor whether, instead of beginning their tour via Bern, Basle, Strasbourg, Nancy, Metz, Paris, they could alter it via Lyons, Marseilles and Toulouse.

"Would you then find it easier to leave Toulouse than now not to visit it?" asked the tutor. "I do not know" replied Milord, too weakly for my liking. "After six months in Paris you can go where you like" continued his relative.

Cécile begged me to take over her hand, saying she was too preoccupied with the journey ahead to play her hand seriously . The Bernois offered to lend us his chaise and horses to take us to the country and to have his coachman ask a dairymaid (who comes into town each day) whether he could be of service to us during the day.

"Not so," said Milord to the Bernois. "Whenever the weather is reasonable I shall go to visit the ladies and ask for their orders which I will then convey to you."

"That is correctly spoken," said his relative. "We poor for-eigners have only our zeal to offer."

Madame X, wife of my cousin the officer, seeing the crowd round us approached and addressed her husband thus: "And you, sir, now that these ladies depart you may decide also to take your-self off. You will have no further excuses to make such as letters to write, or other pretexts. For a week already" she laughed mirthlessly, "his trunks have been secured to his carriage ready to leave."

Everyone was silent. "Well, come on, sir," she urged. "When are you leaving?"

"Tomorrow, Madame, or this evening," he replied and running towards the door, having shaken the hand of his English friend, he left the room and the house there and then, his journey lit by the moon and the snow.

The following day, last Monday, and the day following, I was busy and wished to see no one, but on the Wednesday we were in our carriage – Cécile, Fauchon, Philax, myself – and on the road to our new dwelling. Assuredly we had given orders ahead to open up the apartment, to make up a fire in the dining room where we expected to make only a simple dinner of a milk soup and eggs; witness our surprise, therefore, to see movement and a bustle of activity, windows open and fires in all the rooms vying with the sun to dry out the apartment. Arriving at the door, Milord and his relative helped us to step down from the chaise and carried in our boxes and packages. The table was laid, pianoforte tuned, a popular piece already open on the music-stand. A cushion had been placed ready for the dog by the fireplace; there were vases of flowers on the mantelpiece. There was nothing so gallant or so well arranged! We were served with an excellent dinner, we had punch to drink, and we were presented with provisions: a pâté, lemons, rum and goodness knows what else! They begged us to allow them to come once a week to sup with us! "As for taking tea with you, Madame," said Milord, "I would not need to ask your permission for that since you would refuse this to no one."

At five o'clock their horses were brought round. They let them be led by their grooms, and as it was a fine day, though cold, we accompanied them on foot to the main road. At the very moment of their leaving a beautiful Great Dane approached us, dragging its muzzle in the snow and staggering at its last gasp, trembled and fell at Cécile's feet. She caressed it whereupon

Milord sought to pull it away; she assured him it had not got rabies, but had only lost its master and was half dead with cold, hunger and tiredness. She continued to caress it and the grooms were sent back to our lodgings to fetch milk, bread, whatever they could find. These were brought, the dog ate and drank, and licked the hands of its benefactress. She cried from pleasure and pity then, measuring her pace to that of the tired animal, she took it home and spared not a glance for her departing swain. All the evening was devoted to the dog: to warm it through, console it, to name it, to discussing how it came to be abandoned, to console Philax and avoid any jealousy. On returning, Cécile had made a bed of her own clothes and this poor animal became the happiest dog in the world.

That was last Wednesday. Now we are well ensconced in our retreat and Cécile gives no sign of being bored, not having had recourse to even half of her resources; her books, needlework, the prints all remain in their drawer.

Thursday came and went: flowers, the dog, her piano took care of the morning. In the afternoon she visited the farmer who occupies part of the house. She caressed his children and talked to his wife, noticing that they were taking milk out of the kitchen and enquired the reason. She learned that they were taking it to a sick man, a negro dying of consumption left behind by the previous English tenants. They had been obliged to leave him in the care of the farmer and his wife and instructed a banker in Lausanne to make weekly payments to them for his support and sustenance for as long as he should live. Cécile came to tell me this and begged me to go with her and to speak English to him, to see if there was anything we could do to help him.

"They say he speaks no French, Maman. Who knows whether these people, good though they are, divine his needs?"

We went to see him and Cécile spoke her first words in English to him. Some of what she had learned through love was now being used in the cause of humanity. He seemed to hear her with pleasure. He was not suffering but there was little life left in him. Gentle, patient, quiet, he seemed not to want anything – and he was still young. Cécile and Fauchon hardly left him. We gave him sometimes a little wine, sometimes a little soup. I was sitting next to him with my daughter on Sunday morning when he died. We stayed a long time in our places without moving.

"So that is how we end, Maman?" said Cécile. "He who feels, speaks, moves, ceases to feel, to hear, to be able to move? How strange that this man was born in Guinea, was sold into slavery by his parents, perhaps worked on sugar plantations in Jamaica, went as a servant to the English people, only to die in Lausanne!* Yet we have brought some peacefulness into his last days. Maman, I am neither rich nor clever, and I shall never achieve great things, yet perhaps I can bring some good into those events that may cross my path? This poor negro! But why do we say 'this poor negro?' Whether he dies in his own country, or in another, to have lived a long or only a short life, to have had more or less pain or pleasure, there must come the moment when even the King of France will be as this negro ..." "And I too," I added, "and you ... and Milord." "Yes," she said, "and now let us leave here because I see Fauchon returning from church and she must be told."

Today the negro will be buried. Thus we have experienced a death of great simplicity, not fearful or solemn, no pathos, no relatives in attendance, no mourning, no weeping – sincere or pretended. Thus has my daughter experienced no doleful impression of death. She has returned to the body two or three times a day, insisting that he remains covered and untouched in his bed and

---

*   Emancipated thinkers were beginning to protest against slavery and Belle is here
      clearly declaring herself a part of that movement. Wilberforce's bill against the
      Slave Trade was not to be passed until 1807.

that the room should still be warmed. She has read and worked there. Her example has inspired in me her own reasonableness.

NINETEENTH LETTER*

You seemed to be so sad yesterday that I feel obliged to question you as to the reason. Perhaps you will not wish to enlighten me but you can hardly think badly of me for asking. Since yesterday I have had your countenance in my mind.

Milord comes almost daily to see us though generally of brief duration. Does it seem to you that the people of Lausanne are gossiping about this and that I may be blamed for receiving him? You know him better than anyone. You also know his parents and the way they think about life. I do not doubt that you have read into Cécile's heart. Advise me as to how I should act. I am, sir, your very humble and obedient servant.

TWENTIETH LETTER

Madame, it is indeed true that I am sad. I am so far from thinking badly of you for asking that I had intended anyway to recount to you my story. I prefer to write it; it will give me something to do and will act as a distraction, the only one of which I am capable. So far as Milord is concerned, Madame, I can only say that he is without vice. I am not sure that he loves Cécile as deeply as she deserves, but I am fairly certain that he regards no other woman with interest and that he has no other attachment of any kind. It

---

* This is really the place where the two tales start to diverge. The mother's letter that follows to the English tutor (William D.) is a departure from her previous letters to her relative in the Languedoc. In the next three letters the plot moves over to the tutor's earlier life and that of Caliste.

is but two months that I wrote to his father that his son seemed to be becoming attached to a girl with no fortune but whose birth, education, character and looks left nothing to be desired. I asked the father whether I should find some pretext to cause us to leave Lausanne, though to have done so would have been to suggest to Milord that there are better things than beauty, wit, kindness and grace. I had more reason that most men not to undertake such an odious and, indeed, senseless task. Milord's father and mother both wrote to me that providing their son loved and was loved equally and might marry from love and not from honour, they would be content. They thought that my description of the young lady, and of her mother, invoked no fears such as they might have had. Nevertheless, I counselled the young man to beware of the shame and despair inherent in an engagement entered into through a drunken or misguided moment, certain as I am that he would always honour his responsibilities.

I do not believe, Madame, that people find his visits to you to be strange; he spoke of his making them before you left. In his studies he is assiduous and his evenings are spent with friends.

From Lyons I have had news of your cousin, the officer, who arrived there safely despite riding day and night on roads covered in snow more deeply than usual at this time of year. He is not a happy man.

I shall write to you again, tonight perhaps, and have the honour to be, Madame,

William D.

TWENTY-FIRST LETTER

My story is as sad as it is romantic, Madame, and you may be disappointed and surprised that its unlikely events revolve round what is only an ordinary man.

My brother and I were born during the same hour, and our birth caused the death of our mother. The confusion that reigned due to the double birth, and the distress experienced by my father resulted in our identities being lost; it was never known which of us was born the elder. One of our relatives always believed my brother to have been the first-born, but this she never affirmed positively; nor was it ever challenged so a sort of presumption grew up that my brother came first. It counted little with me either way, and nothing with my brother. He always promised to share everything with me, and not to marry if I married. I made the same promise so that we would have only one family between us, and therefore the same heirs. In this way the law would never have to decide between our respective rights or claims.

If fate had decreed complete equality between us, it had only copied nature; and our upbringing and education only served to affirm these affinities. Our features resembled each other as did our turn of mind; our tastes were the same; we shared the same tasks; we liked the same sports; one did nothing without the other and our friendship was based on our instincts rather than choice, so much so that we did not need to remark it. Others remarked it but we became aware of it only when there was talk of separating us. My brother was destined for a place in Parliament and I to serve in the army. He was to go to Oxford and I to study under an engineer. But at the moment of his parting our distress and protestations were heard and I was allowed to accompany him to the university where I shared in all his studies and he in mine. I studied law and history with him; he studied mathematics and military engineering with me. We shared a love of literature and the fine arts. We revelled in our close links which spurred us on to mutual action and achievement. Our heroes were Castor and Pollux, Orestes and Pylades, Achilles and Patroclus, David and Jonathan. We believed that to have such a friend meant we could be neither cowardly nor vicious because the fault of the one would rebound on the other. One brother must always suffer and blush for the other. And what motive would inspire us anyway to an evil action? Reliant one upon the other, what fortune, ambition, even mistress could tempt us to risk guilt? We sought in history, in books, for friendship; we valued friendship as the greatest virtue and happiness.

Three years went by. The war in America had begun; my regiment, whose uniform I now wore, was under marching orders to leave. My brother came to tell me of this and in speaking of my regiment's departure I was surprised that he said *we* instead of *you*. I stared at him.

"Do you think I would let you go alone?" he asked. He saw I was about to protest. "Do not object," he said. "Spare me the first vexation you could cause me!"

We went to spend some days with our father who, together with other relatives, tried to dissuade my brother from his intention. He was immovable and we departed together. The first campaign went in our favour and we gained some honours thereby. A second lieutenant in my company was killed and my brother asked for and was granted his place. Dressed the same, of the same height, of the same features and hair, people confused us incessantly despite our usual proximity one to the other. During winter we contrived to continue our studies, to draw maps – and to play the harp, the lute and the violin whilst our companions wasted their time in idle pursuits and women. They are not to be blamed. Inaction is hard to take.

At the beginning of the second campaign ... but what is the use of describing the worst misfortune that could befall me? He was wounded at my side. "Poor William," he said, whilst we were carrying him in. "What will become of you?"

For three days I was in a state of fear and hope; for three days I was witness to the greatest pain patiently borne. During the evening of the third day, seeing his condition worsen from moment to moment, I cried: "Grant a miracle, O God! Give him back to me!" "No! Rather console my brother!" he said in a voice almost inaudible. He pressed my hand feebly and expired.

I scarcely recall the events following his death. I found myself back in England. I was persuaded to go to Bristol, then to Bath. I was an errant ghost and attracted some compassion for the useless half of my existence that remained. One day I was sitting on one of the seats upon the promenade, sometimes opening a book I had brought along, sometimes letting it lie beside me. A woman whom I had noticed beforehand came to sit at the other end of my seat. We stayed silent for a long time: I scarcely noticed her. Then I turned to answer some questions she put to me, quietly and discreetly, and probably through gratitude and politeness I escorted her to her home. But the next day and the days following I sought her company for the pleasure of her gentle discourse and her tender interest which were preferable to my own sad reflections. Caliste, so named after the part she had played to great applause the first and only time she appeared on the stage, was of respectable birth and connected with a rich family. But her mother was a depraved woman fallen on hard times who wished to profit from her daughter's talents. Her face was beautiful and her voice more appealing than any other to strike the ear. The mother destined Caliste at an early age for the theatre and started her off in the role of Caliste, in *The Fair Penitent*.*

At the close of the play a man of considerable status asked, to all intents and purposes, to buy her from the mother, and on the morrow left with her for the continent. He placed her in a famous convent in Paris, under the name of Caliste, and let it be known

---

* The title, given in English in the French text, suggests the role in real life that Caliste is destined to play. The original play by Nicholas Rowe (1674–1718) had Calista as its heroine.

that she was of a good family the name of which was to be concealed for reasons of importance.

She was adored by the nuns and her companions, and the tone of her voice was so little affected by her mother's coarser tones that she was taken to be the natural daughter of the Duke of Cumberland, and therefore cousin to the King. When she was questioned about this, her blushes gave credence to the suspicion though the blushes were due in reality to her knowledge of her true state. Soon she learned the skills of a young lady of style: to draw, to paint, to sing, to play the harpsichord. In dancing she was already adept, her mother having thought of training her as a dancer, but she now perfected herself in this all-seductive art.

I always found her playing of an instrument, or her singing, to be as one speaks or rather as one ought to speak (and as indeed *she* did speak), namely for others and not for herself. Never was there a pleasanter musician nor a greater talent. Italy rather than Paris was where she perfected these skills as it was in Italy that her lover, Lord L., took her to spend two years with him, a time when he concerned himself only with her instruction and pleasure.

After these four years abroad, he brought her back to England to live with him, either at his house in the country or in the town house of his uncle, General D. He enjoyed four more years with her, but happiness and love are no rival of death. He fell victim to an inflammation of the lungs. "I leave her nothing," he said to his uncle on his deathbed, "for I have nothing left. But you are living, you are rich, and whatsoever she receives from you will be viewed as more honourable than anything I might have given her. In this I regret nothing and die content."

The uncle, after some months, gave Caliste the house in Bath where she was now living, and an income of £400. He visited her there for some weeks each year, and when he was suffering from gout he asked her to visit him in London. She resembles you,

Madame, or she *did* resemble you. I am not sure which to say!* In her thinking, her judgements, her mannerisms, and in the way she disregarded things of little moment to go straight to those of greater interest, both in people and in things generally, she resembled you. Her soul was always in harmony with her words, her tone with her thinking; whatever was merely clever did not interest her, discretion was foreign to her and she always said she did not know what reason was. But she could be clever if required, discreet to protect others from pain, and exercise reason to allay wrong thinking and to instil calm into a troubled heart or a misguided spirit. *You* are often gay and occasionally impetuous; she was neither. Vulnerable, adored, despised by some though served by others on bended knee, she had an assured manner that was sad, proud and reserved. Had she been less loveable she might have given the impression of being somewhat sullen and unsociable.

Once, seeing her withdraw from some strangers who had accosted her eagerly, wishing to speak with her and learn her name, I asked why she had done this. "Let us go back to them," she said. "Having asked my name, just see how they will regard me once they know who I am!" We made the experiment which concluded as she said it would. She smiled at me ruefully. "Why does it affect you?" I questioned. "One day it may affect me." She blushed as she said this and it was only much later that I understood her meaning. I remember another occasion when she had been invited to a reception which I was also to attend. She refused to go. "But why," I asked her. "The hostess and all those present will admire you." "Ah! It is not so much the marked contempt that I fear the most. I know myself and do not need to sink

---

*   Suddenly, we are back in Lausanne! Subsequent passages confirm William D.'s mild attraction to Cécile's mother.

to the level of those who express their disdain. No, it is rather the consensus whereby the gathering will *avoid* speaking about the theatre, about kept women, about Lord L. When I perceive the self-imposed constraints that people must suffer on my behalf, I suffer these too. When my lord was still alive I felt a gratitude that made me more sociable. I wished to win hearts for his sake. Were the servants not to respect me, if relatives or friends shunned me (or I shunned *them*) then he would have jumped to my defence. Those who visited us knew my position so well that often, without thinking, they would say something offensive and many was the time that I signalled to my lord to let them speak. I felt at ease that they had forgotten my position, glad that they made an exception of me compared with others of my sort. And indeed the intrigues of other such women, their greed and manipulations did not concern me."

"Why did he not marry you?" I asked her.

"We discussed it once," she replied. "He said to me: 'Marriage between us would be an empty ceremony which would add nothing to my respect for you nor to my permanent attachment to you which I have sworn to observe. Nevertheless, had I a throne to offer you, or a passable fortune, I would not hesitate to marry you. But I am almost penniless, you are much younger than I am, and what good would it do you to be an impoverished, though titled widow? Either I know the public ill – or she who has gained nothing in being my companion except to make him the happiest of mortals would be more respected than someone merely with a name and a title'."*

---

*   Footnote in the original text: "He did indeed know the public ill, and reasoned wrongly." Belle knew her world well. Caliste would have certainly had a better future with a title (and a name, which she lacked) rather than a rather besmirched reputation. There is more than a hint here that "my lord" had used Caliste for his own purposes. We are really witnessing a protest at the inequality of women and men – as will be seen during the rest of the tale.

You may be surprised, Madame, that my memory is so exact and you may suspect me of embellishments but if I have succeeded in making Caliste a reality as a person, through her words, you may not believe what you hear and may not be surprised that I remember minutely the first conversations we had together. These return to me in detail, the words as much as the places.

In order to paint her more exactly for you, Madame, I return to those comparisons that I have not ceased to make ever since I had the happiness to meet you for the first time. More silent than you with those indifferent to her, more caring and loving than you perhaps just because she was childless;* showing perhaps greater concern for those she loved; her wit less audacious than yours; her expression less lively, but softer.

In our country where pictures substitute for natural beauty of landscape,** appealing as they do to the senses and speaking to the heart, so I see Caliste favouring the senses and you the heart! Your house is simple but dignified though not rich; hers had taste with economy. She saved all she could from her meagre income to support girls whom she helped to bring up. She worked as the fairies do, and every day her friends could see in her home some new thing to admire or enjoy. Sometimes it would be a useful piece of furniture that she had made herself, sometimes a vase she had designed which would make a potter's fortune. She painted portraits for her friends and copied old masters for her own pleasure. What talents and means of pleasing did this young lady encompass!

Cared for and distracted by her, my health returned and life no longer seemed to be a burden too heavy or insipid to carry. I was able now to mourn my brother, to speak of him without hindrance, and indeed to cry for him. My tears caused her to cry also.

---

*   As was Belle herself.
**   Belle had visited Surrey and was not impressed by English landscape.

One day she said to me: "I see why you are so tender and gentle though still a man! Most men who have had only rather ordinary companions of their own gender lack delicacy and grace. Those who have lived much with women may want boldness in manly things. They may become demanding, egotistical and melancholic – as women are! All that you shared with your brother, such as games and sports, will have made you robust and skilful. Yet by nature you are sensitive and your close proximity to him will have increased this."

"What a lucky man!" she cried one day when I had spoken at length of my brother. "Happy will be she who replaces this beloved brother!" "And who would love me as he did?" I asked her. "That would not be so difficult;" she reddened at this. "You will never love a woman as you loved him but if you retain only that tenderness so that someone could believe you loved them as you loved your brother ..." I looked at her. Tears fell from her eyes. I knelt at her feet and kissed her hands.

"Did you not see that I loved you?" she asked. "No," I replied, "and you are the first woman from whom I have heard such words of love."

"I am now repaid," she said whilst I regained my seat, "for my constraint and pain in not revealing my love to you until now. I loved you from the first moment I saw you. Before you, I knew only gratitude, not true love. Now that I know it for what it is, it is too late! What a situation is mine! The less that I deserve to be respected the more I need it! I would be affronted if I were subjected to the usual marks of love; humiliated and frightened by the least indecent approach which could only remind me of what I was. I would be unworthy of you in my eyes and doubtless also in yours. I do not wish, ever, to revert to my earlier life. Ah! I have only known an untarnished life and reputation since knowing *you*. How often have I cried to see a young girl, even the poorest, who is nevertheless chaste and still innocent. If I were such a girl, I would have devoted my life to you, served you in whatever fashion you required. I would have known only you, you could even have married someone else and I would have served your wife and children, and been proud to be your slave and to suffer for you.*

"But what can I do? What can I offer you? Known as debased I can become neither your equal nor your servant. You see that I have thought it all through? For so long now I have thought only of my love for you – the misfortune yet the pleasure of loving you. I have wished a thousand times to withdraw from all the unhappy consequences that I foresee – but how to escape one's destiny? At least, in telling you how much I love you I have given myself a moment of happiness."

"Let us not foresee unhappy consequences," I cried. "I see none. I see only you and you love me. The present is too delight-ful to torment myself with the future." And, in speaking, I pressed her to me. She tore herself away.

"I will also speak no more of the future," she said. "I cannot hurt those whom I love. Go now, let me collect my thoughts, and you must reflect seriously as to our situation, yours and mine. Perhaps you will be wiser than me and not wish to continue a liai-son that bodes little happiness. Do not delude yourself that you can always leave me and not be distressed. *Today* you could leave me without being cruel, even though I could not be easily con-soled. But you would not need to reproach yourself. Your health is recovered, you could leave Bath. If you return to me tomorrow it will be to tell me that you have accepted my heart. Never again, despite any remorse, can I be wholly unhappy. Think," she said whilst pressing my hand, "I repeat, you can leave, your health is

---

* And repeat the same mistake? Belle is always even-handed in her attitude to social questions. So she defends Caliste in some measure, but also underlines her delicate situation vis-à-vis society.

mended." "Yes," I replied, "and it is you that I owe for this." And I left her.

Not deliberately, but as though some force restrained me, I left my house very late the following day to present myself at her door. Heavens! What joy I saw shining in her eyes! "You returned! You returned!" she cried. Who could have denied himself such happiness! After the long night, dawn rose promising felicity: how could I deny it?

Sitting opposite me, her hands clasped, crying and smiling in equal measure, she repeated: "He returned! ... but the end will not be happy. I dare to hope nevertheless that the end is still far off. Perhaps I will die before becoming destitute. Promise me nothing but receive my solemn oath that I will love you always. I am certain of always loving you and even if you cease to love me I shall never cease to love you. Let the moment when you have cause to complain of my love be the last of my life! Come, let us go now and sit on the same seat where we spoke to each other for the first time. Twenty times already had I wanted to speak to you, but did not dare to do so. That day I was bolder! Bless that day! Bless my boldness! Bless the seat and where it stands. There I shall plant a rosebush, a jasmine and a honeysuckle" – and she did exactly that. The plants grew and prospered and are all that remain of that sweet liaison.

I cannot paint adequately for you, Madame, her inexpressible charm, tenderness, tact, how she matched love with love mastering the senses with her soul, replacing excesses with subtlety, over-riding her own presence with her individual *esprit*. On occasion I complained of her reserve which I likened to indifference but was caused by uncertainty as to my father's attitude to our marriage. Whenever I wished to go and ask him for his consent she would reply "Just so long as you have not asked him, so we still have the joy of believing he would be in favour of it." Lulled by love and hope I lived as happy as one can with uncertainty, filled with a passion to which I had been a stranger. "Oh! Brother mine! What would you say in all this? You are no longer here – but who else could be more worthy than she to take your place?"

I was not entirely idle otherwise. The regiment in which I had served had been destroyed in the disgrace of Saratoga and if I were to return to America it would have to be in another corps; but my father, desolated at having lost one son in a war of which he disapproved, swore that he would not allow his other son to return to America. The capitulation of Saratoga enabled him to plead that ill health only had prevented my return to the original regiment, now disbanded. In effect I had left the service. I therefore prepared afresh for a career in Parliament or the civil service. To this end I resolved to study law and history as well as to improve delivery in my own language: I had decided that eloquence lay in persuasion if not in conviction, necessary in such a career. Following the example of Lord Chatham I set myself to translate Cicero and, above all, Demosthenes, destroying a thousand such attempts in the fire. Caliste helped me to find the correct words and phrases even though she knew no Latin or Greek. Following my literal translation she was adept in discovering the sense of the original better than me. And in translating Pascal or Bossuet she was of even greater assistance.

For fear of neglecting any of my tasks, we had arranged that, in the event that I permitted unsatisfactory work to be done, I should pay a fine for the benefit of her poor *protégées*. I rose early and two hours of the morning were given to a walk with Caliste; hours too brief, walks of poignancy to two spirits both tranquil and enchanted. We walked with our mutual admiration of nature which we could appraise together as a third love. Then I studied until dinner,* dining at my home but drinking coffee with Caliste.

---

*   Dinner was really lunch, at about 3 p.m. Supper was at any hour up to 10 p.m.

I would find her dressed; I would show her my work, we would go through it and when satisfied I would write the fair copy at her dictation. Then I would read to her from recent books enjoying good repute, and fall back on Rousseau, Voltaire, Fénélon, Buffon, and other works that pleased us in your language. Then I would go to the public rooms from fear, as she said, that people would otherwise think she had buried me, the better to hold on to me! Having passed an hour or two there I was permitted to return and not to leave her again.*

According to the seasons, before supper we would walk, converse, or on occasion we would hold a concert at her house where players of great skill would perform and English or other foreign musicians would share their genius with us. They were moved to give of their best due to their admiration of their hostess rather than financial reward. We enjoyed these concerts alone, though occasionally men of the highest rank asked leave to attend. Once some ladies asked also to attend but were refused. On another occasion some young people heard the music and entered boldly. Caliste told them that she supposed they had made a mistake but that they could remain providing they observed total silence, not to return again without permission. You see, Madame, that she demanded respect and her lover was the most submissive and the most enchanted of her admirers.

After the concert we gave supper to our musicians and any guests. I was allowed to pay for these suppers but was never allowed to pay for anything else. These were gay occasions with our polyglot musicians speaking their foreign tongues in a riot of witty sallies. With anyone other than Caliste these could have been formal affairs but with her they were always gay and charming.

---

*   "… *et de ne la plus quitter.*" The implication might be here that the rest of the day and night would be spent with her, yet the tenor of all that follows denies this. She is determined to resist her own impulses, and his, despite her true inclinations.

Caliste had found that the hours after supper lay heavily on our hands, unless the moon shone to invite us outside or some book demanded to be finished. She had taken to inviting to play for us a little violincellist, dirty and drunken but very skilful. When this gnomic creature appeared I was upset and cursed him and made to leave but at a sign from Caliste I would remain, and often with my hat on my head and leaning up against the door I would be captivated by Caliste singing to her harpsichord alongside the instrument of the evil genius. At other times I might grumble but would take my harp or violin and play until she sent us both on our way. Thus passed weeks, months, more than a year and you can see that these delicious memories have kindled a flame of joy in a heart that is otherwise overwhelmed by grief.

Finally, I received a letter from my father. He had been told that my health was quite recovered and there was no need for me still to remain in Bath. He wished me to return home and marry a young girl whose fortune, education and birth were all that could be desired. I replied that I was certainly cured, and told him of she to whom I owed my recovery. I spoke of her frankly as the erstwhile mistress of Lord L. and said I would marry no one but her. I begged him not to be prejudiced and reject my plea and pleaded that he should make wide enquiries in London, Bath and elsewhere as to the conduct of her whom I wished to give to him as a daughter. "Yes, her conduct," I repeated, "and if you discover that prior to the death of Lord L. she behaved in a manner lacking in decorum, or following his death that she was in any way rash, I will renounce my request. If you hear anything except praise of her I will deny the only person who might give me the happiness to live and conserve my reason." Here is the reply from my father.

"You are of age, my son, and you may indeed marry without my consent. As to my approval of it, you may never have that for the marriage you propose. Should you contract it I will never wish to see you again. I have never sought preferment and you know that I have allowed the younger branch of our family to solicit, and obtain, a title without attempting to procure one for ourselves. But honour is as dear to me as to any man, and never will I willingly allow the honour of my family to be impugned. I shudder at the idea of a daughter-in-law before whom one could not speak of chastity, and to whose children one could not speak of virtuousness without causing their mother to blush. And would you not blush, also, when I exhorted them to favour honour above passion? Not to give in to passion but to master it? No, my son, I will not give to this daughter-in-law the place of she whom I adored. You may give her your mother's name, certainly, and may cause me to die of sorrow in so doing; I shudder at the idea , and so long as I live she will never sit in your mother's place. You know that the birth of my two sons cost her her life; you know that the friendship between you and your brother cost him his life; and only you can now decide if my remaining son is to be spirited away by a foolish passion. For in that event I shall have no sons left to me if you can take only such a wife."

Caliste, seeing me return to her later than usual, and with an air sad and defeated, guessed immediately the content of the letter. She took it, and in reading it I could see each word pierce her heart like a dagger. "Let us not altogether despair," she said to me. "I will write to him myself tomorrow but I am too upset to do so now." And sitting next to me on the sofa she cried and caressed me with an abandon she had not shown before. I was too upset to take advantage of it. I have translated her letter as best I can and transcribe it for you to read.

"Permit a suffering woman, Sir, to appeal to your heart rather than to your judgement, and to plead her cause with you. I accept the force of your reasoning but please be so good as to ask yourself, Sir, whether there may be considerations in my favour that outweigh those that may reprove me. Consider whether complete devotion, the greatest tenderness, gratitude wholly felt, do not weigh in the scales that I ask you to reflect upon in this case. Deign to ask yourself whether your son could expect to find these sentiments in another woman to the same degree. Consider other marriages, those that may appear the best matched and the most advantageous; in these there usually appear drawbacks and unhappiness greater and more hurtful than those you fear in the marriage desired by your son. Will you not then be more indulgent towards his, rather than your resolution? If an honourable birth, a pure life, an intact reputation were all that were required to give your son happiness, if virtue were all, if my passionate love for him, unique as it is, were as nothing – then, believe me, I would act generously and silence the wishes of my heart.

"You find me unworthy to be the mother of your grandchildren. I must accept, with pain, your views which are based assuredly on public opinion. If however you would incline to your own judgement, if you deigned to see me, know me, your verdict might be less severe. You would come to see with what docility I instructed my children according to your wishes, in lessons that I did not myself receive. And just suppose that such blandishments lost some of their force through being spoken by *me*, you would be able to judge nevertheless of my correct behaviour and honesty. You may believe, Sir, that any disgrace you might see in me has been offset by my being sheltered from any licentious sights or sounds – unlike other women of whatever rank or position.

"Is it so very difficult for you to form even a reasonable opinion of one who loves your son so tenderly? I finish by swearing to you that I will never consent to anything you may condemn, whatever might be the thinking of your son, though that is unlikely for he would never forget the respect he owes you. We share that view, Sir, your son and me, and I send you for my part my humble and sincere assurances."

While waiting for my father's answer, much of our converse was concerning Caliste's relations, her upbringing, journeys, her history in a word. I posed her questions I had never done before. I had avoided questions up to now that might be painful for her. Now she removed such scruples and I was able to delve deeply into her past and was pleased to see how that helped her to know herself. She told me that, by virtue of his supreme tact, nobody could ever affirm positively, and in any country, that she had been Lord L.'s mistress. She said that she had never suffered the least ill humour on his part, nor negligence, nor refusal of any wish she might have. What woman was ever so treated as a divinity for eight years! I asked her once whether she had ever had the thought of leaving him.

"Yes, once," she said. "But I was so struck by my ingratitude that I recoiled from any justification of such an act. I was nearly the dupe of so-called virtue whereas vice was its true name."

Three days we awaited my father's letter when I left to one side my studying and outside activities. Instead I went to her each morning. Sorrow had made us more familiar without making us less restrained. On the fourth day Caliste received her reply. Instead of transcribing or translating it, Madame, I am sending it for you to translate, and you may wish to show this to your cousin some day. I do not have the strength myself to translate it.

"Madame,

I apologise for having to say things that are unpleasant to a lady of, I may add, great merit. I have not troubled to seek information about you, which I would anyway have disregarded, but have nevertheless heard much good of you. Once again, I am sorry for having to say disagreeable things to you, but to leave your letter unanswered would be even more rude than to refute it. – which I must now do.

"Firstly, Madame, I must tell you that I have no proof of your attachment to my son except what you tell me and a liaison such as this may not prove to be permanent. But, supposing it proves as deep as you say it is, and I admit that I believe it to be so, why should I not think that another woman could love my son just as much as you do? And even supposing that another woman whom he married did not love him with the same tenderness nor with the same devotion, is it certain that such a depth of attachment would be desirable for him? Would he always need such great sacrifices from his wife?

"But let us assume that to be so. Is such an attachment everything? You speak of frictions that are evident in marriages but is it not correct reasoning to suffer such inconveniences because these exist in every *ménage*? To rise above all such frictions that may present themselves in order to avoid others not yet foreseen, to adopt a course that may be bad because there may be others even worse? You asked if it is difficult for me to entertain a good opinion of she who loves my son? Perhaps you may add: 'and who is loved by him.' No, certainly not, and I have such a good opinion of you that I believe you would set a good example to your children, and far from invalidating the lessons you gave them, these might be given with even greater zeal and care than by another. But do you not see that on a thousand occasions I would see you suffer for what was being said (or not being said) to your children or about them, or on a thousand other occurrences? And do you not think that the more I become attached to you through your goodness, honesty and amiable qualities, the more I shall suffer (or imagine that I see *you* suffering) to see you unhappy, especially as you deserve above all to be happy yourself?

"In truth, Madame, it goes against the grain for me not to show you the greatest tenderness and consideration that are your due, but which it would be impossible for me to extend to you, except possibly for brief moments when I forgot that this beautiful, amiable woman before me was my daughter-in-law. And whenever I heard you being called by the same name as my wife and mother (forgive my sincerity, Madame) I would turn against you, and I would perhaps even hate you for having been so amiable that my son could love and marry only yourself. And if I thought to hear someone speaking of my son or children I would imagine them to be saying: 'he is the husband, they are the children of a woman of *that* sort.' In truth, Madame, that would be intolerable and even now, when it is not a reality, I find it to be so.

"In no way do I scorn you, that would be unjust, and I am in fact predisposed to think quite differently. The promise you made me at the end of your letter places me under an obligation to you – and I do not blush for that obligation. I have the greatest faith in your promise, though I do not know exactly why.

"To repay your honesty and the respect you show for the ties that unite a father and son, I undertake to you, and to my son, not to attempt to separate you from him; also, not to reopen with him ever again the subject of another marriage, even if a princess were proposed to me for a daughter-in-law. – on condition that neither of you ever speak to me again of the marriage in question. If I allowed myself to soften I know I would have bitter regrets; and to resist further entreaties as I know I would, might inevitably displease and afflict a son whom I love dearly and who merits my love. This could store up even more trouble for me for the future, for an affectionate father can reproach himself (and this without reason) not to have conceded to even the most unreasonable requests from his child. Believe me, Madame, that it is not without pain that I must distress you both by my reply."

I found Caliste sitting on the floor, her head leaning against the chimney breast. "This is the twentieth position I have tried in the last hour. I am where I am because my head feels on fire." She pointed to my father's letter which lay open on the sofa, where I sat to read it. She moved to lay her head on my knees. Absorbed as I was in my thoughts, regretting the past, deploring the future, and not knowing how to survive the present, I scarcely felt or saw her. I made her sit beside me. Our tears intermingled.

"Let us at least come closer to each other, " I said, so quietly that it was as if I feared she might understand my words. She made no sign of having heard me. I hoped she would consent but I was not sure. She did not answer and her eyes stayed closed. "Let us change this moment of sadness into one of rapture," I said. "Ah!" she replied, opening her eyes and looking at me with sadness and fright. "So I must return to what I was!" "No," I replied after some moments of silence, "you are not obliged to do anything – but I thought you loved me." "And do I *not* love you," she replied putting her arms round me: "do I *not* love you?"

Imagine , Madame, if you are able, the turmoil of my heart. Finally I knelt to kiss her knees and ask her pardon for my impetuosity. "I know that you love me. I respect and adore you and you must be for me only what you want to be." "Ah! I see that I must revert to all that I found distasteful or lose you which would be a thousand times worse." "No, you wrong me, you are mistaken, you will not lose me for I shall always love you."

"You may love me but I shall lose you nevertheless," she said. "And by what right could I keep you? I am sure I will lose you." She choked on her tears to the point where I thought to summon help but she restrained me from fear that we would no longer be alone together. She calmed down. But from that moment she was no longer the same. Anxious when I was not there, trembling if I left her as though fearful she might not see me again, transported with joy when I reappeared. Fearing to displease me, joyful when she had pleased me, she was invariably more amiable, more caring, more ravishing than she had been in the past. But she had lost some serenity, and the particular appropriateness in all her actions that had so distinguished her. Her actions were either less or more pronounced, never the same as before and therefore not the same either to her or to others. Heavens! What struggles and torments did she not undergo! Moved by my least caresses, which she now sought rather than avoided, she was nevertheless watchful of her emotions. Fearful that I might escape from her, yet reproaching herself for having drawn me to her, then pushing me gently away, then annoyed for having done so. Fear, tenderness, passion, reservation – these succeeded each other in swift progression by her movements and looks, changing so swiftly that they seemed to fuse into each other.

As for me, by turns on fire, then cold; irritable, charmed, loving, resentful; I was hopelessly confused. "Let us finish it," I said one day, overcome by love and anger, and locking her door I led her from her harpsichord. "I know you would do me no violence," she said in a voice that disarmed my frenzy. Whereupon I took her on my knees, inclined her head against my shoulder, and covered her beautiful hands with my tears. I asked her pardon and she thanked me in such a manner that she showed me the fear that she had had. Yet she loved me passionately and suffered as much as I; she wanted in reality to give in to me, to be my mistress (*"… et pourtant elle aurait voulou être ma maitresse."*)

"You cannot resolve to give yourself – yet you wish that you could do so," I said to her (*"vous ne pouvez vous résoudre à vous donner, et vous voudriez vous être donnée."*) "That is true," she replied. This avowal showed me no way forward, nor that I should even attempt it.

Do not imagine, Madame, that all our moments were painful, that our situation was not without its joys. Our privations induced their own caprices. If a quarrel threatened, to ask the other for some small service caused the disagreement to vanish. This was our way out of trouble and it never failed. Her caresses, if I am truthful, caused me more fear than pleasure but our intimacy was delightful. Treated sometimes as a brother, or indeed as a sister, I valued this above everything.

Caliste developed, and this will not surprise you, a remorseless insomnia. I was opposed to her taking remedies that could affect her health irretrievably, and I arranged that her maid Fanny and I would take turns to read to her in bed so as to induce sleep. Once asleep, I, and more especially Fanny, would withdraw quietly with care, and on the morrow as a reward I had the joy of sleeping at the foot of her bed with my head on her knees. One night I fell asleep whilst reading to her; Fanny, as usual, brought her mistress breakfast at daylight (we abbreviated the nights as much as possible) and took care not to wake me for a while; I awoke to find them both smiling at me. "You see," I said to Fanny – "all is as you left it – table, lamp, the book fallen from my hand." She saw my embarrassment at leaving the house in broad daylight and said to me: "Go, Sir, even though the neighbours will see you, it is of no matter. They know full well that Madame is unwell, we have explained that you live as brother and sister: if we were now to tell them otherwise they would not believe us. "Do they mock me?" I asked. "Oh, no, Sir. They are amazed, that is all. They love and respect you both."

"That they are amazed is not surprising," I said. "And if we were to surprise them less, would they still love us?" "Ah, Sir, that would be a different story!" "I can hardly believe that, Fanny" I said, "but if they did not know …" "Such things can only be hidden, Sir, if they do not exist" she replied naively. "But," I replied. "There are no 'buts', Sir. You could hide nothing from James* and me that we would not guess. James would say nothing, but he would not serve Madame as he does at pres-

---

*   A manservant who has suddenly appeared. These protestations on the part of her maid expose Caliste's reputation to the world at large. The painful struggle between the "brother and sister" to remain chaste is here brought to the breaking point.

ent – as the first lady of the land, proof of his great respect for her. And I would say nothing but I could not remain with Madame for I should always be thinking: 'if it became known one day I would be reproached all my life.' And other servants, who have always heard me praise Madame, would begin to suspect; and the neighbours, who know the goodness of Madame would suspect also, and then would come another lady's maid who loved Madame less than I do – and soon the word would be out. So many people like to gossip! Whether they praise or they blame it is all one as long as they can gossip. I can hear them now: 'You see' they would say, 'you cannot trust appearances. She *seemed* to have reformed. She gave to the poor, she went to church ...' What they admire about you at present would then be treated as hypocrisy. And, Sir, you would be forgiven even less than Madame for, seeing the extent to which you are loved by Madame, they would say: 'why does he not marry her?'"

"Oh! Fanny, Fanny," cried Caliste sadly, "how you do speak truth! What can I say" she continued to me in French. "Why must I have left it to her to prove to you that I could not change my conduct however strongly I might wish to do so." I wanted to reply but she counselled me to leave.

A neighbouring shopkeeper was up earlier than most as I walked down the street. I passed by him expressly so as not to appear to be avoiding notice. "How is Madame?" he asked. "She sleeps very little," I replied. "Fanny and I read to her at night to try and get her to sleep, and she wakes with the dawn. Last night I read to her so late that I fell asleep myself." "Have you breakfasted?" he asked. "No, I thought to throw myself upon my bed to try and sleep for an hour or two." "That would be a shame on such a beautiful day," he replied. "You do not appear tired, Sir. Why not come and have breakfast with me in my garden?" I accepted with the thought that this man was not one to speak ill of Caliste, and indeed he informed me of so many good deeds she did – of which I was ignorant – that I was amply rewarded for my complaisance.

That day Caliste received a letter from Lord L.'s uncle (General D.) who was repeatedly asking her to visit him in London. I resolved to pass the time of her absence with my father and we left Bath at the same hour.

"Will I see you again?" she asked. "Is it certain that I will see you again?" she repeated. "Yes," I replied, "just as soon as you wish it, if I am not dead ..." We promised to write to each other at least twice a week, and never was a promise so well kept. Neither of us had a thought or an experience that we did not wish to share with the other, and the difficulty lay in *not* writing more often.

My father might have greeted me coldly if he had not been satisfied by the manner in which I had spent my time studying. Others now praised me to him, and by good chance there were those around him who were able to judge me, and whose approval I gained. Opinion had it that I had learned very well to express myself, and success was predicted for me which pleased a father already disposed to regard me favourably. I renewed my acquaintance with the paternal home which I had hardly taken note of since my return from America, at a time when I noticed very little. I got to know neighbours and friends of my father with whom I shot and hunted, happy enough to please them. "I saw you on your return from America," said one of our family's oldest friends. "If your father sees you today in such an improved state, he should out of gratitude allow you to marry the woman who has brought this about."

Those women I happened to meet received me flatteringly. How easy it would have been to succeed with any of these of whom my father approved, rather than with the one so scorned! I swear to you, my soul was so much in need of solace that at certain moments I might have succumbed to one of these ladies.

Caliste was so little disposed to jealousy that to cause her pain through this might not have occurred to me. Any distraction must be an infidelity, but since I saw no one remotely comparable to her there was no danger of my becoming unfaithful. And it must be said that other ways of distracting me were preferable than to dally with ladies. Sometimes I wanted to use my faculties to better purpose. I did not realise at the time that my wish to serve the public was only an illusion; that unseen events and circumstances have little effect on changing nations for better or for worse; and that the good intentions of a citizen however virtuous never influence the well being of his country. I did not see that to be the slave of ambition is even more puerile than to be the slave of a woman.* My father wanted me to present myself for a seat in Parliament at the next election. Pleased to comply at least once with his wishes I acquiesced.

Caliste wrote to me: "If I still feature in your plans, which I flatter myself is the case, you could do worse than embrace a project which would oblige you to live in London. A brother of my father wished to see me and has just told me that in eight days I have given him more pleasure than he has received from all of his other relatives and their children in twenty years, so much so that he intends to leave me his house and fortune. I am to repair and decorate the house in using the fortune, rather than his other heirs who would demolish the one and squirrel away the other. I recount to you all this so you do not blame me for being in no fashion opposed to his wishes; and I have as much right to this inheritance as any other person and indeed none of his other relatives are in need of it. My father's brother is rich and very old; his house is well situated close to Whitehall. I will avow that the idea of receiving you there or of lending it to you gives me great

---

* It is not clear here whether the woman in question may be Caliste herself, or is impersonal. The cynicism about public service is Belle at her best.

pleasure. If you fancy to spend money on, say, a beautiful picture or a handsome horse, please satisfy such a wish, because the will is made and the testator so self-willed that he will certainly not revoke it. Therefore I feel rich already and would like to become your creditor."*

In another letter she said: "Although I miss you at this distance, although all that I do seems useless and insipid unless I can give an account of it to you, I see that you are finding repose away from me. On the one side you seem to experience impatience and boredom, on the other satisfaction and repose! What a contrast! I do not complain, however. If I were vexed I would not dare to say so. If I saw another woman come between us, I should be vexed without a doubt but would not dare, or deserve to say so."

And in another letter: "I believe I have seen your father. Struck by his looks which reminded me of you, I stayed immobile and looked at him. It was certainly him and he looked at me also." In fact, as he told me later, he had seen Caliste during a visit he had made to London. I do not know where he encountered her but he had asked who that beautiful woman could be. "What," said someone. "Do you not know the Caliste of Lord L. – and of your son?" "Without that first name," he said to me … and he stopped. "Wretch that you are! Why did you ever tell me her name?"

I began to be concerned as to how I might return to Bath. My health was no longer a pretext and although I had no other plans it might have appeared strange for me to revisit there so soon.

---

*   A useful coincidence in that she is suddenly an heiress? As "creditor" to William she remains an independent lady of means. To excuse Belle for the seemingly improbable coincidence of the unexpected inheritance, the uncle in question might have been hinted at on p. 215 when Caliste was said to have come from a "rich family." Though of her own father we have up to now known nothing, and shall know nothing as the tale progresses.

Caliste felt this, also, in a letter she wrote announcing her own departure for Bath. She mentioned having met other acquaintances at Lord L.'s uncle's house. All were speaking of going to Bath. "It would be terrible," she wrote me, "to see everyone there except the one I most wish to see." Happily, or so I thought at the time, my father suddenly announced his intention to spend several months in that city. Whether he was persuaded in this out of curiosity to encounter more closely she whom he had rejected, to hear and learn more about her, perhaps also live with me there and to make my stay less obtrusive, I did not know but could hardly contain my joy at the way events were turning out. Heavens, I told myself, if I can unite my father, my duty to him, Caliste, her happiness and mine …! But no sooner had my father's intentions become known than a young woman, widowed by the death of one of our relations eighteen months earlier, wrote to my father begging him to take a house large enough also to contain her, as well as her young son of some ten years. I found this proposal somewhat strange and was not sure whether my father was pleased or displeased by it – but he could hardly refuse.

In consequence I was sent off to Bath to arrange lodgings for my father, for me, his cousin-by-marriage whom I did not know, and her son. Caliste was already in Bath. She delighted in helping me to find, and decorate, the lodgings I had settled on and spared no effort so that when my father and Lady Betty B. arrived they praised all that they saw. And showed me a gratitude that I did not deserve. They admired the taste and elegance such that they had never seen before! All this worked somewhat to the disfavour of Caliste and caused Lady Betty to believe, from this moment, that my intentions towards her might be those as befitted someone of her fortune, countenance and rank, as well as her young age. She had married very early and was not even seventeen when Sir Harry was born. I cannot blame her for these ideas, nor for their consequence. I am only surprised at my own reaction to her caprices. I was not exactly flattered by her attention but my attachment to Caliste certainly lessened. She became less precious to me. I believed that all women shared a propensity for love and that it was only chance, or destiny, that determined the object of their passion. Caliste quickly saw a change in me. Change? The word is too strong. Nothing had altered in my heart nor in my thoughts. But we are inconsequential beings and I cannot account for any change in me that caused my weak and feeble behaviour.

Lady Betty's son was a charming child and resembled my brother at that age, and the games we played then, so that my eyes would fill with tears when I beheld him. He became my pupil and my companion. I never went out without him, and I took him daily to see Caliste.

One day when I had visited her on my own, I found with her a handsome country gentleman who was watching her draw. I concealed my surprise and my displeasure and waited to remain after he had gone; but this proved not to be possible because he asked her to give him supper. At eleven o'clock I affirmed that nothing harmed her more than late nights and forced my rival, for that is what he was, to withdraw, as I did. For the first time the hours did not pass quickly with Caliste. The name of the man was not unknown to me: it was the name of an ancient family from Norfolk whose members had brought neither fame nor splendour to it. But it was a family of consequence. He knew Lord L.'s uncle and, seeing Caliste with him at the opera, had asked to be presented to her, and subsequently to visit her. This he had done two or three times and now believed he had encountered such a goddess as seen before only in books of classical literature. After his third visit he had asked the General for information about her, her fortune and her family. He asked whether he would advise him to marry her. The reply was straightforward. "Without doubt if you can win her. I would give this advice even to my son, or to the son of my best friend. There is an imbecile who has loved her for a long time but who does not dare to marry her, because of his father who will not consent to it and who does not even dare to meet her for fear of becoming predisposed in her favour. They will repent this all their lives. But be quick because they may change their minds!"

Such was the man I had found with Caliste. The following day I visited her early and expressed to her my displeasure and impatience of the day before. "What?" she asked. "That caused you pain? Before, you used to suffer whoever it was with me, a workman, even a woman; but for some time now you have always brought the little boy with you and I have come to believe this was on purpose so that we should not be alone together." "But he's only a child," I said. "He hears and sees as well as another," she replied. "And if I don't bring him any more, will you cease to receive the man who annoyed me here yesterday evening?" "You can always bring the boy," she replied, "but I cannot dismiss anyone who has a claim on me. My benefactor the General introduced him and asked me to receive him." "He is in love with you," I told her, striding round her room with big steps, "he has no father, he could ..." I could not go on. Caliste made no reply and the man in question was announced. Shortly afterwards I returned. I determined to become acquainted with him rather than banish myself from my own hearth – for so I considered it to be. I called more frequently thereafter but stayed a shorter time. Sometimes she was alone and I rejoiced when this was the case.

I no longer took the boy with me and after a few days he complained of this bitterly. Lady Betty was there when he addressed his complaints to my father, begging him to take him to see Mistress Caliste since I no longer did so. The boy's manner, even the name, caused my father to smile favourably though somewhat embarrassed. "I do not visit her," he said to Sir Harry. "Will your son not introduce you to her?" replied the boy. "Ah! If you had only been to her house you would want to return there daily as he does." Seeing my father moved and affectionate I was on the point of throwing myself on his mercy. But the presence of Lady Betty or my unlucky star held me back, or was it my wretched weakness? Oh, Caliste, how much braver you would have been at this moment! You would have persuaded him – and we would have enjoyed our lives together which was not to be. Irresolute, uncertain, I let the moment pass. James, Caliste's servant, called at this moment to ask Lady Betty whether her son might be allowed to dine with his mistress? I had informed her of his complaints. The little boy hardly waited for the reply and rushed away with James. That evening and during the days that followed little Sir Harry spoke incessantly of Caliste, which irritated Lady Betty but noticeably weakened my father's resolve. Who knows what this might have produced? But my father was obliged to go home to London for a few days to attend to business and these moments of goodwill were interrupted, not to return.

Sir Harry became so established at Caliste's house that I no longer found her alone with my rival. He must have been as discountenanced by the child as I was by him. On these occasions she used skill and resources such as I had not seen her use before. The country squire, unable to converse freely with her, wished at least to be entertained by her singing and harpsichord. He asked her for French and Italian airs, and extracts from opera. Caliste, believing that these would be repetitive for me and not pleasing to the boy, and that I would not be prepared to accompany her as usual on my instruments, turned to inventing songs for which she composed the music and I the words. The boy sang the words and my rival judged the result.

She also wished to teach Sir Harry to draw. She obtained copies of pictures by Rubens and Snyders in which children disport themselves with garlands of flowers. We all made copies of these and spread them round the room so that the result was joyful. If the child was the most pleased we were all entertained. Alone with her and Sir Harry, I praised the inventiveness of the room and commented that she had never excelled herself so well, and was it to impress Monsieur M. as to the greater beauty of the house?

"Ungrateful wretch!" she exclaimed.

"Yes, you are right, I am indeed ungrateful, but who could remain unaffected by a display of talent that used to be for me alone, now available to others and of even greater brilliance?" "It is their swan song," she replied.

There came a knock at the door. "Prepare to receive a certain Monsieur M. from Norfolk," said little Sir Harry, as if he had understood more than had been said. It was indeed our Norfolk squire.

We continued in the same way for some days but my rival did not intend always to share Caliste with me and the boy. He came to tell her, one morning, that after learning all he could of her from General D., and from public hearsay, but above all from his own observation of her, he had resolved to follow the dictates of his own heart and offer her his hand and his fortune.

"I will," he said, "make an exact summary of my affairs so as to render a full account of these. Then I wish your friend, General D., to whom I owe the happiness of knowing you, to examine and judge with yourself if my offers are acceptable; but that when you have so examined everything you will not delay your response."

"I wish that I were more worthy to receive your offers," Caliste said to him, as much agitated as if she had not expected his declaration. "Go, Sir, I am indeed sensible of the honour you do me. I will consider deeply whether I can accept and will give you your answer on your return." Sir Harry and I found her an hour or so later so pale, so overwrought that we were frightened for her. Is it believable that I still did not decide, even then? I only had to speak one word. I spent three days from morning to evening with her, regarding her, dreaming, hesitating – and I said nothing. The evening before the day when her swain was due to reappear I went to her after dinner, knowing she would be alone in the house until the following day. She held a casket filled with small jewels, engraved stones, miniatures that she had brought from Italy or had had given to her by milord. She made me look at them and observed which I preferred. She put a ring on my finger that milord had always worn and begged me to keep it. She hardly said a word. She was tender but resigned and sad. "You have not promised that man anything?" I asked her. "Nothing," she replied, and this is the only word I remember of that evening, a word that has recurred to me since a thousand times.

But I shall never forget the manner in which we parted. "What," I said looking at my watch, "is it really nine o'clock?" I wanted to leave but ... "Stay," she said. "I cannot," I replied; "my father and Lady Betty are waiting for me." "You will have supper with them very many times still," she said. "You will have nothing to eat yourself?" "I will have supper; I have been promised ices." "I will give you ices," she said – the weather was excessively hot.

She was only lightly clad. She stood up against the door through which I would leave. I kissed her and moved her a little to one side. "I shall not let you pass," she said. "You are cruel," I replied, "to excite me in this way!" "*I cruel?*" she answered. I opened the door, I went out, she watched me go and in shutting it behind me I heard her say "It is all over!" Her words pursued me, ringing round my head so that I returned after half an hour to demand an explanation. The door was locked. She called to me from an upstairs room that she was having a bath and could not open the door as there were no servants in the house. "But what if you needed something," I asked. "I need nothing," she replied. "Are you sure you harbour no sinister design?" I queried.

"None," she replied, "unless it is to find you in another world than this one. But I am getting hoarse from shouting and cannot speak any more."

I returned home, slightly easier in my mind but with "It is all over!" still with me and which will never leave me. The following morning I returned to her. Fanny said her mistress could not see me and, following me into the street, asked "What has happened to my mistress? What sorrow have you caused her?" "None that I know of," I replied. "I found her in a terrible state, " she went on. "She did not go to bed at all last night. But I must go back to her. If it is all your fault … you will have no peace for the rest of your life." Fanny went in, I left, exceedingly anxious.

One hour later I returned. Caliste had left. I was handed the casket with a letter: "When I wanted to hold you back yesterday, I was unsuccessful. Today I sent you away and you obeyed immediately. I am leaving to spare you from committing further cruelties that would poison the rest of your life – if you were ever to comprehend them. I am also sparing myself the torment of contemplating in detail a misfortune and loss the more painfully felt because I have no right to reproach anyone for them. Keep, in memory of my love, these trifles that you admired yesterday; you need have no scruples over this for I am resolved to keep all of the assets that I have received from milord and his uncle."

How can I persuade you, Madame, of the depth of dejection into which I sank? Of all the puerile, absurd and confused considerations which flooded into my thoughts? Was I now incapable of sane thinking? Was this a return to the breakdown caused by the death of my brother? I wish you to believe this for, otherwise, how could you have the patience to continue reading this? I wish to believe it myself – or that the memories of that day be for ever obliterated.

She had been gone for only a half hour. Why did I not follow her? What held me back? If there exist other intelligences that are witness to our deepest thoughts, let them explain to me what held me back. I sat at the desk at which Caliste had written this letter, I took her pen and kissed it. I wanted to write to her, in my turn, but her rooms were being tidied by the servants and I withdrew. I walked out into the country, then returned to shut myself in my room at home. An hour after midnight I lay on my bed, still dressed and slept. My brother, Caliste, a thousand sad ghosts assailed me. I woke with a start covered with sweat. Planning to tell Caliste how I had suffered that evening and recount to her my dreams. Tell Caliste? She had gone, it was her departure which had caused me this pain. She was no longer available to me. She was no longer mine, she belonged to another.

No! Not yet! I called for the horses and my carriage. I went to ask the servants whether anything had been seen of Monsieur M. I was told that he had arrived at eight o'clock that evening and at ten had taken the road to London. That was the moment that I wanted to take my own life. I began to confuse things, I thought Caliste was dead. My father's concern for me brought a doctor to bleed me which alleviated somewhat my disturbed mind. I found myself in my father's arms; he sought to care for my health, and at the same time to conceal from the world at large the low state of my mind. Unwise precaution! If the world at large had known the low state of my mind, no person would have wished to unite themselves with me.

The next day I was brought a letter. My father asked if he might open it. "… That I may see, although it is too late, just what sort of a woman this was." "Read it," I said, "for you will see nothing that it is not to her credit."

"It is now certain that you have not followed me. Three hours ago I still had hope. Now I am happy to think that it is no longer possible for you to arrive, happy because it could only have resulted in fatal consequences. But I might still receive a letter. There are moments when I still deceive myself. Habit is so strong. Anyway you cannot hate me, and I cannot ever be the same as others for you. I still have an hour of freedom. Although all is in readiness I can still retract. But if I hear nothing from you I shall not retract. You have no more need of me. Your situation with me has grown too predictable; for a long time now you have been wearied by it. I made a last attempt. I almost believed you would hold me back, or follow me. I will not enumerate the other motives that have swayed me – they are too confused. I intend now to seek repose and the happiness of others in my new life and to conduct myself in a manner that you will never have to blush for me. Adieu, the last hour is running out and in a moment they will come to tell me that it has passed. Adieu, you for whom I can find no name; adieu for the last time."*

The letter was spotted with tears, those of my father fell to join hers, mine … I know the letter by heart but I can now no longer read it.

Two days later Lady Betty read from the gazette: "Charles M of Norfolk, with Maria-Sophia …" Yes, she read out these words and I had to hear them. Lady Betty cannot be blamed for any insensitivity in this. I believe she considered Caliste as an honest girl, for one of her sort,** with whom I had lived and who loved me still although I had ceased to love *her*. Now that I had detached myself from Caliste and could not marry her, I might choose, albeit with some sadness, to marry Lady Betty so as to bring matters to an honourable conclusion. Lady Betty certainly attributed my sadness to pity and far from thinking ill of me, she

---

*   In her own marriage, Belle exacted a pre-condition from Monsieur de Charrière that she was free to renounce her betrothal right up to the last moment in the church. She, as Caliste, went through with the ceremony with a resigned reluctance.

** "*une fille honnête pour son état* …" The derogatory meaning is clear in the original: *état* translates accurately here as "sort."

thought better of me for this. These judgements were quite natural and differed from the truth by only a small degree which she could not possibly divine.

A week passed; during this time I was scarcely alive. Restless, distracted, running always as if in search of something, finding nothing, seeking nothing in particular, wanting only to escape from myself, and from all that met my gaze! Ah! Madame, what a state I was in! And there awaited me an even more cruel event. One morning during breakfast Sir Harry came up to me and said: "I see you so sad and I am afraid you will go away as well. I have had an idea. People talk about Maman getting married again and I would prefer it to be you rather than someone else, to become my father. In this way you would always be with me, or at least I would accompany you if you went away." Lady Betty smiled. She gave the impression that her son had merely proposed what I had been considering for some time. I did not reply. She believed I was embarrassed, too timid – but my silence lasted too long. My father answered for me: "That is a very good idea, my dear Harry. I am of the opinion that some day or other everyone will think the same." "Some day or other!" said Lady Betty. "You take me for being over-modest! I would not need time to consider an idea that would please you, as it would me, and our two sons." My father took my hand and led me from the room.

"Do not punish me," he said, "for not having yielded to strong arguments over those that were weak. I may have been blind but I believe I have not been hard. Nothing in the world is so dear to me as you are. Deserve my affection right to the end. Certainly, I would not have wished to exact such a sacrifice on your part but now that that has occurred, accept it for your own sake and for mine. Show yourself to be a tender and generous son and engage in a marriage that will appear advantageous to everyone except yourself. Give me grandchildren to interest and amuse my old age, to make amends for your mother and your brother, and indeed for yourself, because you have always failed, and may continue to fail to be your own man."

I re-entered the breakfast room. "Please forgive my lack of eloquence," I said to Lady Betty. "And believe that I feel more than I can express. If you will allow me to make a journey to France and Holland lasting some four months, and keep this as our secret, I will return to ask you to fulfil my honourable intentions which are so advantageous to myself." "In four months?" she said. "And to keep it a secret? Is this secret to humour the sensibility of that woman?" "Whatever my motives, those are my conditions," I replied. "Do not be angry," the boy said, "Maman does not know Mistress Caliste." "I shall be marrying you also if I marry your mother!" I said, embracing him, "and I promise you tenderness and faithfulness!"

"Madame is being only too reasonable," said my father, "not to agree to keeping it secret. Why should you not marry secretly before your departure? I would be pleased to see you married – you could leave as soon as you wished following the celebration. In this way nothing will be suspected. And if rumours do start then your departure will correct this. I quite understand that you prefer to travel as a bachelor, that is, alone; in the past it had been planned that you would travel with your brother following university, but the war interfered."

Lady Betty was so appeased by my father's suggestion that she agreed to it all, and thought we should be married before a certain ball that was to be given a few days hence. "It will be amusing for us both to see the mistake that people will be making," she said. With what speed was I hurried along! I had known Lady Betty for five months; our marriage was discussed, agreed and decided in an hour! Sir Harry was overjoyed but I doubted whether he could stay discreet. He said four months was too long for him to remain silent, but that he would do so until my departure if I took him with me.

Thus we were married. Nothing untoward occurred except that contrary winds prevented my departure by several days, spent at Bath rather than in the country. The wind changed, I left leaving Lady Betty pregnant.

In four months we visited the main cities of Holland, Flanders and France. As well as Paris we visited Normandy and Brittany. I did not hurry because of my young companion, but neither did I dawdle, not wishing to stay long in any one place. I did not need or seek society; all that I saw of women caused me no distraction from my loss. I preferred buildings, theatres, pictures; hearing or remarking something noteworthy, I looked for *her* to share it with, she with whom I would have wished always to share every-thing, she who had helped me to judge, to feel all that we had viewed together in the past. A thousand times I took my pen to write to her and a thousand times I desisted: how could I write a letter that would give me little pleasure to write and none for her to receive?

Without little Harry I would have found myself alone in even the most crowded cities, yet with him I was not entirely alone even in secluded places. He loved me, he made me no trouble, and I found a thousand ways to get him to speak of Mistress Cal-iste even if I did not mention her name. We returned to England, first to Bath then to my father's and finally to London where our marriage became public, Lady Betty judging the time was now right for her to be presented at Court.

In the past my brother and I had been spoken of as a supreme example of friendship. Subsequently I had been spoken of as a young man rendered of interest through the passion of a charm-ing woman. My father's friends had said that I distinguished myself by my knowledge and my talents and, in their turn, men of talent praised my taste and sensibility for the arts. In London now I was seen as a silent and sad young man. The dedication to me of Caliste, the choice made by Lady Betty – these were viewed with amazement. And even if the earlier judgements on me had not been entirely false, later opinion about me was just – yet I took no notice of it. Lady Betty, on the other hand, became aware of public opinion. She found herself not to be as popular as she would have wished, and all of this justified her in loud complaints. She found consolation in a sort of contemptuousness on which she prided herself.

I did not find any of her reactions to be unjust; I could not be offended by them or confront them. I was too indifferent to be angry. She did what she wished, and she wished to please and shine in society, aided as she was by her handsome face, her charm and that repartee of which women always have the knack. All this made it easy for her and she passed from a general coquetry to one rather more special – to the one man in the kingdom with whom all women would be flattered to be seen, though the least able (or so I thought) to induce or inspire passion. I appeared to see nothing, to be opposed to nothing and after the birth of her daughter Lady Betty gave herself up unreservedly to all those amusements that fashion or her own taste deemed desirable. Little Sir Harry was happy with me because I looked after him all the time and he remained faithful to me. The only unhappiness I suffered was when his mother insisted he be left behind to board at Westminster School when, after the birth of her daughter, we repaired to the country.

It was about this time that my father, walking with me near the house, spoke openly as to the life being led by milady. He asked whether I should not oppose her conduct before it became entirely scandalous. I replied that I could not add to my other griefs those of criticising someone who had given herself to me with greater advantage apparent to me than to her and who, in fact, had a lot to complain of. "There is no one," I said to him, "who does not need their *amour propre* to be enhanced. Women of the people have their domestic difficulties, in particular their children whom they must care for themselves; genteel ladies, if they do not have a husband to whom they are everything, and *vice-versa*, find recourse in parlour games, gallantry or religious devotion. Milady does not like games, and she is too young and attractive anyway to play at them. She has every right to complain, and it does not afflict me sufficiently so that I should, in my turn, also complain. I do not wish to indulge myself in ill humour, and attract the ridicule which is the outcome for a jealous husband. If she were sensitive, serious, capable in a word of listening to me and believing me, if there were between us a true harmony of character I might become her friend and advise her to avoid scandal and impropriety so as to spare herself pain and alienating the public. But as she would not listen to me it is better that I preserve my dignity and she remains in ignorance of my reticence being deliberate. She will commit some imprudences the less if she believes she is deceiving me. I know that I can be criticised for tolerating disorderly living but I could only prevent this by not letting my wife out of my sight. Who would wish such a task on me? And I would invite any man who said he would not tolerate any abuses in his marriage or in his house or family – I would invite him to throw the first stone."

My father saw I was not to be moved and kept silent. He sympathised with my point of view and always got on well with Lady Betty. During the short time that we were still to be together he showed his affection for me daily. I remember one dinner party we held when a bishop, who was related to Lady Betty, half seriously, half jokingly uttered some rather commonplace views on marriage and authority within marriage. These remarks could be taken as ecclesiastical pleasantries of a general sort but which might have a particular relevance to present company. After letting him run on to the end of his pet subject I said it was up to the law to keep wives in order, but failing that religion or its ministers should do so; and that, if husbands were to be charged with the task there should at least be a dispensation for those who were excessively busy and hard-working, as also for gentle, lazy husbands who would find such a duty unpleasant. If they did not grant us such an indulgence, marriage would suit only busybodies and idiots, or those who had lost their sight. Lady Betty blushed. She had for some time now believed I lacked all spirit and was clearly surprised at my words. Perhaps all it needed for me to return to her favour would have been the admiration of some other pretty woman.

It seems, even though it may not always appear to be the case, that women have great confidence in each other's judgements and tastes. A man is a commodity who circulates amongst women, passing from hand to hand, his price rising each time, until he suffers a decline which is total and usually thoroughly deserved.

Towards the end of September I returned to London to see Sir Harry. I hoped also that, being the only one of our family in town during a month when it was deserted, I would be able to move about unhindered and might encounter, in some café or tavern, someone who could give me news of Caliste. We had now been separated for a year and a few days. If this was not successful I would visit General D. and the old uncle who had made her his heir. I could not live any longer without knowing what she was doing: the void she had left in me grew more painful with each day. We are wrong to think that a severe loss is felt with greater pain at the outset. At that time we do not yet fully appreciate our loss, we have not yet come to terms with it, we do not yet realise there is no remedy for it. We believe at the beginning of a cruel separation that it is only a temporary absence. But when the days that follow do not produce the person we crave, and it seems that our anguish is confirmed for eternity we can only repeat: "It is for ever!"

The day after I arrived in London was spent with my small

friend and in the evening I went alone to the theatre, thinking to nurse my feelings in solitude. There were few in the audience owing to the heat of the evening and a storm threatened. I entered my box and, distracted as I was, thought I was alone. Then I saw that I was sharing the box with a lady whose face was hidden behind a large hat. She had not turned to look at me and appeared to be sunk in the deepest reverie. I do not know what it was about her that reminded me of Caliste: the real Caliste must have been miles away in Norfolk, gone there with her husband and not spoken of since. So I gave it no more thought. The piece began. It proved to be *The Fair Penitent*. I cried out in surprise; my neighbour turned towards me; it was Caliste.

Our astonishment, emotion, delight – these cannot be described. Every sentiment we had been feeling yielded in this moment to the sheer joy of our encounter. My mistakes fell from my shoulders, regrets vanished, I had no wife, she had no husband. We had found each other again. Even if only for an hour or so.

She looked pale and more carelessly dressed but more beautiful than I had ever seen her. "What a happy chance" she cried. "I have come to see the piece at the same theatre that determined my future. This is my first visit since then, I had never had the courage to do so before but newer regrets have overtaken that particular shame. I came to relive my start in life. And I find *you* here, the real you, not just the constant subject of my thoughts and memories, but you, the sole interest of my life whom I did not expect ever to see again."

It was long before I replied. We just looked at each other, steadfastly, as though each wanted to be sure that the other was real. "Is it really you?" I asked her finally. "I came here with no particular plan. I would have counted myself lucky to have gained some news after asking about you everywhere, but now I find the real you, and alone, and we can count on at least an hour or two of pleasure where before we had an infinity of time together!"

I suggested we should each recount the events that had transpired for both of us since we separated. Thus might we learn about the other and be more at our ease. She asked me to begin and hardly interrupted me till the end, only to excuse me if I accused myself; if I spoke of her she smiled with understanding; if she saw me upset she showed me pity. The lack of feeling that was evident between Lady Betty and myself caused her no pleasure, although neither did it induce any pain.

"I see," she said, "that I have never been entirely disdained, nor quite forgotten. That is all I could have asked for, and I give thanks to heaven that I have learned it. Now for my tale of the last sad years.

"I will not tell you all that I went through on the road from Bath to London, trembling at the smallest sound I heard behind me, fearing to look round for fear that it was *not* you in pursuit to be convinced of the truth, then my hopes raised again, then dashed once more. Enough! If you cannot guess at my feelings, then neither can you comprehend them! Arrived in London, I learned that my father's brother had died some days before and had, as promised, left me everything. With legacies paid it amounted, apart from the house, to thirty thousand pounds. The event moved me very deeply; the death of an old man of eighty-four years is less of a surprise than his age, but I realised that such an event determined that I was now obliged not to forego my marriage. I had, after all, received Monsieur M.'s declaration and for me now to reject him when I had a fortune to give in exchange for a name and an honourable position seemed impossible for me to inflict. I would have felt dishonourable. He arrived the next day and showed me an account of his fortune, clear as was the fortune itself, and a marriage contract by which he gave me three hundred pounds a year for life plus a dowry of five thousand pounds. He knew nothing of my inheritance; I informed him of it and refused his proposed income [but accepted the dowry].* I demanded that if the marriage were to take place (a phrase I repeated several times) I reserved the right to retain and enjoy the ownership of all that I held, and might hold in the future, from Lord L.'s uncle, General D. I also said Monsieur M. must accept that I remained free of any promise to marry him until the moment when I said *yes* at the church.**

"'You see, Sir' I had said to him, 'how confused I am. I prefer that any promises I may have made should count as nothing, and that you give me your word not to reproach me if I should retract up to the last moment of the ceremony being concluded.'

"'I promise it,' he had said, 'if you do this of your own wish. But if someone else causes you to change it must be his love or mine.‡ A man who has known you for so long and could not bring himself to do what I am proposing does not deserve to be the one preferred.'

"After this speech the very thing that I had hoped for up till now seemed the one I should fear the most. He returned with the contract altered as I had wished. He gave me five hundred pounds for my property – my jewels, furniture and pictures. The clergyman had been alerted, the licence obtained, the witnesses were ready. I asked for one more hour of liberty and solitude. I wrote to you and sent you the letter via James; but none came in return. The hour ran its course, we went to the church, we were married.

"Let me take breath for an instant," she said. The tears she was shedding could have been interpreted by others in the audience as

---

*   The author does not specify that the dowry was to remain with Caliste but this is the implication which is borne out later.
**   See footnote on p. 246.
‡   i.e., a duel.

the result of the acting being witnessed on the stage. She continued after a little while, "Some days afterwards all matters regarding the settlement having been arranged, my husband took me off
to his country seat. Lord L.'s uncle, General D., on my saying my
farewells, made me promise to return to see him when requested.

"I was well received at my future home. Servants, tenants,
friends, neighbours even the most highly born (or who had the
right to be so-called), all were anxious to make me feel welcome
and I could only imagine that they had received me with good
reports. For the first time I began to wonder if your father may
have been mistaken and whether indeed I would have brought
dishonour in my train.* For my part, I neglected nothing to give
pleasure in return for their civility. My old habit of adapting to
others my actions, my words, gestures, voice, even my countenance returned and served me well.

"I swear that in those four months Monsieur M. had not one
disagreeable moment. I did not utter your name, the clothes I
wore were different, the music I played was not the same as in
Bath. I had become a second person bent on silencing and con-
cealing the first. My husband had a veritable passion for me and
this helped the illusion that he believed himself to be the most
loved of any man. He certainly deserved all the happiness I could
give him during a long life – but his happiness lasted for only
four months.

"We were seated at the table of one of our neighbours when a
man, who had come down from London, spoke of a marriage
that had been contracted some long time ago but only made public in the last few days. He could not remember your name, then
remembered it. I said nothing but fainted clean away and was
unconscious for two hours. Various untoward events occurred to

---

*   This must be Caliste's most poignant remark. It strikes at the heart of the book
     and its prejudices.

follow this, resulting in a dire miscarriage which brought me twenty times to the brink of the grave. I hardly saw my husband. A local woman who knew my story, and sympathised with my situation, kept him away from me so that I would not see his anguish nor hear his reproaches and at the same time she neglected nothing to console and appease him. She did even more for me.

"I had come to believe from this that you had been secretly married before I left Bath, and that you were already engaged before you returned there; that you had deceived me in saying you did not know Lady Betty before her arrival there; that you had let me arrange your lodgings there to impress my rival and pay court to her; and that when you evinced ill humour at seeing Monsieur M. in my presence you were already engaged, perhaps already married. The lady who had befriended me knew of these conjectures which returned to haunt me a thousand times and she made it her business, without telling me, to inform herself of the truth of the previous happenings: of the impression that my departure had made on you; of the conduct of your father; of the actual moment of your marriage; of your departure delayed through bad weather; of your behaviour during your journey and after your return. She fathomed all of the truth by speaking to different people around you and Sir Harry and her information proved to be correct because it tallies exactly with all you have now told me. I was consoled and thanked her with my tears. Alone at night I could say to myself: 'I need neither despise nor hate him; I have not been the plaything of a plot, of a premeditated betrayal. He has not played a game with my love or my blindness.'

"Yes, I was consoled. I recovered sufficient health to return to my usual life and hoped to make my husband forget his grievances by virtue of my solicitude and amiable attention. I was unsuccessful. Estrangement, if not actual hate, had taken the place of love. He only took notice of me if my illness seemed to threaten my life, but on any improvement in my health he fled from the house and on returning would shudder to see the one he had once loved. I struggled for three months to correct this wretched frame of mind, more for affection for him than love of myself. Always alone, or with the lady who had so helped me, working as I did ceaselessly to run his home for him, neither receiving nor writing letters; with my anguish, my humiliation (his friends had all abandoned me) – all this I thought must surely touch him. But he was embittered beyond recall. He spoke not one word of reproach and this allowed me no opportunity of excusing or justifying myself. Once or twice I wanted to speak but I could not bring myself to utter a word.

"Finally, I received a letter from the General to say he was ill and asking me to visit him, alone or with Monsieur M. I showed him the letter. 'You may go, Madame,' was all he said. I left the next day, leaving Fanny so as not to appear to desert the house, nor to be banished from it, and I left open my cupboards and caskets so they could be examined by everyone. But I do not believe anyone deigned to look at anything of mine, nor to ask the least question on my behalf.

"So now you see returned to London the lady that was loved by milord; and by you; and today I find myself here once more unloved and more friendless than when I played in this same theatre and belonged to nobody except a mother who bartered me away for money."

Caliste did not cry when she had finished the recital. Rather, she seemed to reflect on her fate with astonishment more than sadness. I withdrew myself into the blackest of thoughts.

"Do not vex yourself over me – I am not worth it" she told me with a rueful smile. "I knew, and said always, that the end would be unhappy. But I have had such sweet moments! The joy of seeing you again would alone make up for a century of suffering.

Who am I, in truth, but a kept woman that you have honoured more than she deserved?" In a quiet voice she asked me for news of Sir Harry and whether he cared for his little sister. I asked her about her own health. "I am not at all well," she said, "and I doubt that I shall ever return to full health. But I consider sadness will take a long time to put an end to my strong constitution."

We spoke of the future. Should she return to Norfolk where her duty lay, though not her inclination nor her happiness? Should she entreat Lord L.'s uncle to take her to France for the winter? If we were both to spend the winter in London, on the other hand, we could see each other – for how could we *not* see each other?

The theatre finished, we went out having decided nothing, whether we should separate, be together again, where we should go. The sight of James brought me to my senses. "Ah! James," I cried. "Oh! Sir, is it really you? What a lucky chance that you are here! I will call a carriage instead of this chair." Thus it was James who decided that I would have some moments more with Caliste. "Where do you want him to go?" he asked her. "Oh! To St James's Park" she replied, then, after glancing at me, "let us be together for a little while – no one will know. It is the first secret James has been obliged to keep – I am sure he will not betray it. But, if you wish that reports of our being seen together at the play are not to be believed, then you may leave tonight, or tomorrow morning, for the country. It will be thought that it was all one for you to see me again because you would have left me so quickly." Thus a noble and generous soul will put decency before love, will consider as paramount the wellbeing of others.

"But write to me," she added, "advise me, tell me your plans. There can be nothing against my receiving letters from you from time to time." I agreed. I promised to leave and to write. We arrived at the park's exit. Thunder began to growl. "Are you not alarmed?" I asked her. "Let it kill me alone and all will be well.

Let us keep near the gate and we can sit on this bench whilst the carriage waits." And after studying the sky: "No one will be walking out now so we will not be seen here." She felt in the dark for my hair, cut off a lock and placed it in her bosom. She caught me close in her arms and asked: "What shall we do without each other? In half an hour I shall be as I was six months ago, as I was this morning, alone. What shall I do if I have some time still to live? Do you want us to leave together? Have you not obeyed your father enough? Do you not have a wife of his choosing and a child? Let us return to our true ties. Whom will we harm? My husband hates me and does not wish to live with me any more. You wife loves you no longer. No, do not reply," she said, putting her hand over my mouth. "Do not refuse – yet do not consent either. Until now I have been only unhappy; it is better than I should not be guilty as well. I can live with my own faults but not yours. I would not forgive myself for having put you to shame! Ah! How my heart weeps. How much I love you – never was a man loved as you are!" She held me close and burst into tears. "How ungrateful I am to say that I am unhappy; I would not exchange for anything the pleasure that I have experienced today – and am still experiencing."

The thunder was now frightening and the sky seemed on fire. Caliste appeared to see and hear nothing, but James came running and cried: "For heaven's sake, Madame, take shelter. You have been so ill. It is starting to hail!" And taking her under the arm he led her to the carriage and handed her in. I stayed in the dark. I never saw her again.

The next day I left early for the country. My father was surprised to see me return so soon, saw my agitation and asked me what was the matter. I owed him my confidence and told him everything. "In your place – and I do not say this as a father – I would be uncertain what I should do. 'Let us return to our true ties!' Was she right? But she did not want this herself! It was a moment of aberration from which she quickly recovered." I paced up and down the gallery where we were speaking, my father sitting at a table, his head in his hands. The sound of voices put an end to the strange scene.

Milady had returned from hunting. When she saw me she changed colour. She imagined something untoward had occurred in view of my early return, but I said nothing as I left the room. I dressed quickly for dinner and repaired to the table in my usual place. All that I saw persuaded me that milady was happy in my absence and that my unexpected return did not suit her at all. My father was certainly struck by this and on leaving the table pressed my hand and said with as much bitterness as compassion: "Oh! Why ever did I dismiss Caliste? And why did you never make her known to me? Who could believe there could be such a difference between one woman and another? And that the one should love you with such a true and constant passion?"

He followed me to my study where we sat opposite each other for a long time without speaking. There was the noise of a carriage arriving and Lord X was announced. This was a distant relative, the father of the young Milord whom I am accompanying here in Lausanne.* He said to me, speaking forcefully: "I have come to see whether you can do me a great service. My only son wishes to travel abroad but he is young and I cannot accompany him. My wife cannot leave her father and she would die of anxiety and boredom were she to be deprived of both her son and her husband. I say again, my son is very young, but I would sooner he travel alone than in the care of anyone but yourself. Things are not well with you and your wife, your own overseas visit was only for four months. My son is a good lad. I will meet half of the expense. Now then, I find you with your father. I will leave you to talk it over for a quarter of an hour."

---

*   So we have nearly come full circle!

I looked at my father and he took me aside. "Consider this," he said, "as providence coming to the rescue of our weak inactions, both yours and mine. Caliste has to all intents and purposes been chased out of her home by her husband and, in London, will gladden the heart of her benefactor, General D. I will lose you but I deserve this. You will render service to another father and his son of whom great things are expected. I will console myself with that thought."

"I will go," I said to milord, "but on two conditions which I will explain to you after I have taken a breath of fresh air." "Both conditions are agreed to in advance," he said, shaking me by the hand. "Thank you. It is settled." My two conditions were: firstly, that we should start with Italy where my knowledge was paramount; and secondly, that after a year, pleased or displeased with the young man, I could leave him at any moment I desired without disobliging his parents.

The same night I wrote to Caliste and explained all that had transpired. I asked for a reply and promised to continue writing. "Let us not deprive ourselves of any innocent pleasure" I wrote.

I was of the opinion that we should make the journey to Italy mainly by sea. We embarked at Plymouth, disembarked at Lisbon, went across land to Cadiz, thence by sea to Messina where the volcano was active. I recall, Madame, having told you of this in detail. And you know that after a year in Italy we passed through St Gothard to the Valais in Switzerland where we saw the glaciers, baths and salt springs. At the start of winter we came to Lausanne where you were so kind to us and a sympathy sprang up between us. Your house became our refuge. It remains to tell you the reply I received from Caliste.

I received her letter at the moment of embarkation. She lamented my leaving but approved my plan and sent me a thousand good wishes for a good outcome. She wrote also to my father, thanked him for his concern, and asked his pardon for any sorrow she might have caused him. Winter came. Lord L.'s uncle was not making a good recovery from his gout and she decided to stay in London. Sometimes he became really ill so that she nursed him daily and even at night. When he recovered he wanted to entertain her and invited men of the highest calibre to the house. Grand dinners and noisy suppers were held, and gaming went on often far into the night. He liked Caliste to adorn these gatherings until they broke up. At other times he persuaded her to go out into society, saying that to act as a hermit would give the impression that she had been disgraced by her husband; and that on the contrary he would be pleased that she was out in the world and well received. All this, added to the shock of our meeting, damaged her health. Excuse me for saying that she suffered painfully at our fresh separation, as did I. Her letters were always tender and proved her attachment to me.

In the spring came a letter with news that gave me great pleasure but also great pain.

"Yesterday I was at the theatre and had reserved the same box where we met in September. I believe my good angel must inhabit that place. I was hardly settled in my seat when I heard a young voice say: 'Here is my dear Mistress Caliste! But how much weight you have lost! There, Sir, is she whom your son never took to see but now you can see for yourself!' Sir Harry was of course speaking to your father. He now gave me a look, so pained that tears cloud my eyes in describing it. His look had in it such sadness and tenderness. 'But how did you get so thin?' asked Sir Harry 'Many reasons, my young friend!' I replied. 'But how you have grown and you seem to be well and happy' I said to him. 'I am very unhappy that our friend in Italy does not have me as his companion, rather than his cousin. I had more right than he did. But I have always thought Maman did not wish it, and it was she who said I must attend Westminster School. He would willingly have kept me and given me lessons himself which would have been far pleasanter for me – and we could have talked about you! It is so long since I saw you that I must speak frankly. I have often thought that because I loved you so much, and was so upset at your leaving, Maman was displeased. But I will not say any more because she is even now observing us from the box opposite, and may well divine all that I have said!'

"You can imagine the effect his words had on me! Because of the looks I was receiving from Lady Betty I did not dare to have recourse to my smelling salts, and I breathed with difficulty. 'But you are not pale, at least, and I can presume that you are not ill?' 'I have some rouge on my cheeks,' I replied to him. 'But you did not wear it eighteen months ago.' At last your father told him to leave me in peace, then asked if I had news of you and recounted the contents of your letters to him.

"I made myself remain in my seat until the first interval, but piercing looks from your wife and those accompanying her obliged me to leave. Sir Harry ran to look for my carriage and your father had the goodness to hand me in."

In June she was advised to take asses' milk. The General advised her to return to her home in the country to take this, believing that she only had to show her countenance to the man who had once so loved her, to recapture those feelings she once inspired. He said to her: "It was I who, in some measure, was responsible for your marriage. I will accompany you and we will judge whether they dare to receive you badly."

Caliste wrote to her husband to warn him but expected no reply. Waiting for her, however, was this reply: "The General is quite correct, Madame, and you do right to return to your own home. Try to recover your health and engage in your duties as mistress exactly as before. I have given clear orders to the servants, although they are your servants as well. I hope one day to live happily again with you, as in the past, but for the present I feel my hurt so greatly that if we were together you would see only this hurt. To try to lose it I intend to travel overseas for several months and anticipate success because it will be my first venture abroad. You will not be able to write to me as my whereabouts will be unknown, but I will write to you and people will see we are not estranged. Farewell, Madame, it is in all sincerity that I wish you a return to health, and I regret having shown such distress over your involuntary action that you have done so much to ameliorate. But my distress was too acute. You can rely on Mistress G. to help you. She was speaking only the truth when she assured me there had been no secret correspondence, or contract, between you and the man lucky enough to have won your heart. Your surprise at meeting him again was proof of your innocence but I did not listen."

Monsieur M. may have entreated servants and friends to give their full support to Caliste. Initially this was not the case, but she charmed them to such a degree that she was able partly to restore herself with their help. The country folk were as discreet as they were kindly. She wrote me that she had improved and looked better in herself. Then, in the middle of her cure, the General died and she was obliged to return to London and attend to his funeral and other matters. This reduced her health to where it had been. The General had left her capital of six hundred pounds a year in the three percents.

Following his death, Caliste went to live in her house in Whitehall which she had amused herself in decorating the previous winter. She continued to receive Lord L.'s friends and those of his uncle. Once again, she invited the best musicians to come and play. She wrote me all this and told me she had given a home to a singer who had tired of the theatre. Caliste had also helped her to marry a musician who was an honest man "I make use of them both," she wrote, "to teach music to little girl orphans whom I teach as well, so as to give them something of a profession. When it is asserted that I am only training them to become courtesans I remark that I only take those who are poor and pretty. Such a combination in London leads them into almost certain ruin. But being able to sing adds nothing to the danger and, dare I say it, it might be better to begin and finish as I have done rather than walk the streets and perish in a hospital."

All these happenings could not prepare me, Madame, for the terrible letter I received from her a week ago. Return it to me. It will stay with me till my death.

"It is over, my friend. I can now say to you that it is over for ever. I can only bid you my eternal farewell. I will not explain the symptoms that have convinced me of an early release but I am sure I do not mislead you, nor myself. Your father came to see me yesterday. I was extremely touched by his visit. He said to me: 'If in the spring, Madame, if in the spring …' He could not bring himself to add 'if you are still living.' I will myself attend you to Provence, Nice or Italy; my son is at present in Switzerland and can join us there.'

"'It is too late, sir,' I told him, 'but I am no less touched by your goodness.' He could have said more but did not do so out of consideration for me. I asked for news of your daughter. He said he would have had her come and visit me, if she had resembled you. But even at only eighteen months she resembled her mother. I begged for Sir Harry to come and said I would convey to him *via* the boy a present I felt too embarrassed to give him myself. He replied that he would receive with pleasure anything I chose to give him. Thus I gave him your portrait that you sent me from Italy and will give Sir Harry the copy of it that I had already had made. The first portrait you sent me shall be returned to you after my death.

"I have not made you happy, I leave you suffering; and I am to die. I can never say, though, that I wish I had never known you. I cannot, I will not reproach myself. Our last meeting, the memory of which recurs to me constantly, may have been a little foolhardy. People might have talked. One could call it 'braving the heavens.' Will the Supreme Being be angry? If so, I ask him to forgive us both.

"Farewell, my friend. Write that you have received this – just a few words. They may not reach me alive but if I am well enough I will have the pleasure of seeing your handwriting for the last time."

I have received and heard nothing more, Madame. She has said "It is over!". I have waited until it was too late, my father also. If she had only loved another man, and he had had another father, she would be living now. She would not be dying from sadness.

TWENTY-SECOND LETTER

Madame,

I have received no more letters. There are moments when I still hope. But that is not really so. I have in truth ceased to hope. I already think of her as dead – and I am desolated. I had become accustomed to her illness as I had become familiar with her wisdom, with her love. I did not believe she would marry. I did not believe she would die. I must now live with what I could not foresee – or did not wish to foresee.

Before the last blow had fallen, there occurred an event that you may find important. For some days I had lived with my memories, I spoke to no one, not even to milord. But this morning he came to enquire how I had slept and I said to him: "Young man, if ever you capture the heart of a woman who is truly tender and sensitive and whom you feel you cannot love as she deserves, leave her, make her forget you, otherwise you risk exposing her to much unhappiness and lasting sadness." He stayed pensive for a while. An hour or so later he asked me whether I remembered telling him that your daughter might have one of several reasons for withdrawing from Lausanne. I acquiesced, and he then asked if I thought she might have a preference for someone. I said I thought it likely and he asked if it was for him. I replied that sometimes I had thought so. "If that is so, I am sorry that Mademoiselle Cécile is so well born because I am too young to marry. I could not think of it at my age."

This may come to nothing. One does not know. I said no more of the matter to milord. In my time I would have preferred to exchange my liberty for Caliste – but what use was I to her?

TWENTY-THIRD LETTER

What interest can you have, Madame, in a man more unhappy than all others, but who deserves his unhappiness? The past returns to me ceaselessly without my understanding it. I do not know if others who have gone downhill equally feel as I do – if so, I pity them. I seem to have done nothing that another man would have done naturally. Thus I should have married Caliste without asking for a permission that I did not need. I should have prevented her from promising that she would not marry without parental consent. If a thousand attempts had not swayed my father, I should have made her my mistress (in reality a wife) which is what her heart demanded despite any words she may have used to the contrary. I ought to have heeded her when, on that last evening together in Bath, she had tried to prevent me leaving her. And when I returned that same evening I should have forced her door which she had locked; and on the morrow I should have made her see me again, or at least have given chase when she took the road to London. I ought to have stayed single and not given her the pain of believing her place had been filled beforehand, that she had been betrayed or forgotten. Having found her again I should not have left her, and should have acted at least with the promptness and zeal of her faithful James. Perhaps I should not have let her leave alone in her carriage on that last evening after the theatre; I could have hidden myself in it; perhaps I could have entered the household as one of her servants – I was unknown therein. And this autumn ... this winter ... *now*.

I knew her husband was not with her. Instead of dreaming in your chimney corner why did I not return to her, even now, and ease her pain, let her see me during her last days to prove she had not loved an automaton without feelings; and that if I had not loved her as she deserved then at least I could weep for her! But it is too late, so are my last regrets of which she knows nothing. Of which she *knew* nothing I should perforce say because I must summon the courage now to believe she is dead. If there remained any last hope she would have lightened the tone of her last letter – for she knew how to love. Now I am alone in the world, I am loved no longer. I lacked the courage to prevent my loss; I am now without the strength to endure it.

TWENTY-FOURTH LETTER

(from Milord to Cécile's mother)

Madame,

Having learned that you are leaving tomorrow, I wished to have the honour to visit you today to bid you and Mlle Cécile a safe journey, and to tell you that the pain I have at your parting is only softened by the firm hope of seeing you both again. But I cannot leave my relative. The effect on him from a letter just delivered is so immense that Monsieur Tissot has forbidden me absolutely to leave him. He who has come to deliver the letter may not leave him either, and in truth he is about as afflicted as my cousin. I believe he would prefer to kill himself rather than prevent my cousin from doing so.

I beg you, Madame, to retain for me those kind good wishes which I value perhaps more than you realise, and the gratitude which will cease only with my life.

I have the honour to be ...

Edouard.*

TWENTY-FIFTH LETTER

(from Monsieur M. to William D.)

She whom you so much loved died in the evening two days ago. To describe her thus means no reproach; I forgave her a long time ago and, at the extreme, she had caused me no real offence. It is true that she did not open her heart to me but, equally, I am not sure whether she should have done so and had she done so, I believe I would still have married her for I loved her passionately.

She is the only amiable woman I have ever known. If she did not confide in me, nor did she deceive me. I deceived myself. You had not married her. Is it believable that, loving you, she should not have waited or tried to marry you? You must know how cruelly I was undeceived. I now repent of having shown so much resentment and chagrin and I remain amazed that, losing her love and the hope of a child, I showed such immoderation. Happily, we know this is not what killed her. I am certainly not the cause of her death and, although I have been jealous of you, I would rather be in my shoes than yours. Nothing however proves that you have any reproaches to make yourself and I beg you not to take my words in that sense; with reason, you would find me to be unjust and reckless and also cruel, for I am certain you are profoundly afflicted.

---

*   The first indication of his name!

On the same day that Madame Caliste wrote you her last letter she wrote asking me to visit her. I went without losing a moment. I found her room arranged as befits someone in good health, and herself fairly well in appearance except for her thinness. I was glad to be able to tell her that she appeared better than I had imagined; she smiled and said I was deceived by a little rouge that she had put on that morning, and which had already spared Fanny some tears and James some sighs. In the evening I heard her little girls sing, accompanied by her on the harpsichord, music excesssively touching such as I had heard in several churches in Italy. The next days I heard similar music morning and evening.

And finally, she read me her will whilst begging me to make any changes I wished. I changed nothing. She left her estate for the poor in the following manner. Half, that is, the interest of three percent of three hundred pounds, in perpetuity for the Lord Mayors of London to instruct, each year, three small boys, drawn from the foundling hospital, in the trades of pilot, carpenter and cabinet maker. The first of these is to be chosen from the most fearless; the second from the most robust; and the third from the most skilful. The other half of her estate goes to the Bishops of London; each year they are to take two girls from the Magdalen Hospital, and to place them with well-established tradeswomen, bringing with them each one hundred and fifty pounds to buy their way into an equal partnership. She asks that the bishop and his wife should supervise this arrangement.

Of the five thousand pounds I had given her on marriage, one thousand goes to Fanny and five hundred to James. Even so, the capital from her uncle which she had brought me on marriage is worth at least thirty-five thousand pounds. She begged me to retain Fanny and, by so doing, would bring honour to her as well as to her maid who had served her honestly and should not be suspected otherwise. Her clothes and jewels go to Mistress G. of

Norfolk, her house in Bath and its contents to Sir Harry. After all
funeral expenses have been paid, she wishes that any cash and
revenue remaining from this year should be distributed equally
among the little girls she was instructing, and servants in her
employ other than Fanny and James. Having assured herself that
there was nothing in her will that displeased me, or was unlawful,
she bade me and some friends of Lord L. and his uncle to ensure
that the will is properly executed.

After that, she continued her life as well as her fading strength
allowed, and we talked more at that time than we had ever done
before. In truth, Sir, I would have given my all to preserve her
life, if only in the manner in which I had found her, and spend the
rest of my days with her.

People found it hard to believe that she was as ill as she was;
friends continued to send her verses addressed to herself, sometimes in the name of Caliste, sometimes in that of Aspasia but she
no longer read them. I asked whether she enjoyed the esteem in
which she was now held. She assured me that having formerly
been very sensitive to scorn she had never been so to esteem.

"My judges are only men and women," she said, "as I am, and
I know myself better than they do. The only praise that gave me
pleasure was from Lord L.'s uncle, who loved me for being as
people should be (as he said), and if he had had to change this
good opinion of me he would have been much discountenanced.
I would have been annoyed if I had died before he did. In many
ways he needed me to be there for his esteem of me."

She had no one to keep her company at night. I wanted to
sleep in her room but she said this would disturb her. Fanny's bed
was separated from hers by only a partition that opened without
effort and noise; at the slightest sound Fanny would wake and
give her mistress something to drink. During the last nights I
took Fanny's place, not because she complained of being woken
so often but because the poor girl could no longer hear the weak

voice, the breathing so short, without bursting into tears. It pained me no less but I controlled myself better. The day before yesterday she was more oppressed and agitated than usual and wished to have her Wednesday concert as usual but she could not sit at her harpsichord. She asked that pieces from Handel's *Messiah* should be performed, also a *Miserere* sent to her from Italy, and the *Stabat Mater* by Pergolesi. During an interval she removed a ring from her finger and gave it to me. She then called James and gave him a casket and said to him: "Take it to him yourself * and, if it is possible, stay in his service. Tell him that for a long time I had wished that for myself. I would have been content with just that."

After having joined her hands together she raised her eyes to heaven and stayed like this for a few moments, then sinking back into her chair she closed her eyes. Seeing her so weak I asked if she preferred that the music should cease. She signalled that it should continue and summoned up enough strength to thank me for what she called my kindness. The last piece finished, the musicians filed out of the room on tiptoe thinking that she slept. But her eyes had closed for ever.

Thus ended your Caliste, some will say she died as a pagan, others as a saint. But the crying of her servants, the tears of the poor, the consternation of the whole neighbourhood, and the pain of a husband who had believed he had been wronged – these say better than words what she was.

In forcing myself to recite to you the end of this sad tale I have believed, in some measure, that I would please and obey her thereby; and from the same motive and the same tender respect to her memory, if I cannot offer you my friendship I can at least renounce all sentiments of ill-will.

---

* James obviously took the husband's letter as well as the casket to William.

Switzerla) - fairview

21. 4. 01.

INDEX